MW01138833

Girls Girls Girls

Girls Girls Girls

a novel

Shoshana von Blanckensee

G. P. Putnam's Sons
New York

PUTNAM
— EST. 1838 —
G. P. Putnam's Sons
Publishers Since 1838
An imprint of Penguin Random House LLC
1745 Broadway, New York, NY 10019
penguinrandomhouse.com

Book design by Alison Cnockaert

Library of Congress Cataloging-in-Publication Data
Names: von Blanckensee, Shoshana, author.
Title: Girls girls girls: a novel / Shoshana von Blanckensee.
Description: New York: G. P. Putnam's Sons, 2025.
Identifiers: LCCN 2024046955 (print) | LCCN 2024046956 (ebook) | ISBN 9780593718445 (hardcover) | ISBN 9780593718452 (ebook)
Subjects: LCGFT: Bildungsromans. | Queer fiction. | Novels.
Classification: LCC PS3622.O653 G57 2025 (print) | LCC PS3622.O653 (ebook) | DDC 813/.6—dc23/eng/20250113
LC record available at https://lccn.loc.gov/2024046955
LC ebook record available at https://lccn.loc.gov/2024046956

Printed in the United States of America
1st Printing

The authorized representative in the EU for product safety and compliance is Penguin Random House Ireland, Morrison Chambers, 32 Nassau Street, Dublin D02 YH68, Ireland, https://eu-contact.penguin.ie.

For S. J. Kahn, and the broader us

I remembered how good it felt to have the wind in my hair,
even though I was running for my life.

—Kathleen Hanna, *Rebel Girl: My Life as a Feminist Punk*

Preface

Dear Reader,

In the mid- to late nineties, when I was a teenager, before the widespread use of the internet or cell phones, long before social media, before queer people were represented on television or in movies (unless their role was to hurry up and die), I went out in search of queer community the only way possible—feet to the pavement.

Even though I grew up in the Bay Area, I had no way of knowing that the golden era of dyke culture was in full bloom in the Mission District of San Francisco until I stumbled my way into it. And when I did, I was desperate to stay. I'd found my people and my place, and I finally belonged. The problem: San Francisco was a city I couldn't afford. I was nineteen, a college dropout, and had a strained relationship with my family. But I had one thing worth a lot of money: my body. I found a strip club off Market Street, the Chez Paree, and cashed in.

Stripping and sex work were commonplace among queer people in my community at the time. It wasn't that we were all helplessly and hopelessly down and out, we just weren't going back to where we came from—the places in which we had to shrink ourselves—and San Francisco was expensive. I personally chose stripping over "better" options. I could have returned to my family and been fed and housed, but I felt like an alien in my childhood home. Stripping gave me the freedom to stay in my city, and staying in my city made life doable, right at the moment when I felt like I couldn't do it.

Girls Girls Girls is very much fiction, but it began from the seeds of lived experience, and it's taken me almost twenty years to write. Early on I wrote to process the choices I made, the shame I held, and the chasm I felt between myself and my family of origin. As the years went on, the book transformed into a love letter to my younger self, and a love letter to a lost time of San Francisco, the people and places that raised me in my early years.

I've written this book with an eye for accuracy of time, place, and culture. Every location mentioned in the book existed in San Francisco in 1996, and the language used reflects the limited language we had for our identities at the time. It's my hope that I can take your hand and pull you back with me, show you what it was like when there was nothing "cool" about being gay, show you the ways we found one another and wove ourselves into makeshift families. What I hope more than anything is to illustrate this: While we may have clung to each other out of necessity, the fruit of that necessity was a love and devotion uniquely, definingly queer.

Shoshana

Author's Note

This novel uses language authentic to queer culture in San Francisco in the mid-1990s, a time of gender rebellion and exploration that informed today's more roomy and nuanced understanding of gender identity. For this reason, you won't see expansive pronoun use, or terms like *nonbinary*, *trans*, *masc*, or *gender fluid*. Instead, you'll see words like *femme*, *butch*, *dyke*, and *fag*. These words are historically accurate, chosen with intention, and typed with bucketloads of love and nostalgia.

Girls
Girls
Girls

Part One

On the Road.

June 1996.

1

Sam doesn't think I'm weird. I know by the way she rolls toward me, by the way she reaches for me, her fingers tangling in my hair. In the damp of the van, she bites my neck and wraps a leg over my hip, her knee high on my ribs, the weight of her thigh rolling me onto my back. Our sleeping bags have shifted and the industrial carpet scrubs against my skin, the smell of the life it had before us souring the air. She finds my mouth with hers right as the storm cracks, the rain pecking at the roof like gravel. I feel my heartbeat rise into my neck and ask, "What if a cop pulls up?"

Sam doesn't say anything. She sinks me in her hair, still wet from our swim; her warm breath; her dewy skin. She pushes her hips into me like, *Come on. Why are you so scared? Do it.*

I slide my hand between her thighs. I want her more than I'm scared. We aren't in Long Beach anymore. I don't have to listen for the sound of footsteps in the hall. I don't have to double-check the twist lock on my bedroom door.

Even though we left Long Beach early this morning, we've only made it to the swimming quarries on the outskirts of Stroudsburg, Pennsylvania. One of Sam's pockmarked cousins told us about this place, described the graffiti on the turnout sign, marked the spot on our map with an X.

Sam led me by the hand, out of the van and into the woods, through the buggy shade of the birch trees until they stopped abruptly, dumping us into sun. A rocky bowl the size of a football field pitted itself in the earth before us, the sky mirrored on the water. It was like looking into an enormous eye.

We ditched our clothes, scattered them on a boulder, and spent the afternoon spitting long streams like fountain cherubs, jumping into backflips, doggy-paddling wide circles around each other. Treading water in the center, I watched Sam's head ride the surface toward me like a magic trick. We explored a shelf of granite, stood naked on it, shin-deep in warm water. I pushed my short hair back with both hands, closed my eyes, and opened my chest toward the sun, thinking about the last time I'd felt its heat on my naked body. I was four, maybe five years old, decorating the sukkah in the backyard with Bubbe and my sister, Rachel, in preparation for Sukkot. My clothes were itchy and tight, so I'd wriggled out of them. It was late September and my mother had objected through the kitchen window. "She'll get cold!" she'd shouted, eyeing my dress and underwear discarded in the crabgrass. "Nu?" Bubbe said, and shrugged. "So she'll get cold." A frown had settled on my mother's face before it migrated like a bird into my chest.

Sam yelled my name and it echoed through the quarries. I opened my eyes and found her with a half smile, her hands cupped and dribbling, a tadpole circling the pool in her palms, like a turd with a tail doing laps.

"Let's get you pregnant," she said.

"Gross!" I laughed, covering my crotch with both hands. "Marriage before babies!"

"We'll have nine months. We'll get married when we get to San Francisco," she said.

"You're such a dork." I shook my head. "And girls can't get married anyway, not even in San Francisco."

"Who says?"

"The law?"

"Then we'll break the law," she said, grinning. I pushed her wet hair from her shoulders, leaned in, and kissed her. She must have dropped her tadpole, because her hands moved to my waist, her breasts and belly pressing into mine. Away from Long Beach we could do this in daylight. We could swim back across the quarry when the clouds rolled in, make it to the van before the storm. We could find each other in the mess of sleeping bags and wet towels and empty coffee cups. She could pin me against the industrial carpet, and I could move inside her until she quaked in my hands, the sound of her free to rise now, free to lift in the hammering rain.

Sam and I met on the first day of eighth grade when our science teacher, Mr. Jeeter, plucked her from a group of chatty girls and punished her with a seat between April and me. April had crossed her arms over her chest and shot me a smirk that drew a circle around the two of us, a signal that we shared a disdain for this particular type of girl, the overly friendly type who took a crimper to her blond ponytail. But when Mr. Jeeter turned his back, Sam told April she liked her thick black eyeliner, she said it was cool and she wished her mom would let her wear more makeup than just lip gloss. April, disarmed by the compliment, opened her mouth to respond but said nothing. I watched Sam pinch her palms between her knees, cross her ankles and swing them back and forth under her chair, before turning to me.

"And you," Sam whispered. "You have pretty eyes."

I remember sitting there feeling like I'd won a prize, the sleeves of my Esprit sweatshirt pulled over my hands, my long mousy hair matted privately at the nape of my neck. I studied her. She had a gap between her two front teeth and amber eyes with dark flecks in them.

"Yours are amber with little—"

"Little bits of prehistoric insect legs," she said.

That day after class, Sam followed us out to eat our bagged lunches on the field behind the cafeteria. She asked us if we'd heard the new Smashing Pumpkins album, then looked shocked when we told her no.

"Why aren't you sitting with them?" April asked, angling her chin in the direction of the girls Sam had been talking to in class.

"They're fine," Sam said, "for normies. Maybe I like you guys better."

April shot me a glance, this time curious, while Sam explained she'd just transferred in from a Catholic school and was looking for friends who weren't 110 percent lame like the ones she'd had in seventh grade. She said her parents were splitting up and splitting up was expensive. They couldn't afford private school anymore, but it was fine since she'd hated it anyway.

"We're not even Catholic, and dress codes are idiotic," she scoffed. April agreed. I did too. The circle was redrawn.

We spent eighth grade in cahoots, complaining about everyone and laughing at everything: our buzzkill teachers telling us to spit out our gum; George Bush's comments on his distaste for broccoli; the boys who yelled "Booyah!"; and the girls who called the guys "toys," cackling audaciously like they'd really flipped the script.

By the time summer rolled around we were jumping the waves at Neptune Beach with our hands clasped together. We shared Popsicles and popped each other's zits. We passed a single journal between us, taking turns entering long-winded whiny rants and cataloging our big dreams: where we would go and what we would do. *Promise we'll be best friends forever,* April had written. To seal the deal, Sam made us promise bracelets. They were like regular friendship bracelets but better, with beads knotted into the threads. "You hold each one, make a vow, and say our names," she explained, "like rosary beads." She wrapped them around our wrists and tightened them with her teeth.

On the night before we started high school, Sam brought us to her house and painted my nails gold, while April and I hung open our jaws watching the "Pretend We're Dead" music video on MTV. Neither of us had that channel.

"That drummer's a girl," I said.

"They're all girls," Sam said. My eyes bugged wider.

"I can't believe your mom pays for MTV," April said.

"She can't afford it, my dad pays for it even though he doesn't live here anymore," Sam said. "He's an alcoholic. He just moved in with his fake-boobs girlfriend in Manhattan, and I think he feels guilty."

I darted my eyes at April, wondering if she'd say anything about her birth mom, the addictions that had crumpled her childhood up like paper. Instead, she offered, "Well, my real mom doesn't even know who my dad is, and my foster dad is *so* not cool. He's obsessed with baseball and collects Yankees shit and puts it up on the walls like it's decoration."

I thought I could win the Disappointing Dad prize. "Mine died when I was three," I chimed in. "I don't remember him at all."

We looked at each other knowingly.

Once we started ninth grade, I began taking them to Bubbe's after school. We'd sit on the stools at her counter, devour hot apple cake, rugelach, warm challah, while she told us stories about growing up in the tenements, her father schlepping her up and down the stairs on his back until she was strong enough to climb them with her arm crutches. Sam's mom had recently taken a job at a car dealership an hour and a half away in Yonkers, and Sam was hungry for baked goods but also attention. Bubbe provided both. "The three of you eat like soldiers," Bubbe would tease before sliding another serving onto each of our plates. "Samantha, come. See if you recognize who's in here," Bubbe would say, lifting her chin and pointing to the gold locket slung from her neck. And Sam would happily oblige every time, prying it open with her fingernails to coo at the baby pictures of Rachel and me inside.

April, on the other hand, moved shyly around Bubbe. She'd learned the hard way to keep her mouth shut around adults, especially adults as warm and kind as Bubbe. It had been warm and kind adults who'd gently asked about her homelife, the scant contents of her Care Bears lunch box, softly eyeing her dirty clothes, her unwashed hair. April had tried and ultimately failed to protect her mother from CPS intervention and was placed in foster care at age ten. A home with kind Christian parents doing "the good work of God," a foster dad who loved the Yankees, a foster mom who taught Sunday school. At church, adults leaned in to tell her how lucky she was.

"Are people constantly telling you you're lucky?" she asked us once. Sam and I both said no. "They took me from my mom! Why do people always tell foster kids they're lucky?"

"Because they're stupid," Sam offered.

"Yeah. Stupid," I agreed.

Nearly all my high school memories feature the three of us together: the goth foster kid, the awkward Jewish girl, the pretty one who could have been popular if she'd tried a little harder. It was always the three of us, until something shifted. Sam and I shifted.

The summer before our senior year I started to feel Sam's gaze holding me when I wasn't looking, and when I'd glance at her and ask, "What?" she would smile at me until I covered my face with my hands. Sometimes, just looking at each other would trigger a long bout of the giggles. April kept telling us we were being super weird. I could see by the way it quieted Sam, *super weird* was a slight she couldn't bear. That's when she started asking me to hang out alone, without April. Not all the time, but enough that it wouldn't go unnoticed.

When classes ended on the first day of our senior year, Sam and I snuck off, just the two of us, to her house. On the count of three, we fell backward into the hammock that hung between two trees in her yard. She wrapped her legs around me. I swallowed. She took my hands in hers, examining my fingernails, praising the ones I hadn't bitten to stumps, testing the length of each by dragging it across her cheek, then her lips. I couldn't speak.

It went on like this, ditching April a few times a week to sneak off with Sam. April was losing her footing, and she knew it. She'd ask where we'd been, why we hadn't invited her. I'd flush with guilt while Sam stumbled through excuses. And April would pretend to buy them—put on a forced smile, the hurt seeping through her stale grin.

One afternoon, Sam and I sat side by side in front of her closet-door mirror. We made up a game where we pretended to be conjoined twins in one stretched-out T-shirt. The goal: to suck each other's thumbs without laughing. Impossible. It took a zillion attempts, always aborted by someone's cackling. When we finally pulled it off, our eyes caught in the glass and went soft, the heat we'd stumbled upon undeniable. It was silly, but with Sam even childish games had become seduction. When she slept over, the lights would go out and she would pull me closer under the covers, falling asleep with her nose against my back. I would lie awake for hours. My heart thudding, judging the gravity of the situation. I was falling for a girl, and the girl was Sam. There had never been anyone more compelling, or anything more terrifying. I would never act on it, I promised myself, never admit it to her or anyone else.

But then, on a regular old Wednesday in November, Sam and I were bundled in coats, hoods pulled up, sitting in the dirt underneath the bleachers while the sun went down. Her amber eyes practically glowed. She slid her ChapStick over her lips and then held it up in front of me.

"You want some?" she asked.

I said sure. But instead of swiping the tube along my lips like she usually did, she capped it, pinned my head in her hands, and wiped the ChapStick on me with her spearmint-flavored gooey lips. Then she paused, my head still pinned; looked me in the eyes; and kissed me for real. Her mouth was warm and wet and slow, and I melted into it. Even after she pulled away, my whole body continued to hum.

"Did you get enough?" she asked.

I rubbed my lips together, while heat spread across my face, burning my ears. I knew I had turned splotchy and red, and the thought of turning splotchy and red made me more splotchy and red. I looked down at my shoes.

"Why are you blushing, Hannah Banana?" She laughed. I wanted to look up and see if she was blushing too, but I couldn't. The only thing I could do was grin, keep my eyes on the ground.

After that, I was wrecked. Totally dead. At that point I still thought boys were inevitable, and eventually I'd have to find an entire husband, but with that kiss Sam became everything, blotting out the rest of the world. I wanted to tie myself to her like a carnival balloon, string knotted at her wrist. How would I ever find some tolerable Jewish boy, invite him to Shabbat on Friday, when I belonged to Sam? Sammie, Sam, Sam. Sammie with the thick thighs, Sammie with the amber eyes.

The rain has lifted by the time we're dressed and buckled in the front seats of the van. This time I take the wheel and Sam sits shotgun, her right foot up on the dash and her finger on the *Rand McNally Road Atlas* spread across her lap. We stop at a Dairy Queen in a two-block town and order a cheeseburger combo with a side of ranch and a strawberry Blizzard. The burger's for me, and the fries are all Sam's. We share the rest.

"Which would you rather?" Sam asks. "Me, or a million dollars?"

"Shut up." I grin, hooking my ankles around hers under the table.

"Okay, how about *being* the Noxzema girl, or being *with* the Noxzema girl?" she asks.

I lean in. "I thought *we* were together," I whisper. She opens a palm, waiting for a real answer. "I just like her hair! That's all I said!"

"Come on, Hannah."

"Play with her hair, *be* with you."

Sam tries to look annoyed, but her eyes glimmer, a

corner of her mouth turning up and giving her away. She thinks for a minute, sweeping the sides of the empty ranch cup with the last fry.

"My mom on her worst day, or your mom on her best day?"

"Seriously?" I ask.

"You read the letter she gave me, right?" Sam asks, as if this would give me pause. Her mom had written out a laundry list of warnings intended to keep us safe and paired it with a canister of pepper spray.

"Your mom's always trying so hard."

"Trying to scare the shit out of us so we change our minds and stay in Long Beach forever?" she asks, bugging her eyes.

That's not what I mean and she knows it, but she's not interested in discussing it anymore. She turns to look at the menu above the counter. "Still hungry," she says.

I offer her the rest of the burger, but she shakes her head, wrapping her arms over her chest at an angle. I know what she's doing. She's referencing the *New York* magazine cover she had taped to her bedroom wall. Cindy Crawford posed naked wearing only an earflap hat with an anti-fur pin on it. If Sam had any willpower, she'd be vegan. A few months ago, she told April and me that fur for fashion was the next AIDS and PETA was the next ACT UP. I didn't understand why one needed to replace the other. I hated the idea of PETA, with their perfect nude celebrities, dominating center stage. The number of AIDS cases was still rising, no end in sight, I wanted to argue. Instead, I just listened. April had never heard of ACT UP. Sam explained they were activists fighting for more money and research for the AIDS crisis. San Francisco had burned itself into our minds a few months prior when we'd learned about ACT UP from a segment on *PBS NewsHour.* Sam and I had perched ourselves on the edge of the couch next to my mother, waiting impatiently for her to leave so we could take over the TV. She was folding laundry and finishing up *NewsHour* with Jim Lehrer. It ended with a segment on the White House Conference on AIDS. An activist had interrupted Bill Clinton's speech to demand action on the recommendations from the AIDS commission. The segment cut to a newscaster outside holding a microphone in front of a woman who was gripping the corner of an ACT UP banner.

"Can you say a few words about why you're here today?" he asked. My eyes scanned her shirt: *The Lesbian Avengers,* the words circling an image of a black bomb, the sleeves cut off, shoulders square and strong, hair cut short. My heart pounded with recognition. Sam's elbow dug into my ribs. I didn't dare budge, afraid my mother would notice even the smallest shift in expression. I needed to see, and know, without being seen or known.

"My girlfriend and I flew all the way out here from San Francisco to say enough is enough! Our brothers and sisters are dying!" she yelled, her eyes daring the camera to take the first swing. The segment snapped closed, and Jim Lehrer wished us a good night. My mother's mouth shriveled.

She tsked, shaking her head as she stood up to gather the laundry and leave the room, while I imagined a place called San Francisco. A place where you could cut your hair short and have a girlfriend. A place where people believed in the authority of their own hearts. A place where you could blast the injustices of the world with mouths loud as megaphones.

"We need to take pictures," I say as we head back to the van in the Dairy Queen parking lot. I pull my disposable camera from the glove box, and Sam swings the driver's-side door open, puts her foot up on the running board, and tousles her hair in the wind.

"Sammie with the thick thighs, Sammie with the amber eyes," I singsong to her. She smiles wide and laughs, clearly amused. "I've been singing that in my head for a whole year."

"Oh my god, I love you," she says, her eyes shimmering through the lens. Her words light a handful of sparklers in me. We've always said *I love you*, but it's different now. She tips her chin down and her eyes up, closing her lips over her teeth.

"Smile with your cute teeth," I say. She laughs and I snap the picture before she can hide them again. Then we climb back into the van, let out a puff of exhaust when the engine turns, and get back on the highway. Twenty-eight hundred miles to go.

This morning before we left Long Island, Sam and I had met up on our bikes to pick up the van, Sam gliding on her cruiser, hair blowing behind her like a fancy horse, while I looped figure eights around her. At a stop sign, a friend of my mother's from Beth El crossed in front of us, a folded shopping cart with a squeaky wheel in tow. "Gut Shabbos," she said, eyeing my bare legs splayed over my bike. I tugged at the hem of my shorts. "Gut Shabbos," I mumbled back. I wondered if she had heard I was moving to San Francisco. I had been imagining the sound of my name spoken in kitchens across Long Beach for weeks. Kitchens I'd never even been in.

"Gut Shabbos," Sam parroted in a high whisper as we took off pedaling again. I shot her a playful glare. Sam had been the ears for all my resentments, but I could barely tolerate someone who wasn't Jewish mocking a woman as frum as my own mother.

When we arrived at Sam's uncle's garage, he slapped the keys into her hand with a high five and leaned against the hood while explaining he'd fixed up the air-conditioning, rotated the tires, and given it an oil change at no extra charge. "Don't you forget to call your mom," he said as he hugged her goodbye, patting her back a few times. "I don't have time to track you down way out in California."

We'd been saving for this van since we'd hatched our

escape plan in mid-March. Sam had babysat for the family next door twice a week, and I'd picked up a job at Rudy's Wash N Fold on Sunday mornings, folding hot laundry into perfect squares. Our earnings, along with my untouched Bat Mitzvah money and Sam's Christmas and birthday cash, had bought us this white 1985 Chevy Astro. We named her Scooby after the Mystery Machine in *Scooby-Doo.*

"Scooby's a total kidnapper van!" I laughed. "April would love it."

"*I* love it!" Sam said, gripping the steering wheel and peppering it with kisses.

"Are you sure we shouldn't say bye to April?" I asked.

Sam shook her head. "That would be mean. We're doing big things like we always said we'd do. We don't need to rub it in."

April wasn't doing big things. She wasn't doing anything. She was smoking weed and skimming from her foster parents' pain pills, skateboarding in cat-eye sunglasses to the 7-Eleven for chips. We'd fallen out and now she had no one. My heart hurt. I imagined April doing her epic goth makeup, only to sweep it all off with a mildewed washcloth and get back in bed. I knew there was no convincing Sam, so we skipped the April goodbye and headed straight for my house. Once we pulled up in front of my driveway, we sat in silence for a few minutes staring at the front door, my body stiff at the thought of facing my mother.

"Devil's doorway," Sam said, her voice solemn.

"Sam!"

"Donner party doorway where people eat their young," Sam amended.

"I'm pretty sure the Donner party ate their elders, or whoever died first."

"Maybe you could just sneak in, get your stuff, and go."

"What about Rachel?" I asked, kicking the passenger door open. "Plus, my mom would kill me if I didn't say goodbye."

"But you wouldn't be around to get killed!" Sam called as I slammed the door behind me.

I climbed the steps, slid my key into the lock as quietly as I could, and pushed the door open a crack, but I immediately saw my mother, standing in the living room with a hand on her hip, her whole face pinched at the mouth. I froze.

"Leaving on Shabbos," she said, shaking her head. I dropped my gaze. "So you're unhappy, but you think unhappy people aren't unhappy in San Francisco?" she asked. "You'll see, wherever you go, there you are."

I fumbled through an apology, tried to scoot past her to my room, but she followed, airing her grievances. She could never understand. Wherever I went, as long as it was away from here, there I would be, without a witness, without a cage. I wanted to be the magician who escaped from underwater chains and surfaced to air and more air and more air, all the air I could ever imagine.

Rachel came out of her room and brought with her immediate relief. She wrapped me in a hug and rocked me back and forth.

"Goodbye, little sister," she said. She was trying to sound cheerful, but the tone of her voice gave her away.

"Zay gezunt mayn shvester!" I sang back. I would be cheerful for the both of us.

My mother didn't say goodbye. She retreated to her room before Rachel released me from her arms. Rachel looked toward my mother's closed door, then back at me, holding something in her eyes I couldn't decipher, before she put on a smile and offered to help load the van.

"Did you pack your winter coat?" she asked.

"We're going to California!" I protested.

She lifted her eyebrows. "California winters aren't hot, Hannah. Bring it with you. And you have the calling cards, and your driver's license, and your phone book, right?"

I nodded.

"Don't let each other out of view. And remember to call." She hugged me again at the curb, hugged Sam, then returned to me for another. "Promise me you'll be safe," she whispered before releasing me from her arms.

As we drove away, she kissed both of her hands and held them over her head until we lost sight of each other. I felt a punch of guilt leaving her behind. But she had her new job as a teaching assistant at the Jewish Community Center preschool. She had friends. Her life would be easier without me. She could handle Mom. And now she wouldn't have to defend me all the time. Maybe now they wouldn't argue at all.

Our next stop was Bubbe's. Sam and I chased each other

up the wheelchair ramp on the side of the house, swung the screen door open, and startled her in the kitchen.

"Bubbe!" I cheered. I watched her catch herself with her forearm crutches and then lean back against the counter.

"Oy, Hannah, you scared the sh—" she started, before slapping a hand over her mouth. We laughed and she looked thoroughly pleased. "Is this it?" she asked.

Sam answered by throwing her arms around Bubbe.

Bubbe packed a white paper bag full of apricot hamantaschen, mandelbrot, and kichel for us, then gestured with her head for me to follow her. In the living room she pulled a book from the shelf, opened it, and lifted the green velvet cover of its secret compartment to reveal a stack of bills.

"I have this for you," she said, holding the money out toward me. "But this is what you use when you run out of money. You don't spend it on sunglasses or gum. This is bread and eggs money, capisce?"

I looked at Sam, who stood in the doorway. She turned away into the kitchen.

"Go on, take it," Bubbe said, pushing it toward me. "I want to give this to you with a warm hand."

"It seems like a lot of money."

"Three hundred dollars, it won't break the bank," she said.

I pushed the cash into my sweatshirt pocket. "Mom would hate that you gave us money, it's practically wishing us well." I laughed.

She didn't laugh with me. "I *do* wish you well," she said,

taking my face in her palms. I watched her eyes redden and gloss over. I had never seen her cry. I wasn't ready to see it. She was my bubbe, she was my anchor. "She's just afraid, bubbeleh. Have patience," she said. "She's afraid for her child."

I'd told Bubbe about our plans to move to San Francisco before I'd told my mother. We'd go as soon as we graduated. A new place, a fresh start, an adventure. Bubbe didn't like it, chipped away at it with questions, but stopped when she saw my face begin to cave. No matter how much she didn't like it, she could see one thing clearly: I needed this. The move had become the hinge in my mind, on which I'd hung the door—to what, she wasn't sure, but she could see I'd deemed it vital. She wouldn't fight me on it. Instead, she took it upon herself to get to my mother first, tell her my plans, and bear the initial brunt of her rage.

"The answer is no!" my mother commanded, her voice low and stern. I'd come home a couple of days later to find the two of them at the dining room table. I knew immediately what I'd walked into. She stood and sliced the air with the edge of her palm. "You're a child! You can't even keep your bath towel off the floor, you couldn't survive a day out there!"

Her breath was tight and shallow in the silence that followed. I felt Bubbe's eyes reaching for mine, but I couldn't bear to meet her gaze.

"Out!" my mother snapped. "I can't stand your face right now."

I shifted back and forth in my Vans, wondering if she really meant it.

"Gay kocken offen yom!" she shouted.

That's what sent me bolting. Bubbe's voice cut in as I slammed the front door behind me. I stood panting on the stoop, a pressure building in my face, tears readying themselves, but I had nowhere to go. I couldn't walk around crying, waiting to run into the questioning eyes of a classmate or someone from Beth El. This town was suffocating me. Why couldn't she see that? I sat down on the steps, wrapped my arms around my legs, and pressed my eyes into my knees until I saw the splattering of the wide universe across the dark. I rocked back and forth and pleaded for a way into my mother. A way into my mother would be the only way out of here.

A few days after the blowup, I stood outside of her bedroom a full ten minutes before I had the courage to step into her line of sight. "Can we talk about it now?" I asked from the doorway. She was sitting up in bed reading. She put her book down in her lap and leaned back against the headboard, looking worn out already. Maybe worn out enough that this time would be different.

I was lucky, I'd found her in a moment of resignation. A moment in which she explained she wouldn't facilitate this idiotic plan in any way. That I could only go because legally she couldn't stop me. That if we made it all the way to San

Francisco, I would find a synagogue to attend. That when I came home after our inevitable failure, I would return to Beth El with her, I would return to Hashem, devote myself to him completely. That I would willingly try on the life she had hoped for me. It would be like putting on a new stiff coat. The longer I wore it, the more comfortable it would become, and before long I would chill at the thought of taking it off, she was sure of it. I nodded continuously without saying a word. I was a bobblehead on a dashboard. I agreed to everything she asked for.

2

My mother was unaware of the threat she held. She could find out about Sam and me. We had been secretly hooking up since the kiss under the bleachers in November, but our feelings for each other were more difficult to hide, and by January the rumors had started at school. Even though we weren't hanging out with her nearly as much as we used to, April loyally reported back the gossip. Nicholas Fenton had called me a dyke, said I'd probably bring Sam a stuffed bear and chocolates on Valentine's Day. She'd overheard him talking to a group of boys coming out of the gym. April's eyes moved from Sam to me, then back to Sam, as she told us, a question threaded underneath. A long silence followed. They both looked at me, waiting for a response, but Sam's eyes trembled, the tendons in her neck roping under her skin. I laughed at the absurdity of it, and soon April was laughing with me. I called him a dumbass. And Fenton *was* a dumbass, the way he blasted Hootie and the Blowfish from a boom box in the hallways, bobbing his head like a cockatoo.

I seemed to have successfully dodged April's suspicions, but the rumor was still spreading, and I was increasingly terrified it would reach my mother, so I took preemptive action. If she came in the room while Sam and I were loafing on the couch watching reruns of *Saved by the Bell*, my thigh would stiffen, lifting away from where it had lazed against Sam's. I no longer hugged Sam goodbye in front of my mother. I gave a tight wave instead, pushing the door closed as soon as she was on the other side.

But my mother was just existing, in her average brisk and sour ways, folding laundry, chopping onions, sorting bills, laboring in the ways women were endlessly laboring, ignorant of my efforts. She didn't know about Sam and me. She still doesn't. She'd already pinned her disdain on my mediocre grades, my mediocre friends, and my disinterest in Judaism.

I'd lost interest in religion at the same time and at the same pace my mother inched her way from Reform to Orthodox Judaism. I was three when my father died, but it wasn't until I was eleven that she started keeping kosher, that she tried to replace our jeans with calf-length dark skirts, that she tried to move Rachel and me from public school to a Jewish day school, finally giving up after a summer of listening to us beg. It was too late for us. Too late for me at least. I was no good at any of it. By that time I had more than my share of questions, always hesitating at the edge of what I was being asked to believe. And what I was being asked to believe dictated what I was being asked to do. I couldn't do it.

I couldn't keep kosher outside of the house, and I couldn't wear the long skirts to school without flushing with embarrassment. And even though I was failing to meet her demands already, my mother took things to the next level on a Saturday morning in eighth grade, when she forbade Rachel from making us pancakes. Now, she declared, the stove shouldn't be turned on until Shabbos ended. I sat and watched Rachel scrape batter into the trash, stewing over a cold bowl of Cheerios. I vowed from that point on to live a life with Saturday morning pancakes, and tank tops, and goyish friends, and movies she wouldn't approve of, like *Singles* and *Leap of Faith.* I was thirteen, and I could decide for myself. *I* would no longer be pelted with arbitrary rules without putting up a fight. But when I fought, my resistance unleashed a fury in my mother that drew Rachel between us. My head would drop, and I'd retreat to my room, press my ear to the door, listening for the treble of their voices.

Soon after I'd heard Fenton called me a dyke, I noticed Sam talking to him more. I felt her widen the gap between us in the hallway. Her eyes would no longer hold mine at school, her gaze instead drifting to everyone who passed. I knew what was happening, but it still hurt. When we were alone together, she cried and apologized. She assured me she was just scared.

I believed her. Until a frigid day in February. I'd called her, but she hadn't answered, so I assumed she was in the garage, which her father had insulated and turned into his "man cave" the year before the split. Lately, she'd been spending a lot of time in there—her "home away from home," as she called it. I walked over to find her.

Cutting up her driveway, I pushed the garage side door open a crack and stopped in my tracks. At first, I only heard it. Then I saw it. Sam pinned under Nicholas Fenton's scrawny body on the corduroy couch, her legs open. I heard her moaning, a sound I both recognized and didn't. It performed itself this time, desperately, like an audition for the only female role. Fenton was grunting and pumping like a dog, and I felt hate boil up inside me. I must have let out some guttural sound, because both of their heads whipped in my direction.

"Fuck you, Sam!" I screamed with every muscle in my body. I didn't wait for a response. I took off in a run, my legs kicking the icy ground, gloved fists punching the air. But I had nowhere to run to. No place that could hold this, no one who could know this.

I ended up at the beach, my hands planted on my knees while I heaved, lungs burning. And then I wept. I knew why she'd done it. Fenton was the path of least resistance, the easy road that distanced her from the rumors about me, the only plausible road in front of her. I took off my beanie and wiped my face with it. But there was no road for me without Sam. Sam was my flashlight. She was the only way I could see in this world. I felt the lights go out. I decided I would never speak to her again.

I couldn't unsee what I'd seen in the garage, and for days I was twitchy and electric with rage. I wanted to tear the world to pieces with my teeth. Godzilla through every window, flip all the picnic tables, and flatten Fenton's boom box with my reptile feet. At dinner when my mother recited the Hamotzi, I wanted to sweep my arms across the table, clatter all the food and dishes to the floor, and scream at the top of my lungs. Underneath my sullen exterior, I felt wild and reckless, but I couldn't show it, and I couldn't tell anyone why.

In math, April passed me a note torn from the corner of her handout.

Are we still friends?

Are you and Sam fighting?

What's going on?

All I could do was put my head down on my desk and try to keep the tears in, swallow around the hot coal lodged in my throat. After class, April hooked her arm in mine, pulled a root beer Dum-Dum from her bag, and offered it to me. I shook my head.

"I feel sick," I said.

She pulled her sunglasses out next.

"Here," she said, "don't advertise it."

The following Friday I skipped school and sulked. In the afternoon I tucked into our backyard shed with a mirror, scissors, and a box of L'Oreal Blackest Black hair dye. My breath plumed in the light of the bare bulb over my head. I was freezing, but nothing mattered anymore. I smoked a cigarette April had given me, pulled up the hem of my pants to singe the hairs on my ankle between drags, leaving a trail of pink burns. I'd only had a puff here and there at parties, and smoking the whole thing made me instantly queasy. But at least queasy was different, and I was desperate to feel anything but how I felt. A new look would make me feel different too. I would chop off my shoulder-length hair, like the Lesbian Avenger on the news, like Sinéad O'Connor, furious, unwilling to play the role she'd been given. Then I would dye it. Transform it from the apologetic mousy brown it had always been to a decisive black.

I started by cutting along the edge of the comb like a barber, but soon a recklessness took over. I bent forward and hacked haphazardly, littering the floor with chunks long enough to turn the shed creepy and criminal. When I flipped my head up, I ran my fingers through it, no snagging on tangles. I felt lighter, vaster, freer, but I would pay for this freedom. In the early evening my mother's Buick would pull into the driveway. She would come in and see me, and then she would kill me. But she had nothing left to kill, I reasoned, I had been dead a full week now.

I shook up the dye, and when the chemical stench filled the shed, I stepped out into the yard for fresh air. Rachel's face was framed in the window of the back door, and the shocked look she gave me shocked me right back. She swung the door open.

"Oh my gosh, Hannah! What are you doing! Mom's going to kill you!" she yelled. But it was an amused kind of yell, one that ended in a laugh.

I smiled and shrugged. "I'm sick of having boring hair," I said.

"It actually looks amazing. It's so Winona in *Reality Bites*," she said, reaching to touch it. "Can I help you dye it?"

We moved to the bathroom. I handed her the gloves that came in the kit, read the instructions out loud while she squeezed black stripes across my scalp, working the dye out to my ends. She trimmed the long bits I had left behind, then wrapped my head up in a plastic bag that read *Kosher for Pesach*. It made us both giggle. "Not kosher," she said. "Not kosher at all." We sat on the edge of the tub with the kitchen timer ticking, passing a box of Good & Plenty back and forth.

"Mom's going to lose her shit. She won't get it," she said.

"Do you think if Dad was alive he'd get it?"

She shrugged. "Maybe. I mean, he was the chill one. He was silly and fun. But if he were alive, she wouldn't have gotten all hard-core conservative. If he had never died, she might have gotten more chill like him."

I tried to imagine some alternate version of her, a version that would call me gutsy, run her fingers through my hair and say she loved it. A father I didn't remember next to her shaking his head, amused.

"When you say Mom won't get *it*, do you mean *me*?" I asked. I already knew the answer. Nobody but Sam knew me anymore. Not even Rachel, not even Bubbe now, not entirely anyway.

"I meant your hair. But she thinks you make trouble for yourself, and Jews have suffered forever and you're, like, making up your own imaginary suffering—"

"Ugh, Rachel! Aren't you sick of that? Are we supposed to spend our whole lives feeling crappy about all these suffering ancestors? Like the only way to make it up to them is to follow a bazillion rules and go to shul and marry a Jewish guy? Also, so many people's ancestors suffered, it's like we're trying to win, to be the most suffering sufferers!"

"Hannah! Don't talk like that!" She winced.

"I'm so sick of all of this," I said. "It's too much pressure. I can't even cut my own hair? She already thinks I'm an ungrateful, disrespectful asshole. It doesn't matter what I do anymore."

I watched her recoil at my words and open her mouth

like she was going to say something. But she threw a candy in and closed her lips. She waited a good minute before asking, "Hannah, don't you *want* to marry a Jewish guy? Not Conservative, but like a cute Reform guy?"

"I mean, I kinda do," I said, but looked away when I said it. I saw a Jewish guy with his face blotted out. I tried to position myself next to him, the two of us hand in hand like paper dolls. I wished I wanted to marry a Jewish guy. Couldn't that be good enough?

When Mom came home, Rachel and I were on the couch watching *The Sally Jessy Raphael Show.* We turned to each other with big eyes, before I closed mine tight and pulled my knees to my chest. I heard my mother stop in her tracks.

"Hannah!" she yelled. "No. No. Oy gevalt! No! Hannah, look at me!"

"Winona Ryder actually—" Rachel interjected.

"Rachel, stay out of this," she commanded. "Hannah, lift up your head and look at me." She said it firmly, in the tone she reserved for the worst of the worst. I lifted my head and looked at her.

"I walked into this house and thought, *Who is that on my couch?* You look like a *man*," she said, her jaw clenched, a vein in her neck standing up. "No. No, you actually look like an ugly lesbian, Hannah. That's exactly what you look like."

"Mom—" Rachel tried again.

"Keep out of it, Rachel," she said, before turning back to sink her teeth in. "When will you learn, Hannah? When you refuse to go to shul, when you keep the company you keep, and when you do this kind of thing to yourself, you hurt yourself. You spit on yourself. What you do is shameful for all of us, Hannah."

"Mom!" Rachel's voice was loud, and it cracked this time. I ran to my room and slammed the door before I could hear them get into it. Rachel would protect me. Rachel, always the referee.

A couple weeks later April skipped school, so I was alone all day. I successfully dodged Sam, but after the bell rang, she spotted me and followed me out through the gates insisting we talk. I scrambled for my Walkman, pulled my headphones on, pressed play, and dialed the volume as high as it could go. Courtney Love screamed in my ears, daring me to take everything. I glared at Sam's mouth moving around words I couldn't hear until her eyes reddened and she gave up.

Alone again, I flung my backpack in circles, slamming whatever asked to be slammed, a fence, a telephone pole, a fire hydrant. It was a cold day in March and wind was blowing in from the Atlantic. I let my tears run loose with it, horizontal into my ears. I tumbled out toward the beach.

On the boardwalk I stopped and peered into the steamed windows of the arcade. A group of boys from my school swarmed around a new game, fist-bumping, hooting like baboons. Behind them, in the far corner, I spotted Todd Lobach playing pinball, his pale-knuckled hands thrumming the machine, Adam's apple bobbing in his neck. Todd and I had been paired as reading buddies in elementary school. He wasn't loud and dumb like stupid Nicholas Fenton. He was shy and not popular but also not unpopular. Mostly he wasn't anything at all, and maybe I could like him.

I will like him, I thought to myself. *I will like him whether I like him or not.*

I wiped my eyes and nose on my coat sleeve and cleared my throat a few times before I pulled the door open and stepped into the hot stink of BO. I headed straight for Todd, thumping him on the back with my fist when I got to him. He spun around, his arms up to block his face, until he saw it was just me.

"Why'd you do that?" he asked.

"Put your jacket on," I instructed.

"Why?" he asked, pulling it over his shoulders.

I never answered. I wrapped my hand around his skinny wrist and dragged him from the arcade, down the stairs, and under the boardwalk into the heavy shadows, inhaling the thick, cold smell of damp wood.

I marked that afternoon. Checked it like a box. Lay back in the grit, in the smell of piss, yanking Todd over me.

"What are you doing?" he asked. His breath smelled like Doritos.

"What do you *think* I'm doing?" I said, pulling him on top of me. He looked unsure until I put a hand on his crotch. I told him to take off his pants.

"Here? It's freezing!" he bleated.

"Do you have a condom?" I asked.

I watched him fumble with his Velcro wallet, pulling one out. He yanked down his zipper.

My jeans were shoved to my ankles, tying them together, when he pushed his way inside of me. It burned and I winced. *Please don't try and kiss me*, I begged, but only in my head. I turned away toward the strip of gray beach, gray ocean, gray sky, layered like gloomy sediment. My teeth chattered, and Todd humped me like a dog. A dog just like Fenton. But I wasn't just like Sam. I wasn't like Sam at all.

When I got home I showered, then sat on the edge of my bed wrapped in a towel. How would I do it again and again, forever and ever, for the rest of my life? My room cramped tight around me and took me by the neck. *Who are you?* it asked.

I flopped back, closed my eyes, and felt a tremor rising inside of me, projected out in time in front of me. Not because of what I'd done with Todd under the boardwalk, but because of the answer it gave me. What would this life be like? How would I live, now that I was sure?

By mid-March, it had been over a month since I talked to Sam, more than a month since I'd seen her with Fenton in the garage. With Sam out of the picture, April and I were spending more time together. She tried to cheer me up—brought me a skull and crossbones sticker for my binder, offered me the Capri-Sun in her lunch, drew a heart on the back of my hand—but I'd gone quiet and gloomy, unable to appreciate her efforts or answer any of her questions. I was alone after school one day, walking down Lincoln Boulevard on my way home, when I heard my name called out. I turned around expecting to see April but saw Sam instead, running toward me, her cheeks red and wet. My eyes darted up and down the block. I couldn't risk ignoring her here. She was hollering my name, sobbing loudly, making a scene on a block with Moshe's Deli on one end and Glatt's Kosher Butcher on the other; there were eyes, extensions of my mother's eyes, all around us.

"What's wrong with you?" I demanded in a hush.

She stumbled on her words. She'd recovered a note passed from one dipshit to another. A note about me. I ripped it from her hands and read it:

I heard Hannah slept with Todd

Hannah who?

The one who just cut all her hair off

Dude, she looks like Halloween now

Yeah, I guess she isn't a dyke after all

I tore it in half and shoved it into my back pocket, my face flaming.

"Hannah, is that true?" she asked, grabbing my arm. "Is that true?!"

"Do you care or something?" I yelled back, unable to control my volume. My eyes darted up and down the block again in a panic.

Sam fell toward me sobbing, her forehead pressing into my chest, so that my heart leaned forward inside of me to meet her. We couldn't do this here. I glanced around and spotted a narrow walkway between two brick buildings. I pulled her into it, squeezing us behind a metal trash can. She pushed me against the wall and pressed her wet cheek against mine. Her breath was warm and choked in my ear and I couldn't help it, my arms threaded the place between her sweatshirt and backpack.

"I'm sorry, okay?" she cried. "How many times do you need me to say I'm sorry?"

My eyes welled in her hair. I couldn't help but love her. I loved the mossy smell of her, the dip in her lower back where I pressed my palms.

"But why did you do it?" I implored.

She looked at me. Shook her head, tears running down her cheeks.

"This is everything," she whispered, gesturing to the space between us. "I think about us all the time," she said, wiping her face with her sleeve. "All the time I'm thinking, *What would it be like if we could just be together?* But I know it's a fantasy, we can't just *be* gay, you know?"

"But what if we are?" I asked.

"We can't be," she said again, her voice cracking this time. "I don't like people talking about us like that. And if they knew for sure they'd go crazy with it. They'd be so awful to us, call us horrible names, ruin our lives. Our families would find out, and then what? I don't know what my mom would say, but yours would totally flip."

"So we can't be gay *here*," I said, pointing to the ground. "This is where we can't be gay. We just have to keep it a secret."

She looked at me, exhausted. Our secret had already turned into a blister, always hurting, always threatening to pop.

"We can do it," I pleaded. "We can keep it a secret until we graduate in June. That's only three months away."

Sam cocked her head, her eyes searching mine. "Then what?" she asked.

"Then we run away," I said, the idea lighting in my mind as it came from my mouth.

"What are you saying?" she asked. "You would leave Bubbe?"

I nodded, even though I couldn't imagine leaving Bubbe. Sam wrapped her arms around my shoulders.

"San Francisco?" she asked. "Like the Lesbian Avenger on the news?"

"Why not?" I asked.

"You would go that far?"

I couldn't go that far. But it was how far we would need to go.

"I mean, I would do it. If I was doing it with you," I said.

And this is how it started. A love pact. A gray day. Hoodies and backpacks. Wet faces grinning in a brick alleyway off Lincoln Boulevard. Our fingers weaving together. The electricity between us, firing off in every direction.

3

Sam and I squat and pee between Scooby and a chain-link fence in a dark Walmart parking lot. As we're climbing back in the van I startle at the sight of a racoon slinking toward a dumpster. I have no idea if Hazle Township, Pennsylvania, is dangerous or not, but it's tough to feel safe in a vacant parking lot at night anywhere. After checking the locks twice, I crawl into the back to set up our sleeping bags. Sam falls asleep almost immediately, her arm slung over my hip. But my new mosquito bites from the quarries keep me awake. I itch and sweat and worry, the letter from Sam's mom running circles in my head. *Don't ever sleep in the van. Don't ever leave the doors unlocked, especially if you're in it. Don't ever talk to anyone you don't have to talk to. If men ask you questions, you don't have to answer them. Your pepper spray goes everywhere you do. Everywhere.*

The doors are locked, the windows rolled up, the pepper spray within reach. But I'm still on edge, gearing up to fight whoever might come knocking. Eventually my vigilance is overcome by exhaustion. When we wake up sweaty and thirsty, it's light again. Sam unrolls the windows and we find the parking lot full of cars.

"Well, I guess we can get away with sleeping in Walmart parking lots," Sam says, pulling on her shorts.

"*Sleep* isn't quite the word for what I did."

"What do you mean?" Sam asks.

"I could barely sleep."

"Were you scared?"

I look at Sam, her head cocked like a puppy. Would it never occur to her to be scared sleeping in a van? I shrug, lean in, and kiss her.

"Somebody had to be ready to fight, right?" I ask, trying to sound light, like maybe I'm joking.

Sam wraps her arms around me and pushes me back down onto my sleeping bag, rolling herself on top of me, the weight of her hushing the worry. I hold her face in my palms, smoothing her eyebrows with my thumbs.

"Hannah, what if literally nothing bad happens to us?" she asks. I just look at her. "I mean, what if we do this like a couple of dudes, like we've got this, and we don't have to be scared just because we're girls. Do you really want to walk around cowering your whole life? Can't we be done with that? We're out of Long Beach."

I sweep her long hair behind her ears. "Do you actually believe that?" I ask. "That we're as safe as a couple of dudes?"

Sam thinks for a moment. "No," she says. "But I want to believe it. So I'm going to."

She leans in to kiss me. I want to laugh, but I can't quite get it out and her lips land on my teeth. It's been decided. We're in Sam's world, as safe as a couple of dudes. I run my hands down to her waist as she buries her face in my neck and bites. I feel her tugging my shirt up so she can get both hands underneath it. She cups my breasts in her palms, her thumbs on my nipples. I want to be frei. I've always wanted to be frei.

One summer when I was nine, I spent a hot Friday running through the sprinklers on our front lawn with the neighborhood kids. The grass made my legs itch, and I could feel my shoulders and cheeks burning in the midday sun, but I was untouchable. I was a wild panting animal, frenetic with the joy of my own muscled body. Bubbe came through the screen door, leaned her arm crutches against the house, and positioned herself on a patio chair to watch me play. At first, she just smiled when she caught my eye, but soon she was laughing and egging me on to run faster, leap higher, whooping out loud and slapping her thigh as I sailed over the sprinkler, escaping the two kids trying to tackle me. I loved feeling her eyes follow me. Within her gaze I gained superpowers. I had super strength. She beckoned me over with a finger, and when I arrived wet and panting, she grabbed me firmly by the chin.

"Meshugene meydl, ikh hob dich lib," she said. She smiled wide and pressed her nose against mine. I peered into her gray eyes. "Let me tell you a secret," she whispered. Her breath smelled like black coffee. "You are stronger and faster than all these boys." She flicked her hand in their direction. "When you grow up you can be anything you want to be. You can do anything you want to do. You can be *frei*, mammele."

I beamed in her light. She had whispered so the boys wouldn't hear. And neither would my mother from where she stood in the kitchen window wiping down the sink in preparation for Shabbos, Rachel at her side. For a moment my whole life flipped open and unfurled in front of me. It was expansive, illuminated, made of pure permission. Then she gave me a shove toward the sprinklers, and I stumbled back right as the streams tipped in our direction, the heavy drizzle sending me leaping, escaping again.

I stretch my fingers out the window, look over at Sam singing, driving us to our new life. This is what frei means to me.

The days move along, Iowa disappears in the rearview, and the landscape turns golden and flat. Sam and I talk and talk. We talk about our first kiss under the bleachers. We talk about Todd and Fenton. We talk about Long Beach, and music, and our mothers, and what we imagine San Francisco will be like. Hills surrounded by water. The

Golden Gate Bridge and another ocean we've never met. Gay people walking around like it's no big whoop. Could I kiss her at the movie theater and hold her hand walking down the street? It's so unimaginable and yet we bathe in the imagining, roll around like pigs in it, tell each other stories about it for miles and hours. But every time I think of my family, or Sam's mom, or April, the fantasy cracks, a slash of guilt cutting across it.

"Sammie, at the next rest stop we really need to call your mom," I say, adjusting the sun visor above the driver's seat to shade her eyes.

"I know," Sam says. "It's just she's going to stress me out with questions, and I have to lie about where we've been sleeping."

"Lying about where we've been sleeping is better than not calling. Right now she probably thinks we're dead in a ditch somewhere."

I haven't done much better. I called and left a message on Saturday when I knew my mom and Rachel would be at Beth El. It was such an obvious move.

"I'll call my mom, and Bubbe too," I say. But just like it did with Sam, anxiety washes over me.

In the early evening, we pull into a truck stop, in what seems like the middle of nowhere, but to our surprise it's a fully functional truck stop village, teeming with patrons. There's a gas station, multiple restaurants, fast-food joints, and a convenience store. We find the women's bathroom. It's cavernous. Our voices echo while we do a quick armpit wash in the sinks, giggling at each other when a woman walks in and finds us soaped up in our bras. On the way out, we swing the door open and accidentally smack a guy wearing a Harley jacket and a bandana pulled tight across his ruddy forehead.

"Oops! Sorry!" Sam says.

He acts shocked, grinning at us with wide eyes. "Pretty girls just appear out of thin air around here! Any more of you hiding in there?" he asks, peering behind us into the bathroom. He's waiting for us to laugh.

Sam gives in. "Nope!" she says, her voice cheery. "This is all of us!"

I drag her away by the elbow as we head across the parking lot to a long row of pay phones.

"What?!" she asks. "What's so bad about being pretty?"

When we get to the phones, Sam sighs dramatically, sagging her head and pushing out her lower lip for effect.

"We gotta just do it, Sam," I say.

Sam does a moody walk to the last phone in the row while I pick up the receiver at the other end. I take a deep breath. Then another. I decide to do the easy one first, pulling out the calling card Rachel gave me and dialing Bubbe's number.

"Hello?" she answers.

I'm more excited to hear her voice than I imagined. "Bubbe!"

"Mammele! Tell me all about it! Where are you!"

"Well, we're pretty far along, considering how slow the

van drives, about midway through Nebraska. Every state is so different than I imagined it would be. There's actually so much room the more west we go, but the food options get worse and worse. And Pennsylvania had a million tiny white churches that looked like they were out of a storybook." The words tumble from me. "We aren't spending much money, but the van is a total gas guzzler, so that's where the money goes. But really, we're doing great. Sometimes I look out the window and wish you could see what I'm seeing even when it's not super interesting. I mean, it's all just really different from Long Beach." My heart hurts with the miles between us.

"You are an adventurer, mammele. And you are living in a time when women can adventure. Do you know I've never been that far west before?" she asks.

I didn't know. And worst of all, with all my talking of driving to California, I never asked. Was I just like everyone else and limited her without question? Assumed travel was too hard for her with her disability and never asked where she'd already been? Where she wanted to go next?

"Bubbe, someday I'm going to take you somewhere. We'll travel together. I don't know where, but I promise, we'll do it."

Bubbe contracted polio during the epidemic in 1916. She was only two. It was called infantile paralysis at the time, and the tenement buildings on the Lower East Side were ripe conditions for an epidemic. There was no running water, no corner unused, a toddler asleep under every table. The tenements were packed with immigrants; Bubbe and her widowed father shared an apartment with a much larger family of Polish Jews. Over the course of a few days, Bubbe chattered with fevers, began vomiting, and then went quiet and listless. Her father bundled her in a blanket and ferried her to the hospital, where the doctors took one look at her and, speaking in a language he couldn't understand, pried her from his arms, disappearing her from view. He begged and cried, then resorted to insults, calling the doctor a chazer, a fonferer, a paskudnyak. But still he had to go home without her. The next day he returned with a neighbor who spoke English. This time he was allowed to see her through a glass window. She had been encased in a full-body cast. Her chest and arms in one piece, legs from her hips to her toes in another. Her father was ill with it, and no matter how many times it was explained, he couldn't understand why they would do this to his child. So he went home and came up with a plan. Once she had improved enough to have visits in the courtyard of the hospital, he waited until the nurses left him alone with her. Then he scooped her up, cast and all, and ran out. He ran all the way back to the tenement building, up the stairs, locking the door behind him and securing it with the chain. He put her on the kitchen table and found the razor from his shaving kit and slowly, very carefully, he cut open each cast. When he pulled her out, she was covered in sores and flaking skin, her legs and feet twisted up like earthworms. She always told the story with that same line, *twisted up like earthworms.* But I was always picturing her father in my mind's eye. I saw his wiry hair, his silk yarmulke, his glasses foggy with sweat and grief. And I saw my bubbe through his eyes, body too weak to grip him, too weak to hold her head up, pink and sticky, mewing like a newborn kitten.

"He thought the doctors had crippled me and he was furious. But his love made me very strong," she would tell me. She learned to climb the tenement stairs with arm crutches, lift her chin to the incessant teasing, and when a headmaster took one look at her legs and suggested she be moved to the school for the feebleminded, she pigeoned her chest and delivered the Pledge of Allegiance, in perfect English. Bubbe deserved adventure. She deserved an unobstructed road unfurling like a ribbon in front of her.

When I get off the phone with Bubbe and glance down the line of pay phones toward Sam, she's rolling her eyes, holding the black receiver to her ear, the other hand planted firmly on her hip.

"Mom, we *are.* Why are you so worried!" she whines.

Because she loves you more than she dislikes you, I think to myself, a wiry jealousy twisting inside me. My mother's worry looked an awful lot like loathing. I pull out the calling card again, bite the inside of my cheek, and dial home. Does my mother even love me? I'm not sure. I'm sure I'm an obligation. An obligation that has become too difficult to fulfill.

"Hello?" my mom answers. My heart pounds back.

"Hi, Mom," I say, the words tiptoeing out.

"Oy, Hannah, I'm sick with worry. I thought you would call again sooner. I need you to call more often. It's really too much not knowing where you are. Are you okay?" she asks. She *is* worried. I can hear it in her voice, and it's not plastered behind a wall of anger.

"Yeah, we're fine. We're halfway across Nebraska."

"You might find the middle of America to be very anti-Semitic," she warns.

I can't help but laugh. "Mom, nobody is asking if I'm Jewish! Being Jewish is not this huge thing like it used to be," I say.

She doesn't respond immediately. The silence is too long now, and I know I've taken a misstep.

"You are very naïve, Hannah," she says quietly, but with a bite I can feel through the line.

"Is Rachel there?" I ask.

"No, she's out with her friends at the beach."

I imagine Rachel at the beach. I hope she's rolling up her full-coverage swim shirt, exposing her belly to the sun the way she does in the backyard on the hottest days of the year. Suddenly I miss Rachel so much.

"Tell her I love her," I say.

"It would be nice if you showed it. You hurt her when you don't call," she says.

I feel heat rising in me, the tears following suit. "Mom, I could say the exact same thing to you! I literally have no clue if you love me or not!" I yell. I feel furious.

"Don't be ridiculous! Of course I love you! Look how hard I work to provide for you. How hard I try to guide you down the right path, but you don't listen, Hannah! You don't see how hard I'm trying."

"*You* don't listen! And *you* don't see how hard *I'm* trying!" I yell back at her, and then I hang up the phone. I stare at my knuckles, watch them blanch with the force I use to hold the receiver down. I've never hung up on her like that, and I feel the fear of repercussions, despite the distance. I stand motionless for a moment trying to loosen the breath caught in my throat. I'm not going home to her today, or tomorrow, or anytime soon. There are no repercussions, I remind myself. My hands are sweating and shaking. I slide them up and down on my shorts, trying to dry them.

I look back toward Sam, but she's gone from her pay phone. My eyes scan the parking lot and find her leaning against Scooby pouting. I need to shake it off, shed it like a snakeskin. I head toward her.

She opens the passenger door, creating a barrier between us and anyone who might walk by, then wraps her arms around my waist and leans her head on my shoulder. I look around, hesitant, but no one's in sight. I pull her in close to me.

"I hate my mom. And I love you," she says. "You're the only one I want to talk to ever again."

Nebraska is flatter than a thin-crust pizza, and the towns become less and less appealing the deeper in we get. Sam makes the same joke every half hour, saying, "Oh look, we're home now!" and gesturing to places like a broken-down shack in the shadow of a megachurch, or an abandoned trailer sunk low in a field of tall grass.

At the state line, we get out so I can take a picture of Sam under the *Welcome to Wyoming* sign. Big rigs drive by honking at us. This country gets whiter and less populated the farther in we go, and I don't know if it's because we only go to rest stops and gas stations, but there seems to be a disproportionate number of men. The world appears to be made up of white men in big rigs and trucks and RVs. They wave at us from Harleys, wink at us in fast-food restaurants, ask us what we're doing and where we're headed. They crack jokes and roll their eyes up and down our bodies. They call us *sugar, sweetheart, honey.* Sam says if we had a dollar for every leering man, we could stay at a nice hotel every night.

By the time we hit Salt Lake City, Utah, Long Beach has finally detached from us, like the caboose of a train. Sam doesn't call her mom again, and neither do I. Which means I don't get to talk to Rachel. But I still call Bubbe, give her the play-by-play of the landscape, everything we've seen and experienced, minus the leering men and the sleeping in the van.

By the time we're heading into Reno, Nevada, the landscape is dry, hot, and vacant. Red, rocky mountains lift in the distance, but mostly the road is taut and straight like a tightrope disappearing into the horizon. In the afternoon a city rises from it. I squint, the shimmer of a mirage obscuring my view.

"That's Reno!" Sam yells, her finger anchored on the map. As we get closer, we can see it's twinkling in colored lights like a Christmas tree.

We pull off the highway and head to the main strip, passing under a lit-up archway that reads: *RENO The Biggest Little City in the World.*

"Well, that's quite a claim," Sam says. "I guess they mean like me? Like, short with a big personality?"

"I can already tell I like you better than Reno," I say, peering up through the windshield at all the flashing signs. Everything is exaggerated, glitzy, and alive, but there's a sad down-and-out feel to it. At a red light, I watch a guy scoop handfuls of water into his mouth from a fountain in front of a casino.

Farther down the strip we approach a hotel called Circus Circus, marked by a three-story glowing neon clown advertising twenty-seven-dollar rooms and a five-dollar all-you-can-eat buffet.

"Oh my GOD!" I say, peering up at it.

"SOLD!" Sam shouts.

"Really?!" I ask. "This one?!"

"Yes! Look how creepy and awesome!" she says, leaning her head out to stare.

I pull the van into the circular driveway, under a pink-and-white-striped awning.

It turns out Circus Circus is a family-friendly hotel. It's crawling with kids, and inside, there's a ghoulish county carnival with merry-go-rounds and cotton candy and popcorn stands and a very small Ferris wheel.

Our room is magnificent. Better than magnificent. It makes Scooby look like a dumpster. Everything is magenta, neon orange, and maroon, and there are so many different patterns my eyes nearly cross just looking at them. I turn to Sam and cross them on purpose for effect. She shoves me onto the bed, and we squeal and wrestle with glee.

By the time we're showered and dressed, we're beyond starving and head downstairs for the five-dollar buffet. The host who greets us is a man in his forties with tidy hair, pencil-thin arched brows, and a skintight crushed-velvet suit on. Sam elbows me and gestures to him as we follow him to our booth.

"Thank you!" she says to him. And then loudly to me, "This is so romantic!"

He hands me a drink menu and I thank him before covering my face with it.

"Well, aren't you two cute," he coos.

After he leaves, Sam repeats it back to me, in a low sing-song voice: "*Well, aren't you two cute.*"

Sam fills her plate with eggplant parmigiana, fettucine Alfredo, potato salad, and fruit salad coated in something white. I eat bowls and bowls of oversalted chicken soup, bloated noodles floating belly-up. For dessert, Sam gets a fat slice of chocolate cake, and I grab some soft-serve covered in sprinkles with a side of tapioca pudding. We eat until our bodies refuse to carry us back to the buffet for another round.

"We got our money's worth," Sam says from where she's slumped low on her side of the booth.

Our host returns to ask how our meal was.

"It was great, we're stuffed," Sam says, patting her belly. "And we also have a question for you."

I'm already dying. Whatever the question is, I want to slide under the table and hide while she asks it.

"So . . . we want to go to a gay bar. Are there gay bars in Reno?" she asks.

Her boldness scares me. Suddenly I'm hot from head to toe.

"Do you want to go to a lesbian bar?" he asks, leaning in.

Sam looks at me. I think we're both surprised there is such a thing.

"Yeah, a lesbian bar, that's what I meant."

"Okay," he says, standing up tall again. "There's a bar called the Blue Cactus on West Fourth near Summit Ridge Drive. You can pick up a map at the front desk but if you're taking a cab, they'll know."

"Thank you, kind sir!" Sam says.

"Have fun, ladies," he says, giving us a wink.

"I know what you're thinking," Sam says after he's out of earshot. "You're thinking we can't go because we don't have fake IDs, but they might not card us and we could at least try," she begs, clasping her palms together.

"I wasn't thinking that," I lie. "Let's go, it'll be fun."

It isn't just the IDs. My mind has already snagged on my first paranoid thought. One that has been darting in and out of my mind for the last year. That my mother somehow installed surveillance cameras in my eyes, and she's just witnessed Sam asking about lesbian bars. If we went, she'd witness whatever, or whoever, we might find in a lesbian bar. I try to imagine a bunch of lesbians, but all I can come up with is the Lesbian Avenger. I multiply her by forty and feel my palms slick with sweat. I need more than just Sam to get me through the door of a lesbian bar. I need someone who understands how phenomenally weird and socially awkward I can feel at the drop of a hat. Someone who won't ditch me to dance under a spotlight. *I need April.* April with her gifts and words of encouragement: a skull and crossbones sticker, my hand held in hers as she drew hearts on it. April asking me what's wrong and sticking around even when I can't answer. *I need April. And April needs me.*

Late last fall, April, Sam, and I went to Pancho's Cantina in Island Park after school one day. Sam had wanted to go alone with me, but I'd insisted we include April. I'd been feeling guilty for following Sam's lead, letting her leave April out so much since the school year started. "We can't *never* invite her!" I'd argued. Pancho's Cantina was a cute little place with booths and dusty red, white, and navy streamers still hanging from when the New York Giants won the Super Bowl in 1991. They had dollar-taco Tuesdays. For ten bucks, the three of us could eat until we were achingly full.

Sam and I got in line while April took off to the bathroom. We ordered and planted ourselves in a booth. By the time our tacos arrived, April still hadn't come back. I craned my neck. There was a line forming outside the door. Distracted, I was barely taking in what Sam was telling me, something about the plot of *Party Girl* with Parker Posey, her movie star crush. "Should I go check on her?" I interrupted.

"Maybe she has diarrhea," Sam giggled, shaking a bottle of hot sauce before uncapping it.

We were halfway done eating when April meandered out, apologizing to everyone in line. She trudged back to us, slid in next to me, and looked down at her food in the orange plastic basket.

"Thanks. Sorry, guys," she whispered, before her eyes slipped closed and her face sank slo-mo into her tacos. Sam and I looked at each other, alarmed.

Adrenaline flared in me as I pulled April up by her shoulders. A wonky heart of orange grease stained her cheek. "April, what did you take?" I begged.

"Is she that trashed from her pills?" Sam asked, kicking April's shins under the table.

"Hey! Stop kicking me," April slurred before she drifted away again.

I looked around. Nobody seemed to be paying attention. I didn't know if I should be screaming for help or trying to hide her to keep her from getting in trouble.

"April, wake up, wake up, wake up," I pleaded, my lips brushing her ear. She made an attempt to respond, but her mouth oozed words that held no shape. I pulled her closer and her head flopped on my shoulder, the weight of her whole body following.

"What if she's dying?" I whispered to Sam. I was panicking now. "Do we need an ambulance?"

Sam kicked at April's shins again. We watched her flinch and grimace. "We don't need an ambulance. She's just fucked up. Sometimes my dad used to drink so much he would pass out," Sam said with a sigh. "We just have to wait it out."

I couldn't eat. I wanted to scream for help, but I didn't want Sam to think I was overreacting. But what if I wasn't? I listened to April's breath and dug an elbow into her thigh each time it slowed. Sam finished her tacos and pushed her plate aside, rested her head on her forearms, like this was exhausting instead of scary.

Almost an hour later, when the sun was setting and the light outside had turned low and blue, April started to come to, rubbing her face and grunting at me when I asked her what she'd taken. Even when she was sober enough to stand up, pull her hoodie over her head, and walk out into the cold dusk with us, she still wouldn't answer the question. We walked in the direction of her home while she trailed behind us. Watched her tell her foster parents she got sick and barfed at Pancho's Cantina. Saw their concerned looks as they brought her inside by the shoulders, her foster mom mouthing, *Thank you,* at us before the door closed behind them.

As we walked toward Sam's house, her arm linked in mine, she turned to me and said, "She keeps saying *we're* being weird lately, but it's like she's trying to distract us from what *she's* doing. We really shouldn't hang out with her anymore, Hannah." When I didn't respond, she continued, "I know that sucks, but she's not just experimenting casually anymore, like she was in the beginning. She's stuck on pain pills and who knows what else. It's getting depressing."

I looked at her, surprised, but she looked serious, her eyebrows raised, waiting for me to agree. She was right about one thing. April wasn't trying out pain pills to see what they were like. She knew what they were like, and she wanted to gobble them like Tic Tacs.

"We can't just drop her entirely," I said as we turned onto Sam's street. "She's *us.* And she's sad, and she already feels left out. If we bail on her, she'll have nobody. Who will make sure she's safe and walk her home when she's all messed up?"

Sam put her arm around me. "We aren't even helping, we're just covering for her. I'm not going to rat her out, but if her foster parents knew, they might actually help. And if she didn't have us fixing things and bailing her out, they *would* already know. I'm not going to keep doing it and you shouldn't either. We need to set boundaries."

Sam sounded so certain. So clear. I nodded and listened. She'd been in a program for kids of alcoholics, where she'd learned to "set boundaries." She'd spent her childhood trying to help her dad, throwing away his whiskey and then hiding when he wandered around looking for it, putting a blanket on him when he fell asleep on the couch, making excuses for him when her mom had had enough. Setting boundaries had made sense with him. She was a kid feeling responsible for a grown man. But she barely saw him anymore. And now she didn't think we should hang out with April. Kicking the leaves as we walked, I wondered if "setting boundaries" was a fancy term for cutting people off.

I couldn't do it. I kept hanging out with April. But less often. Both of us were making less of an effort, not just me, I reasoned. It felt like a car window was rolling up between us.

On a cold day in May, April and I walked to the beach. I planned on finally telling her about San Francisco, the words waiting, worrying inside me. We planted ourselves in the sand. April smoked a cigarette cross-legged next to me while I snapped Necco wafers between my teeth. *Just say it already*, I told myself.

"Sam's uncle is fixing up an old delivery van and selling it to us for pretty cheap," I explained. April lit another cigarette from the butt of her last. "And we're thinking of just taking Eighty straight across to San Francisco, doing a little van camping along the way and staying in cheap hotels when we need showers."

April nodded, turning away toward the ocean.

"When we get there, I'll probably just get another laundering job, hopefully at a fancy hotel, because Rudy said he would vouch for me, and Sam can babysit or whatever, and we'll try and find a little studio apartment once we know something about the different neighborhoods."

I paused, watching April burn circles into the leather of her Doc Martens between drags.

"I'm going to miss you a lot. But I'm sure I'll be back to visit soon, maybe in the fall, or for Hannukah—if not, then definitely for Passover. My mom would kill me if I missed Passover. She's losing her shit right now."

April took a long haul on her cigarette before crushing it in the sand. With her eyes still cast down, she said, "You, like, fully handed Sam your leash, didn't you?"

"What?" I asked. My skin prickled and stung. "We planned it together," I said, stumbling. "It was actually my idea to leave."

Her gaze was cold when she lifted her face to me. She looked paler than normal, the fingerprint of concealer on her chin zit a warmer shade of white. Her expression was familiar, I'd seen it on my mom a hundred times. I disgusted her.

"She runs your shit, Hannah, and you let her. You're practically obsessed with her. Are you in love with her or something?"

"I—"

"God, you're so pathetic," she said, standing up and looking down at me. "I knew it. I knew the second Sam was done with me, you'd be done with me too. You barely hang out with me anymore and you don't tell me anything. You need to get a fucking spine, Hannah." I could see tears pooling in her eyes, but she wouldn't stick around for me to watch them fall.

She pulled her hood on and headed off down the beach. I couldn't tell if I wanted to scream something back at her or flop into the sand and sob. I did neither. I sat there watching her shrink into the distance until she was the size of a splinter. Until she disappeared completely. Until she was the kind of splinter you can't see at all, but you feel it. You can't stop feeling it.

We didn't speak again. At graduation I tried to catch her eyes, but each time she turned away. I never said goodbye.

4

The Blue Cactus is inconspicuous—the door is closed and covered in flyers, and a neon Open sign shines in the window, despite its otherwise shuttered look. My palms go slick again standing this close to the door of an actual lesbian bar.

"Sammie, there are probably lesbians in there," I joke. She gives me a shove and I let out a nervous laugh.

"Don't be weird, okay?"

"What?" I ask, offended. "I won't."

Sam gathers her hair in her hands and finger combs it into two long columns down her chest.

"Are we even officially lesbians?" I ask. Sam laughs but doesn't answer. It's a real question. I know I don't like boys, but I've also never had a crush on anyone but Sam. Maybe I'm a Sambian.

"Ready?" she asks. I tell her yes even though I'm not. I

swing the door open and extend my arm so she'll go in first, my discomfort masquerading as chivalry. She sees right through it and glares at me as she walks in. The Blue Cactus is all wood, well lit, and sturdy, like a cabin made of Lincoln Logs. As I follow Sam to the bar, all five heads in the room turn our way: two bartenders, two younger women playing pool, and a middle-aged woman with a sour face sitting alone at the end of the bar, pint glass in hand. My brain yells, *Lesbians! Lesbians! Lesbians!* I glance at each one, averting my eyes quickly so they don't think I'm hitting on them.

Sam throws out a friendly "Hello!" I lift an open hand but can't quite get it to wave.

One of the bartenders, a woman who looks to be in her thirties with feathered blond hair, walks toward us with a smile, wiping her hands on her towel.

"You girls are over twenty-one, right?" she asks. I look at Sam. She seems about to answer when the woman says, "It's a yes-or-no question." She's still smiling, she's practically winking at us.

"Yes!" Sam blurts. "Of course."

"What can I get you?" she asks.

"Um," Sam starts, looking at me for help. But I'm useless. We've had her mom's wine coolers. We've had our share of Zimas, the drink of choice among girls at high school parties. We both hate beer. The only mixed drink I've ever had is grape juice with a splash of red wine on Passover. "Two rum and Cokes," Sam says. It's her uncle's usual. When the bartender looks away, Sam grins, and we plant ourselves at the bar.

"Where are you two from?" the bartender asks, sliding our drinks toward us.

"Long Beach. We're slowly making our way out west," Sam answers.

"You mean north and then east?" she asks. "Long Beach, California, right?"

"No, Long Beach, New York."

"You girls drove all the way from New York? Just the two of you?"

She sounds impressed and suddenly I feel proud.

"Yeah. We're moving to San Francisco," I say.

"Deb!" she yells to the other bartender. "These girls just drove all the way from New York and are headed to SF."

Deb turns to look at us and smiles. "You can have those drinks on the house. You're going to need every penny in SF."

"Wow, thanks," Sam says.

"Thanks," I parrot.

I feel elated, like we're being awarded a prize for the tenacity and gall of our plan.

Then Sam is up, drink in hand, walking over to the two younger women playing pool. I can tell she wants to make friends, but I'd rather die than try. I stand, unsure if I should follow.

"Do you two want to play the next round with us?" one of the women asks.

"Sure!" Sam says. I pick up my drink and take a quick sip before I join them. It tastes like cough syrup, and I feel my face twist up, then flush with embarrassment. I'm mortified I exist at all.

Their names are Jamie and Becca. I'm guessing they're in their twenties. Jamie has long brown hair and Becca has short bleached spiky hair, but other than that they're twins: identical black eyeliner, tight white tank tops, studded black belts, and Levi's. They tell us they live together in an apartment complex a block from here. I think it's safe to say they're a couple, although I listen carefully for full confirmation. I put my arm around Sam as if it feels totally normal to do this in public. I can't stop wondering how they met, how they knew they were gay, how they have sex.

Jamie and Becca kick our asses. I only get two attempts and fail at both. They play pool with serious faces and all the moves, and they make it look so cool I decide I'll make time to practice once we get settled.

After the game, we stand around answering their questions about where we've been and what our plans are when we get to San Francisco tomorrow. When they ask what we'll do for work, Sam babbles on about babysitting, saying she hopes people in our new neighborhood will need child care. I glance at Jamie and Becca, who nod and listen. I'm pretty sure they think we have no clue what we're doing. I feel us shrinking. Our plans sound so much better when it's just the two of us whipping up our big dreams.

"Listen," Jamie says to me, pulling a long drag on her

cigarette before continuing. "The Castro is mostly gay men, but you could look for a job there to start. You want to be somewhere like the Castro, the Mission, South of Market. Stick between Market Street and Army Street, anywhere from SoMa to Noe Valley, and you'll be good."

The smoke billows out of her mouth as she speaks. I have no idea what she's talking about, but I nod like I know all those places. Like I have a map in my head that she's pointing to. I glance at Sam, hoping she'll try to remember some of the names Jamie just rattled off, but she's too busy monologuing at Becca.

"We need real jobs right away when we get there, babysitting's not going to pay the rent," I say to Jamie, like I knew better all along.

"Yeah, you do. The city's fucking expensive," Jamie says.

"What do you do for work?" I ask.

Jamie smiles at me, takes another drag of her cigarette, but doesn't answer. Then she elbows Becca.

"Hey, Hannah here wants to know what we do for work," she says.

Becca laughs, eyeing Jamie before answering. "Well, I have a boring job. I work at Sears over at the Meadowood Mall. I'm a sales associate in kitchen appliances. It sounds dull as fuck, but it's kinda fun when you make that commission."

There's a long pause before Becca turns to Jamie and asks, "You want to tell them what you do, babe?" I think *babe* confirms it. Officially hanging out with a lesbian couple.

What would it feel like to call Sam babe? *Hey, babe. Come here, babe.*

"I strip at the Wild Orchid," Jamie says.

"You *what*?" Sam asks.

"I strip," Jamie says clearly. "Like, I'm a stripper."

"Oh!" Sam says, giggling. "Cool. That's funny, I thought you did something at, like, a flower shop that specializes in orchids."

"I kinda do, right?" Jamie says with a smirk. We're all giggling now.

Jamie looks back at me. I'm not sure what to say. She cocks her head like she's waiting for a response. *Don't be weird,* I remind myself. I clear my throat.

"Yeah, that's cool," I say.

"Jamie's my sugar mama," Becca says, hooking two fingers into the top of Jamie's jeans and giving a suggestive tug. "She takes me to Cancún for Christmas every year."

"Dang," Sam says. "I want to go to Cancún for Christmas every year."

I have a thousand questions, but I wouldn't dare, that would make us look immature, naïve to the real world. I glance over at Sam, who looks like she's about to ask something, something embarrassing, I'm sure.

I jump in before Sam can get a word out. "Should we play another round?"

We lose the second game faster than we lost the first, despite Becca's coaching and Jamie's cheering. Every time we take a turn Becca hollers, "So close! So close!," even when we're way off. I start to relax a little. I want to be just like them minus the stripping and the boring sales job. Jamie buys us a round of drinks. It's our second free drink of the night. Pretty good for our first time in a lesbian bar.

"Do you guys want some coke?" Becca asks. I watch her hands twist Jamie's hair up into a bun, then drop it loose to fall back over her shoulders.

"What?" I ask. Sam's arm wraps around my waist, her fingers pressing into my hip to signal something, I can't tell what.

"Do you two want some coke?" Jamie asks slower, her eyebrows lifting.

"Coke?" I say back to her. *She's talking about cocaine, dummy.* I look at Sam, who has no guiding expression on her face. I'm pretty sure Sam does not want to do coke.

"No, thanks, we're trying to save every penny," I say.

Becca laughs a loud short laugh, followed by a cough against her closed fist.

"We're not trying to sell it to you," Jamie says. "We're offering it to you."

I turn to Sam.

"Do you want to?" she asks me quietly. She probably wants me to be the one to say no, so she can be the cool one. The cool one with the uptight girlfriend. But what if *I* want to be the cool one? And maybe I kind of want to do it anyway, make terrible choices, far from the view of any scolding eyes.

"Do you?" I echo back.

Sam shrugs.

I shrug.

I feel Becca and Jamie watching us ping-pong the question back and forth.

"Okay, yeah," Sam says.

My stomach drops. I must look bewildered. Sam's eyes tell me I'm wearing the wrong expression. *Wipe it off, nod and agree,* they say. I wipe it off, nod and agree.

All four of us head to the bathroom and into the handicap stall. My palms are sweating and I reach for Sam's hand to see if hers are too, but she gives my fingers a pinchy squeeze, letting go before I can find out. Becca sits backward on the closed toilet lid and cuts lines with a razor on the top of the toilet while the rest of us keep talking about San Francisco, like this is all totally normal. Then I hear Becca take a deep inhale. I turn to see her head bent low before she flips it up, snorting loudly. I guess that's why they call it "snorting" cocaine. You actually snort like a pig. And then you fiddle with your nose for a bit I think, watching Becca fiddle with her nose.

"Here," she says, handing me a rolled-up dollar bill.

Becca points to the longest line of coke. Why does she want me to have the longest one? To be nice or to be mean? Her eyes glint at me almost flirtatiously. I find her confusingly appealing, not pretty, but charming, handsome under the dim bathroom lights.

When I look to Sam for some kind of reassurance, she won't meet my eye. I sit down backward, facing the wall just like Becca did. We don't need them to know we've never done coke before. We've seen it done in movies. Sam and April and I snuck in to see *Pulp Fiction* at Long Beach Cinemas, watching Uma Thurman snort lines the size of chopsticks. She thought it was coke, but it turned out it was heroin, and she almost died—two trails of blood running from her nostrils to her lips. I glance back at Becca. She's explaining the train system in San Francisco to Sam. Becca's standing up, eyes open, not bleeding or dying. Not yet at least. I turn back, lean forward, and do it quick, sucking up the whole line in one go. Then I tip my head up and feel it drip down the back of my throat. It tastes weird, bitter, chemical, and it's true, I do want to snort like a pig and mess with my nose.

When I hand the rolled dollar to Sam, she appears to be scanning me for information. Information I can't give with only my eyes. I turn back to Becca. Her mouth is moving fast. Too fast. An articulation to her jaw I didn't notice before, chattering out names of cafés and restaurants, an old piano bar called Martuni's where the queens sing show tunes. Sam's quick sniffs distract me, and I lose track of what Becca's saying. Sam sounds like a little kid at the end of a big cry.

It's Jamie's turn. She swings her leg over the toilet like she's mounting a horse. Sam and I lock eyes and try not to giggle. Becca shakes her head and tells us Jamie makes everything hotter. "Isn't she a babe?" she asks, but it's not really a question. We both nod enthusiastically. *Babe, babe, babe.*

When we come out of the bathroom, I notice the bartenders' expressions have changed. Shifted down a gear. I smile at the one who gave us free drinks, but she responds with an uneasy tick of the chin, the corners of her mouth pulled taut, unwilling to reveal the frown I detect underneath. She knows. I've disappointed her, and now I think of my mother, and just picturing her sweeps me with shame. But as quickly as it comes, it's gone, and a new feeling sweeps in. A feeling I hardly recognize. I feel great. Amazingly great. Sam is gorgeous, and I deserve her. Becca looks at me while she chalks a pool cue and I look right back. Maybe I'm gorgeous too.

"You start, Hannah," she says, handing me the stick. I'm pretty sure she likes me—the way she gives me the biggest line of coke, chalks my stick, puts me first. I line up my sight, imagining the break cracking in every direction, finding pockets on the first shot. My vision is crisp on the table, and just beyond, where things begin to distort, Sam's thumbs tuck into the belt loops of her jeans, a blurred flare lighting her cigarette. I hear myself explaining how Sam and I met in middle school, telling it like a comedy routine, and I'm feeling cocky, like a real winner, while Sam gives me woo-woo eyes, her ash dropping onto the green felt.

Part Two

San Francisco,
California.
July 1996.

5

"I can't believe we did that," Sam says. "I never thought I'd do coke in my whole life."

It's three in the morning and today is the day we've been waiting for—the day we arrive in San Francisco. I should be excited, but instead my heart races, and self-doubt crawls under my skin like spiders. We're on our fourth episode of back-to-back reruns of *Silver Spoons*, and even old sitcoms can't placate me.

I take her hand under the covers, but it's sweaty, so I move to her forearm.

"It doesn't have to be such a big deal," I say. "It was one time. It's not like it makes us bad people."

"We just did coke with a stripper!" she says, tossing her eyes to the ceiling.

I push her in the arm half-heartedly. "Stop it, Sammie. She was totally sweet and normal, right?"

"I guess. I mean, I don't know what I thought a stripper

would be like, but definitely not gay, and not trying to list off all the great bookstores in San Francisco."

"Do you think it's sad she strips?" I ask.

Sam pauses to consider. "Not really. She doesn't seem sad at all, but I feel like we're supposed to think she's sad and feel bad for her or something," she says.

"It's kind of messed up, right?"

Sam nods. "I feel bad about myself right now."

I tuck her into the crook of my arm. "Why?" I ask, pushing her hair behind her ear.

"I feel guilty about doing drugs with them," she says. "I can't stand it with April and my dad, and then the second a couple of cute girls offer us drugs, I have no morals."

"Do you think drugs are about morals?" I ask.

She doesn't answer. The *Silver Spoons* marathon is over and an infomercial for Beverly Hills cubic zirconia tennis bracelets starts.

"Don't you feel guilty?" Sam asks.

I press my lips against her forehead, mulling before I answer. "If I think about my mom I do. But how do I know how I actually feel when my mom's always popping into my head?"

We're quiet for a moment.

"I guess I feel weird." I continue, "I felt like me, but a better version of me, and that felt good, but now I feel like a worse version of me, and I wish I could just fall asleep until it's over."

I think about April. I wonder if she got herself stuck like a scratched CD right at this moment.

"Let's never do drugs again, okay?" Sam says, pushing up onto her elbows.

"You sound so Nancy Reagan," I tease.

She doesn't smile. She holds out her pinky for me to promise.

"Maybe okay," I counter. She frowns, refusing to put her pinky down. I should promise, but a part of me doesn't want to. A little bit of coke every now and then wouldn't be the end of the world.

"Can you just promise me?" she asks, irritated. "Just promise me you won't do it again, okay?"

I hesitate for a moment before I wrap my pinky around hers. Is this the leash April was talking about? But I love Sam. I *want* to give her what she wants. She squeezes my finger tight with hers, jerks our fists back and forth, sawing the promise into the air.

We leave Reno with Sam in the driver's seat, while I navigate, squinting as I count out our remaining money on the dash. The world is too bright. My head is killing me. We have $638.74 left. Sitting in silence, we pass a can of ginger ale back and forth. We need jobs. Immediately. Today.

Hours stretch and the farmland begins to ripple with hills, homes and strip malls closing in. We rattle over a bridge. I slide my thumb across the map to find us. The Benicia-Martinez Bridge. By the time I've registered where we are, the bay opens to our right, a shimmering sprawl of blue-green water, vaster than I ever imagined, and across it, San Francisco and the Golden Gate Bridge lift into view.

"That's the Golden Gate Bridge!" I scream. The thrill of seeing the place we've been dreaming of overpowers my headache. The Golden Gate Bridge runs taut across the opening of the bay, as if the land would spring apart if it let go.

"Oh my god oh my god oh my god," Sam says, gripping the steering wheel and rocking herself back and forth in her seat.

We merge onto the Bay Bridge with the water spreading wide underneath us, islands puckering the surface to the right, red freight ships floating like Legos to our left.

"A tunnel through an island!" Sam yells as we hurtle into its open mouth. I find it on the map.

"It's literally called Treasure Island!" I say, laughing. It's cartoonish and absurd, straight out of a storybook, and we both giggle until we're red-faced, tears popping from our eyes. The freeway glides into a downtown spiked with tall buildings, a Coca-Cola sign pulsing in white bulbs. San Francisco holds out an open palm for us. We've arrived.

When we get to the Castro we circle until we find a spot blocks away, on a hill I've never seen the likes of. The parking spots run perpendicular into the street, I'm assuming so the cars don't slide down the hill. Still, I feel afraid poor Scooby might come up with a whole new way of falling, rolling on her side, tumbling like a tin can. We get out, lock up, and head down the hill, our feet thumping in an unfamiliar way that makes us laugh.

When we get to Eighteenth and Castro, I loop my arm around Sam's and pull her close. The Castro is brimming with people, 90 percent of them men I'm guessing are gay. Tight jeans, fresh haircuts, sleeves rolled evenly on both sides. Even the ones with messy hair and untucked shirts look tousled on purpose. My brain does it again, pointing to each one, yelling, *Gay! Gay! Gay!* Even the businesses look gay: we see glittering thongs and leather pants on headless male mannequins displayed in shopwindows. Business names like Hot Cookie, the Tool Shed, Orphan Andy's. And above us, extending from the telephone poles, rainbow flags billow in the wind. Sam grabs my hand and skips forward while I stumble behind her ogling everything I set my eyes on. There's the Castro Theatre with its elaborate marquee, and Twin Peaks Tavern on the corner featuring enormous glass windows like a fish tank, an assortment of well-groomed older men on display inside.

"Let's get something to eat and fill out job applications at every single place here," Sam says.

We stop at a café called Josie's Cabaret and Juice Joint. It has a pink stucco front and large, rounded windows. We stand by the propped-open door reading the menu while a girl in her twenties with pink pigtails and cat-eye glasses watches us from behind the counter. She's wearing a spiked dog collar as a choker, and I try not to stare. The food is pricey compared to Reno, but I'm too self-conscious to tell Sam we should leave. Instead, we step in and I suggest we split a sandwich. Sam wants the vegan cheese and sprouts, which sounds super gross, but it's the cheapest one on the menu, so we order it.

"There are so many rainbow flags here," Sam says to the pink-haired girl. I wince with embarrassment. Pink-Haired Girl nods like a kind kindergarten teacher, encouraging Sam to continue. "We just drove out from New York and saw zero rainbow flags the whole trip."

Pink-Haired Girl smiles a toothy smile, pinning it on Sam with her eyes, while she pulls two slices of grainy bread from a bag. "Well, it was Pride yesterday," she says matter-of-factly.

"It was Pride yesterday?" Sam says, before turning to me. "Oh my god, we missed Pride by one day?"

"It's not as good as it used to be in like '93 and '94. Capitalism is trying to fuck it up. Coors sponsored it this year," Pink-Haired Girl says, pushing her glasses up the bridge of her nose with the back of her wrist and grabbing a handful of sprouts from a plastic tub. The sprouts look like a ball of fur. She pats it into our sandwich. "The Dyke March is way better. It was on Saturday." I feel a jolt of humiliation hearing the word again, even though it's delivered with affection this time.

"The Dyke March was on Saturday?" Sam asks, as if she'd heard of the Dyke March before a second ago.

I'm trying to wrap my head around it. Is that what we call ourselves? *Dykes*? But in a good way? I play with the word like it's a marble, roll it this way and that in my head.

"I can't believe we missed everything by only two days," Sam says.

"Next year," Pink-Haired Girl says nonchalantly.

"Yeah, next year," I say, trying to sound like I don't care. Sam makes a wide-eyed sad face at me, then turns back to the counter.

"Hey, so we need jobs and an apartment, but for tonight do you think there are any hotels where we could get a room for thirty-five dollars or under?" Sam asks.

Pink-Haired Girl laughs. "You can't get a hotel room in San Francisco for under thirty-five dollars unless you want bedbugs and head lice down in the Tenderloin."

I can't hide my disgust. Scooby suddenly seems safe and appealing.

"You can fill out an application here, but unless you have café experience it's not going anywhere. I don't do the hiring," she says with a grin.

Sam and I look at each other. Neither of us has café experience. How do you get café experience if you need café experience to get café experience? Are we already boxed into our dead-end career paths? Babysitter and laundry folder forever? Pink-Haired Girl slides us a plate with the sandwich on it, and adds a chocolate chip cookie on the side.

"It's vegan," she says to Sam. "On the house."

"Hey, thanks!" Sam says, smiling back at her.

"Go to Tower Records," Pink-Haired Girl says, "they're always hiring; tons of young queers working there."

Now I'm confused. Are we queers or dykes? Or both? Are all slurs fair game if we take them for ourselves?

We head outside and sit at one of the tables so we can people-watch as we eat. This whole vegan-cheese-and-sprouts sandwich thing is not a thing on Long Island. The sprouts smell vaguely like dirty socks, but I'm so hungry I eat every little hair of my share. Even after gobbling half the cookie, I'm still starving, but I tell myself we have peanut butter and bread in the van. Across the street, I spot a phone booth next to a flower stand. I want to call Bubbe so badly but I need to save the money on my calling card. I want food and Bubbe. I want what used to be free.

When we've picked every crumb off the plate, I go back inside and stack our dish in a brown tub by the door. Just as I'm about to leave, I turn back to Pink-Haired Girl. "If you were going to sleep in a van in San Francisco, where would you go?" I ask, feeling shy without Sam at my side.

"Go way out to Ocean Beach," she says. "It's quiet out there. Less likely to get messed with."

Sam and I go business to business asking to fill out job applications. We start at Tower Records, then head to a clothing store called NaNa, where they sell platform shoes and gothy dresses. "I want to work here!" Sam whispers at me, picking up a platform Mary Jane with a boxy toe.

We explain to everyone we don't have a phone number or a mailing address to put on the application, but we can check back every day. They look at us like we're morons, until a waiter at Baghdad Café barks, "Get a fucking pager! You're never getting a job with a blank application!" We scurry out the door, humiliated.

We trudge in silence for a couple blocks.

"I don't even know how to get a fucking pager," Sam says quietly.

"Me neither," I admit. There's so much we don't know. "Let's go," I say, defeated. I hook her arm in mine. "Let's find a place to sleep before it gets dark."

By the time we get to Ocean Beach, find a parking spot, and walk out onto the sand, the sun is setting, and the sight of the ocean fills me with longing. My chest swooshes and brims, salt water spilling from my eyes.

"Why are you crying?" Sam asks. I shrug. We walk toward the water barefoot with our hoods over our heads, strings tied tightly at our chins. It's windy and cold. The sun is slipping like a penny into the horizon.

"It's a different ocean, but doesn't it still feel like home?" I ask. I realize I miss Long Beach. The beach itself, but also the walk to Bubbe's, warm challah on Shabbos, Rachel. Rachel, whom I haven't spoken to in more than a week. How can I miss a place that's so wrong for me? Sam knows what I mean. She's crying too, wiping her nose back and forth on her sleeve. We walk to the water and let it rush over our feet. It's freezing but I don't flinch. I like the icy bite of it. I want to walk in deeper, let it pummel the heartache from me.

"I can't really believe in God," I say. "But I can believe in the ocean. I feel like the ocean knows us. It's like, *Hello, friend, long time no see,* you know what I mean?"

Sam laughs, wiping her eyes and nose on her sleeve again. I step behind her to wrap my arms around her.

"I *really, really, really* don't want to go back to Long Beach," Sam says, threading her fingers with mine over her stomach.

"Let's not go back," I say. "Let's just decide we're going to make this work no matter what." Sam pulls my arms tighter around her and squeezes. I bury my face in the crook of her neck.

"Okay," Sam says. "No matter what."

Sam and I spend the next five days back at it, filling out applications, answering Help Wanted signs, checking in with the places where we've already applied. We call the numbers on every Apartment for Rent sign too. But when we do get in touch with landlords, they start talking about credit scores, paycheck stubs, references, and first and last month's rent. We're salmon trying to swim upstream.

At night, we find a place to park and sleep along the

Great Highway, which borders Ocean Beach. We fall into an exhausted spell of despair, hungry for more than just peanut butter and bread. We can't get jobs without job experience, and we can't get an apartment without pay stubs. There's no entry point in the equation. One morning, I see a pay phone at a gas station and crack. I wanted to call Bubbe when I had good news to share, but now it's been days and I need to call regardless so she doesn't worry. When she answers I try to sound cheerful. But immediately she asks how the search is going, and I fumble, stuttering through vague explanations of what might work out, what should have or could have or maybe will. She listens quietly. She knows.

On Friday afternoon, Sam and I stop at a place called Happy Donuts on the corner of Ellis and Taylor. We tell each other we deserve donuts even though we've also agreed not to spend more money, but at this moment, the donuts have won. We push the door open, and the bell jingles as we step into the warm smell of sugar. The place is empty except for two disheveled-looking men sitting with big backpacks in the far corner. The display case is lit up and full of sweets, the glazes so thick they shine. Sam orders two old-fashioneds and one cup of coffee in a Styrofoam cup, then we slide into a booth near the counter.

"I'm not even happy at Happy Donuts," Sam says, pulling an old-fashioned from the bag and setting it on a napkin. She leans in and says with a hush, "San Francisco is full of people looking so broken, I just wonder if that's going to be us in a month." She tips her head toward the guys in the corner.

"Stop it, Sammie. Maybe they're happy. We don't know," I whisper. Sam shakes her head; she's not buying it.

Sam's right. It's like the down-and-out scene in Reno but worse, because it's hundreds, maybe even thousands, of people, and everyone else walks by like it doesn't matter, like they've got a bunch of half-wit pigeons at their feet. The bell on the door jingles, and a round man with a gray beard pushes in, calling to the guy behind the counter.

"Hi, Li Wei."

"Mr. Patrick," the guy behind the counter calls back. "Such a long time!"

"Had to come in. I'm down a tenant. Can I put a sign in your window?"

Sam's eyes jump up at me. I give her the *NO, I'm too shy* look.

"We're looking for an apartment," Sam pipes up, spinning toward him so suddenly he startles. He looks at her as if he hadn't registered anyone else was here, then at me, then back at her, gauging something. He probably thinks we can't afford it.

"These are real small efficiency studios, barely big enough for one person. They're nothing to get excited about."

"How much are they?" Sam asks.

"Cheap. Three hundred fifty dollars a month, but they're

only about two hundred square feet, and this neighborhood isn't the greatest." He moves closer to our table, sliding his hands into his pockets.

"Would we have to pay a deposit?" Sam asks. "We just moved here and we're looking for jobs right now, but I know we'll find them."

"You have three hundred fifty dollars?" Mr. Patrick asks.

"We do, but we don't have enough for a deposit too, and it would help so much to have an address and a phone number for job applications," Sam explains.

He looks from Sam to me again, then back to Sam. "How old are you girls?" he asks, a crevice pitting his forehead.

"We're eighteen. We just graduated high school in New York, and we drove out here right away because we wanted to be somewhere where we—" Sam stops, glancing at me, reconsidering. "Where it doesn't snow," she says.

"Your parents know where you are?" he asks.

"They know we're here," Sam says, tucking her hair behind her ear, "but they aren't exactly happy about it."

"I bet," Patrick says, his brows pinched. I feel like we're being scolded. "I don't think you're going to want it after you see it, but I'll show it to you."

"Oh my god! Thank you!" Sam says, smacking her hands together at her chest.

"Don't thank me until you see it," Patrick says, unclipping the massive key ring hooked on his belt loop.

We follow him out to the building next door, where he unlocks a metal gate and a heavy door set inside. The hallway is dark and musty, and it smells like someone isn't following the No Smoking signs posted in the entryway. We go up a flight of stairs and he puts a key into the first door on the right, marked with a brass 1.

"Number one!" Sam says to me, pinching my arm.

The door swings open, and we see light pouring in from two windows facing the street below. We learn quickly that an "efficiency studio" means an apartment the size of a large walk-in closet and a tiny bathroom with a stall shower the size of a coffin. In the corner there's a mini fridge, a hot plate, and a sink, all in a row. A twin bed with a mattress sits under the windows on the far side. I kneel on it and peer outside.

"It's perfect," I say.

"Yeah?" Patrick asks.

"It's perfect for us, but like I said, we don't have money for the deposit—" Sam starts, but Patrick puts his hand up to interrupt her.

"Listen, I'd be willing to give you a month for three hundred fifty dollars cash if we're clear it's not a rental agreement. If you can come up with the three-hundred-fifty-dollar deposit and three fifty for August rent, then we'll talk about a lease."

"Are you serious?" Sam asks.

"Yeah, but don't ask me again or I'll change my mind."

"Oh my gosh! This is so helpful. Thank you! I can't even tell you . . . ," Sam gushes.

I pull our cash from my backpack, count it out, and hand

him the money, watching him count it out again while he throws questions at us. He seems concerned, not creepy, the way men who don't hit on you want to be your dad instead. He asks things like, "You know this neighborhood isn't the safest, right?" "You know you can't walk alone at night around here, right?" When he's done, he sucks in his stomach so he can shove the roll of cash deep in his pocket, then holds out a ring with two keys and drops them into Sam's hand.

Keys. Sam is holding *our keys.*

As he's letting himself out, he says, "I'm serious, August first I need seven hundred dollars and then we can talk about a lease."

Sam locks the door behind him, leans her back against it, and lets out a high-pitched squeal. She takes me by the shoulders. "That was wild, right? No paycheck stubs or credit scores or anything!"

I squeeze her around the waist and pivot to launch us both onto the bed before I think better of it. "We should check for bedbugs and lice," I say. "Remember what that girl said?"

Sam agrees and leans her forehead into mine, pressing her body against me. I kiss her slowly in the light of the windows, a current moving from her lips into my chest. We suddenly, miraculously, have a home. I hear Bubbe yelling "Mazel tov!" in my head, and I can't wait to tell her. It's ours. All for us. We can have sex whenever we want, eat what we want for dinner, walk around naked, stay up late.

It's everything we imagined when we dreamed it up in the alleyway off Lincoln Boulevard. It's real now, and it blooms inside me as I kiss Sam. She moves her hands into my hair and her tongue into my mouth, and I know she feels it too. It's wanting and having at the same time, a brand-new feeling I didn't know existed.

6

"Hannah, look at that giant leg!" Sam says, whacking me in the arm and pointing down the block.

By the time we got everything into our apartment, parked Scooby out by the beach, and took the train back, it was ten p.m. and we were exhausted. But not too exhausted to poke around the neighborhood, despite Mr. Patrick's warnings.

Halfway down Mason on the right-hand side of the street, a massive leg lit up in bright bulbs kicks out above the sidewalk. A yellow high heel, and a ruffled skirt rimmed in red lights lifted to the hip. On the thigh and calf, *The Chez Paree* is written in neon, and below it on the awning in all capitals, *LIVE NUDE GIRLS*.

"It's a strip club, Sam," I say. "But it totally has your leg. Look at that thigh, that's your thigh!" I reach down to squeeze hers. She doesn't respond; she keeps her eyes locked on the club. "Come on, let's keep going to Union Square," I say, pulling her by the arm. She doesn't budge.

"What are you doing?" I ask.

She looks lost in thought. "Should we go and just check it out?" she asks.

"What? No! Are you crazy?"

"Would you call Jamie crazy?"

"Not crazy, but not us. Okay? We aren't strippers."

"Strippers aren't just one thing. Look at Jamie! We could go see if it's something we could do. Temporarily. Just while we get settled."

"No fucking way, Sam."

"We could go to Cancún for Christmas," she says. I can't tell if she's joking.

"Sam, that's not even funny. We can't be strippers. We aren't even stripper material."

"There's no such thing as stripper material."

"I actually think there is," I say, crossing my arms over my chest.

She holds me by the shoulders to pin me down with her eyes.

"Hannah, what if we could make the rent money fast? When we get real jobs we'll have to wait two whole weeks for a paycheck. We barely have two weeks of money left as it is. All I'm asking is to check it out."

Her eyes tell me she's serious-serious.

"Sam, are you ready to dance around naked in front of a bunch of men?"

I can see her thinking, her mouth pinching at the corners. "Not really," she says. "But am I willing to run out of money and call my mom and ask her to fly me home? Can you imagine, Hannah? Calling your mom?"

Just the thought churns my stomach. The thought of getting this far and failing, having to go back to hiding what we are to each other, and this time, having to commit to modest clothing and shul, makes me ill. "I don't want to go home either, but can you imagine me," I say, pointing to myself, "*me* dancing around naked?"

Sam laughs. "Not really, but it won't be the real you. You don't have to be Hannah. You can pretend you're somebody else," she says.

"Even if I could pretend, I don't think I have a nice enough body for *that*."

"You just don't *think* you have a nice enough body for that," Sam says.

"That's what I just said," I say, irritated.

We stand in silence. I think of Sam's mom, who never thought to put this on her list of no-nos. Then I think of Jamie, who seemed so normal. I think of Becca, and their life together, never worrying about rent or grocery money. I want that for Sam and me. Maybe it isn't crazy. It's like making a bad choice for a really, really good reason. If it's for a really, really good reason, maybe it's more complicated than just a bad choice.

"Remember we said we'd make this work no matter what?"

I don't answer.

"This is the 'no matter what,'" Sam says.

"Okay, fine, but we're only checking it out," I say. "Promise me?"

"I promise," Sam says, holding her right palm up.

Sitting in the doorway of the Chez Paree is a bullish-looking bouncer wearing a long black coat, holding a flashlight. The sign behind him reads *Ten-dollar cover!*

We watch a middle-aged man in a Blockbuster Video polo stamp out his cigarette before stepping inside and disappearing behind a black curtain. Sam pulls off her hair band, shakes her head, and sweeps her hair over one shoulder. I know what she's doing. I don't have long hair to tousle around all flirty-like. My hair has no shape; it's hardly past my jaw. It hasn't been cut since I hacked it in the shed in late February. Three inches of brown roots, followed by three inches of jet-black split ends. I run my fingers through it. I'm not stripper material, inside or out.

The bouncer pulls the curtain open as we approach.

"Oh, we don't work here," I say, confused.

"I know you don't work here," he says. "Ladies don't pay the cover."

Sam looks at me and smiles, like *I told you so, going great already,* as we push through two curtains into the club. It takes a moment for my eyes to adjust. It's dark, but the stage is glowing in warm lights. There's a bar with a man behind it washing glasses and a heavyset woman talking on the phone, hand on her hip. Onstage, a girl with bouncy red curls in tall white patent leather heels and a pink gingham bra and G-string set rests her back against the pole and slides down with one leg extended while she unhooks her bra. Once she's on the floor she tosses it toward the mirrors at the back of the stage, sits on her knees, and leans toward a man in the first row. He's leaning in too, so far forward I wonder if he might climb on the stage with her. He holds a five-dollar bill in front of her face. I watch them, my mouth open, as she takes the cash out of his hand with her teeth, arches her back, and pushes her hips toward him. Bubbe always told me to never put money in my mouth. My stomach hurts. Just thinking about Bubbe right now feels wrong. This is certainly not what she meant by frei. My mother enters my mind next, bringing with her a hot wave of panic.

Sam and I move to the farthest open table, away from any other patrons. We sit close together holding hands between our chairs. The girls are mesmerizing. The way their bodies roll as if they have no joints, the way they bend over and fold flat like paper, breasts to shins. As we watch, I begin to see the pattern. Each girl dances her first song in a dress or lingerie, second song topless, and third song completely naked except for heels. Some of the girls have amazing acrobatic pole skills, while others seem to slink around with enough sex appeal to get by. Others do a kind of energetic, flirty cheerleader thing, engaging with as many of the guys as possible. I lean into Sam and whisper, "How did they learn to do this?"

"I literally have no idea."

"Hey, girls." We turn toward the voice and see the redheaded dancer standing over our table.

"Hi," Sam squeaks back.

"Any chance either of you want to go in the back for a lap dance?" She leans her palms on the table, locking her elbows so her boobs squish together. As soon as I realize I'm staring, I shift my gaze up, gluing my eyes to her face, embarrassed. She's giving us a half-turned smile. She's flirting with us. I watch, stunned. Does she think we're gay? And if she does, is she straight but pretending to be gay for us? Or gay pretending to be straight for everyone else?

"We would totally want a lap dance," Sam says slowly. "But we actually just—"

"But we don't have any money," I interrupt. I feel Sam's hand on my thigh telling me to shut up.

"We actually just moved here," Sam continues, "and I'm wondering if it would be hard to get jobs dancing if we've never danced before."

I feel my jaw clench and punch her thigh under the table. She shoots me a glare and elbows me back.

We hear a laugh from the redhead as she releases her boobs from their squish and stands. Her entire demeanor shifts. She drops her sex appeal like a load of bricks, the muscles in her stomach softening, and smiles a regular old smile. "It's not that hard to get a job here," she says to Sam. "This isn't the Gold Club or something. We don't make as much money but it's chill. We're all nice to each other for the most part. Just go talk to Mama Beth." She points to the woman behind the bar. Mama Beth looks up, still on the phone. She doesn't smile, but she does tip her head in some kind of recognition. "Mama Beth manages the dancers," she says as she turns and walks away. I watch her ass sway side to side waving goodbye as she crosses the room to approach an elderly man. She takes the cane hooked on the arm of his chair and holds it in both hands like she's going to perform an old-fashioned number. I watch her giggle and hear him chuckle back, his shoulders bouncing.

Sam and I go back and forth for a good thirty minutes about whether we should talk to Mama Beth or not. I can argue for all the reasons why we shouldn't, why we can't possibly. But Sam's right: even if we land jobs tomorrow, we won't see paychecks for two weeks. It's a fact I can't argue with. When I rack my brain for other quick-money plans, all I can come up with is dealing drugs, an even more dangerous and implausible option. I return to the argument that I'm just not stripper material.

"My body isn't even cute, Sam. It's just lanky and embarrassing."

Sam looks annoyed. "Can you at least let Mama Beth decide?"

I'm quiet for a moment. Sam studies my face. She knows she's wearing me down.

"Okay, listen," I say. "We're just going to talk to Mama Beth. That's it. And *you* do the talking."

"Deal," she says.

When we get up the nerve to approach the bar and talk

to Mama Beth, she doesn't really want to talk, she just tells us to come in to audition for her at two p.m. the next day when the club's closed. Before I can register what she's said, Sam has agreed to it. I'm mad all over again. We head back to our table. I keep my mouth shut and my arms crossed over my chest, while Sam gives me some kind of backward apology explaining why she *had* to say yes the instant the offer was made. The thought of getting naked in this place, even just for Mama Beth, makes me want to toss chairs and bolt. When the redhead returns to ask if we're going to audition, I answer, "Maybe." I'm now standing solidly in the land of maybe. She proceeds to give us tips on where to get the best gear, a place called Foot Worship & Felicity's Fetiche. And by the end of the night I have reluctantly but technically agreed to show up and dance for Mama Beth.

On the walk home I wonder if I'm a whole different person in San Francisco. Long Island Hannah would have never even considered this. Long Island Hannah wouldn't have done cocaine in a bar bathroom in Reno either. If I'm a different person here, then which person is the real me?

The next day, at Foot Worship, we stand in a curtained dressing room, staring at our reflection in the mirror. We've settled on matching sexy Catholic schoolgirl outfits with shiny black stilettos.

"We look like the twins from *The Shining*," I say.

"We do not!" Sam objects. "We look like Liv Tyler and Alicia Silverstone in that Aerosmith video."

"'Crazy'?" I ask. "Don't they run away from Catholic school and go work at a strip club?"

"Exactly. We're them."

Back at the apartment we shave and practice. The shaving takes me forever, so Sam offers to help. She positions me on a towel with my knees splayed. I'm slathered in shaving cream while she goes to work, dipping the razor into a bowl of hairy water after each pass.

Practice, on the other hand, goes as terribly as I imagined it would. Sam is light-years ahead of me in balance and bendiness, sexy faces and hair flips. I feel mortified even trying, even if it's just Sam watching from the bed, her eyes peeking up from behind her knees. I beg her to stop laughing. My stilettos keep rolling out from under me, threatening to snap my ankles, and I can only take a few steps before I break into a wobble and drop to the floor. Sam suggests I embrace the floor, pick a slow song and crawl around on all fours like a dog. A hot dog. "You're one hot little doggie," she says, giggling.

"I'm going to die of embarrassment before I make a penny," I tell her.

"Either way, if we make lots of money or we die, we won't have to go back to Long Beach," Sam points out.

The club is closed when we get there, but when we knock on the door Mama Beth answers and lets us in. I wouldn't call her cheery or bright, but she has a kindness to her I like. She checks our IDs to make sure we're over eighteen, pours us ginger ales from the tap at the bar, and talks to us before we dance, asking the same questions everyone does: Where are you from? Why'd you leave? What are your plans?

After we finish our ginger ales, she gives us a moment to get dressed and pick songs from the jukebox in the dressing room.

Sam picks "Age Ain't Nothing but a Number" by Aaliyah, and I pick "Wicked Game" by Chris Isaak. We promised we wouldn't watch each other dance, and I'm so glad because I'm sweaty with nerves and preemptive embarrassment.

I sit in the dressing room on a metal folding chair while Sam is out there, her song blasting. I stare at myself in the mirror, at my sexy Catholic schoolgirl outfit and my heavy makeup, two-toned hair gelled into pigtails. I barely recognize myself. I look like a caricature of a caricature. I stick my tongue out to make sure it's me. When I can't stand to look at myself any longer, I turn my chair away to face a wall of tan lockers with stickers on them like *Wild 94.9 FM* and *Go Ahead, Make My Day.* The jukebox sits at the far end of the dressing room, next to a ramp with a curtain at the top that leads to the stage. Sam's song ends and a moment later the curtain swings open. She tromps down the ramp fully naked in heels, all of her clothes balled in her armpit, cheeks pink, sweat gathering at her hairline.

"Oh my god! That was so weird and scary!" she says.

Before I can even respond, my song starts. I run up the ramp and push through the curtain.

Mama Beth is sitting in the dark, and I can hardly see her with the lights beaming in my eyes. I attempt to saunter around in a sexy way, but the first time my ankles wobble, the fear of falling brings me to my knees. I slither around on the floor, roll on my back, and kick my legs in the air while I take my clothes off, ears burning. *I'm doing a terrible job. Big Bird would do this better than me.* After a lot of fumbling, I get everything off and get back up on my feet, holding on to the pole for support. I swing myself around it, gripping tight, jutting out a hip while trying to loosen my expression into something softer and sexier before my song ends. But my song never ends. I picked the longest song that ever existed. I go back to the floor to crawl, sit back on my heels, and arch like I saw the girls do last night. I'm still on the floor when it's finally over, and I sweep my arms around to gather my clothes, then struggle to my feet and stumble for the curtain, stepping behind it before tripping down the ramp into Sam's arms.

"She isn't going to hire me, I look like Big Bird in heels!" My hands shake as I try to get myself dressed, pushing my head through the neck of my T-shirt right as Mama Beth swings the dressing room door open. She sits herself down on the folding chair by the mirror.

"Well," she says. "That was something."

"I'm sorry. I don't know what I'm doing—" I blurt out, but she puts up a hand to quiet me.

"First of all, you don't have to know what you're doing or even how to dance, but you do need to make eye contact and act like you feel like the hottest thing that has ever walked the earth. You have to appear confident and approachable, or you won't get anywhere. You'll figure out the dancing. You'll both be fine. Hannah, you need to do something about that hair. Maybe a wig. You aren't going to make as much money as the rest of the girls with hair like that." My fingers move to my pigtails. "And please practice walking in your heels. You'll be independent contractors, so you won't get workers' comp if you break your ankles." She looks at us like she wants confirmation that we understand, but I've never heard of independent contractors or workers' comp. She moves on, leaning forward to rest a palm on each knee. "You'll need to pick your stage names. And if I find out you're passing out your phone numbers, you're fired. The stage fee is seventy a night. You charge twenty for a clothed lap dance, forty for a topless, and sixty for a nude. No drugs. No drunks. No one is allowed to touch you. You can't give extra services here, and you can't advertise anything you're doing outside of here, okay?" She stands up. "Show up at seven."

"Seven tonight?" Sam asks.

"Does that work?"

"Yeah, yeah, that works for us," Sam says, glancing at me nervously.

"What happens if we don't make the seventy-dollar

stage fee?" I ask. If anyone's going to end up with less money than they came in with, it's me.

Mama Beth laughs out loud. It's the first time I'm seeing her smile. Her teeth are wild—crowded and leaning in all directions like tombstones in an old cemetery. "With your baby faces, you're each going to leave with at least two hundred, no way around that."

On our way out we pass the stage, still lit up, the silver pole glinting at its center, and I imagine a full audience of eyes. Every inch of my skin exposed.

One summer when I was six or seven, Bubbe took Rachel and me to the beach. Rachel and I spent most of our time in the waves playing a game we called Drown. I'd close my eyes and drop under the water, feel it rush through my hair. Then I'd wave my arms around over my head to get Rachel's attention. I would feel her grip tight under my armpits and across my chest. She'd yank me up to the surface and drag me to the wet sand. "YOU'RE GOING TO BE OKAY!" she'd yell over me, her head blocking the sun, salt water dripping from her teeth, and I'd spit and cough and pant and thank her.

Bubbe sat in the sand and read a newspaper. When our game had lost its thrill, we trudged back to her, scorching our feet. I flopped down next to her, wet and spent, and saw she had taken off her long skirt to sit in her swimsuit, revealing her legs, twisted and misshapen, her right foot a curled-up fist. Her arm crutches lay like two skeletons in the sand next to her. Fear churned in me. I'd never seen her body this exposed in public, uncovered on a beach where someone might run by and stare. I pinched my eyes shut. My skin prickled in the afternoon air. Then I felt her warm, dry hand brushing away the wet hair from my face. She leaned in close to my ear and whispered, "I'm not shy anymore. I spent most of my life ashamed of my own body. What a waste of time." She tsked. "I hope you will never be ashamed of yours." I kept my eyes closed, rolled toward her, and wrapped my arm around her sun-warmed belly.

I didn't know I would need this memory. I would need to pull it like a thread and stitch myself up with it, in a future I could have never imagined. It's the only way I can make this future mine.

The first night at the Chez Paree is full of firsts, starting with the first time we've ever picked our own names. Sam chooses Lavender after her childhood pet hamster. I can't think of a name, but when Sam puts a deep wine lipstick on me, she gasps and says, "Scarlet. It's perfect. We can dye your hair red. We'll both be named after colors." I can't come up with anything better, so it sticks, like a piece of toilet paper to my shoe. I feel embarrassed to say it out loud.

When I have to get onstage, sweat drips from my armpits. Sam suggested we divide and conquer. She said she couldn't flirt with men in front of me. I thought I couldn't flirt with men without her. I'm left alone, trembling at the bottom of the ramp. A girl named Jade with dark hair curtaining her bare breasts sees me and pulls out a silver flask, offering a swig.

"What about Mama Beth?" I ask, eyeing the door.

"What about her?" she asks. I pause, wondering where a swig fits into "No drugs. No drunks," but also wondering if Sam would object. I need to loosen up or I can't do this. I take a quick fiery gulp, then another, and push the flask back into her hands.

Onstage my palms sweat and leave handprints on the glass. I know better than to walk on my heels unsupported, so when I move away from the mirror, I drop to my knees. My heart is hammering. I've been watching the other girls all night and now I copy what I can, trying to ooze like honey, arching, crawling, rolling my head back, a shaky smile plastered on my face. I'm supposed to be handing out bedroom eyes like party favors, but I can't make eye contact. I can't look anywhere but down. The men in the audience are noisy, and I can't tell if they're into me or making fun of me. Halfway through my second song, the whiskey hits, and I feel something shift inside, more light and liquid. I drop my shoulders, feeling a knot in them come undone, and I lift my chin, catching my reflection in the mirror. Sam was right, she doesn't feel like me. She doesn't look like me either. That girl I see is somebody else. Scarlet.

After dancing, I come out of the dressing room and see

Sam leaning into the ear of a stocky bald guy in a suit jacket. A current of worry runs through me. What if he's a serial killer? She catches me staring and gives a sheepish half smile. I drop my gaze and walk over to Marla, the redhead.

"You just got offstage, this is when you work the crowd," she says to me.

"I just walk up and ask if they want a lap dance?"

Marla nods. I can't imagine talking to anyone in here. She aims her elbow at a man in the corner. "That guy, he's super shy and nice. Normal vanilla guy. His name's Eric. He teaches computer science at the community college. He only gets the twenty-dollar lap dances with bras and panties on, only one song, so you're not going to get a lot of money from him, but he's easy and reliable."

I look over at Eric. He looks middle-aged, in khaki cargo shorts and a waffle-knit long-sleeve shirt. He looks generic, not like a serial killer.

"What should I say?" I ask Marla.

She laughs. "Just say, 'Hi, Eric, I'm Scarlet. It's my first night, and Marla says you're really sweet, so I wondered if you wanted a lap dance.' And then he'll smile because he got called sweet and say yes."

"Will you come with me?"

"To meet him?"

"No, to do the lap dance with me."

Marla laughs again. "We'll be splitting twenty bucks! Unless I can talk him up for two girls," she says.

"You can have the whole twenty, I just need to understand what I'm supposed to be doing back there," I say.

Marla looks at me, then over to Eric. "C'mon," she says, taking my hand and leading me toward him, her hips swinging the whole way. I pull my stomach in and try to copy her motion, limiting my sway to keep my stilettos upright underneath me. When we get to him, Marla flips her hair to one side and leans in to whisper in his ear. His eyes lift and he smiles at me briefly before dropping his gaze. It's a shy smile. A kind one. Totally normal.

When we get to the curtained booth, Eric sits down on the vinyl bench. Marla grips the backrest and swings her thigh over to straddle one of his legs.

"Do what I'm doing," she whispers to me.

I straddle his other leg. She leans toward his face like she's going to kiss him, but when she's almost touching his lips, she slides her body up and forward, pinning his shoulder with her hips. I do the same, lean toward him, then slide up, pinning his other shoulder with my hips.

I follow Marla's movements, the ooziness of her, for the rest of the song. Arms out wide across the backrest, Eric sits frozen, a goofy smile gummed on his face. When it's over he thanks us like we've passed the stuffing on Thanksgiving, then hands us each a twenty.

"Do you want to stay for another?" Marla asks.

"No, thank you. Not tonight," Eric says politely, adjusting his pants before pushing his way out through the curtain.

"Does he ever talk more than that?" I ask.

"Not really. He's kinda weird but in a good way. I wish all the weird ones were Eric's kind of weird."

I look at Marla. I want her to say more, to tell me about the other kinds of weird, the bad weird. But she's done teaching. She saunters off toward a young guy with floppy jaw-length hair, a pukka shell necklace too tight on his thick neck. I scan the crowd and spot a middle-aged man with a clean side part and a brown blazer hanging on the back of his chair. He looks Eric-esque, but preppier and richer. I swallow and straighten up, try to swing my hips the way Marla does as I head in his direction.

"This is insanity," I say, looking at the stacks of bills spread out on our bed. We've been working at the Chez Paree for the last four nights, feeding bills into the slats of our locker, dialing the lock open at the end of the shift, cash tumbling out like we robbed a bank.

It's three a.m. We've both showered, and we're sitting in bed eating Dunkaroos, drinking milk from the carton, and counting our haul. Two thousand one hundred eighty-six dollars. More money than I've ever seen in my life.

"How long before we quit and try to get regular jobs again?" I ask. "We've got way more than the seven hundred we needed."

Sam doesn't answer. I know what she's thinking. How do

we go back to begging for minimum-wage jobs now that we know what we're worth?

Every time I dance a set, I get a little better. And now that I'm getting the hang of stilettos, I can focus on the dancing part instead of just the staying upright part. I tell myself a story to trick myself into getting onstage. And tonight was the first time the story felt convincing. Sam had trimmed my hair and dyed it burgundy in the morning, a box dye, Clairol Nice'n Easy. "This is so nice and easy," she'd joked, her gloved hands crinkling in my ears. When I'd arrived at the club, Marla said we looked like redheaded sisters now, and I looked "H-O-T hot." *Hot?!* Suddenly I wasn't lanky anymore. I wasn't awkward and flat chested. I was Pamela Anderson—a ginger-haired Pam—in her *Baywatch* swimsuit. I was *Playboy* hot and button-nosed pretty, with butt-crack-deep cleavage, an orange rescue buoy in hand. I was running in slo-mo, ready to give all the CPR they could ever want. And they wanted it. They came up to the edge of the stage one by one to slide bills toward me, tuck them in my G-string.

Marla was right about the girls. Most of them are kind and funny and shameless in the best way. They call the Chez Paree the "Cheese Parade," which makes Sam and me die laughing when we say it ourselves. And lots of them give us tips, tricks, and insider information like we aren't competing for the same cash. We were surprised to learn Marla's stripping her way through premed at UC Berkeley so she doesn't have to take out loans. She introduced us to Reba, who's raising her baby without any family at all, hiring a sitter on the evenings she works. In the dressing room we watched Reba squeeze milk from her dark nipples into the trash before she danced. "So I don't leak out there," she explained. We learned Jade's real name is Lisa. She was born in Arroyo Grande, California, to fourth-generation Japanese-American farmers, but in the club, she fakes an accent. Sam and I have a favorite dancer, Monique. At first, we thought Monique hated us because she told Jade she was sick of inexperienced white teenagers sucking up her tips, but soon she started giving us a heads-up on which guys to avoid. We love watching her dance. She's got long braids down to her butt and every muscle in her body is cut. She spends all her stripping money training at a circus school, which is obvious when you watch her on the pole—she can literally walk on the ceiling. The entire club erupts in applause when she click-clacks her heels up there. She makes it look effortless. She makes it look like the whole world is upside down. Which it kind of is.

Surprisingly, a lot of the guys are decent and polite, not just reliable Eric. But there are still the jerks who are rude and handsy. There was the groping drunk we looked both ways for when we left the club last night. Part of me thinks we should quit while we're ahead. Ahead of the rape and murder newsreels that play in my mind. But Mama Beth said she'd handle the assholes. She said, *Let me know if anyone gives you trouble.* Marla told us when Mama Beth kicks a guy out, she takes a Polaroid of them and adds it to the sprawling gallery of Polaroids on the wall behind the bar. Above the photos, there's a sign drawn with a red marker: *86'd.*

Sitting on the bed, Sam rubs her swollen foot, her wet hair wrapped up in a towel, while I roll our money into bundles, securing each with a rubber band and stuffing it in a sock. We're listening to a man and woman argue in the apartment above ours, trying to guess what language they're speaking. Sam decides it's not Spanish or Russian. Not Yiddish is about all I can say for sure. When I'm done, I slip the sock in my duffel and tuck the bag in the closet. Then I get in bed beside Sam and gesture for her to put her feet in my lap.

"They hurt so bad," Sam says.

Her stilettos have left an imprint of their straps across the top of her feet. I rub them, trying to avoid the places where blisters have opened.

"Dancing in stilettos is foot torture," I say. Sam winces as I accidentally squeeze a tender spot. "So . . . maybe we start looking for real jobs again?"

She unwraps the towel from her head and throws it on the floor. "My feet will still hurt if I'm standing behind a counter, or doing laps around a warehouse filling orders, or washing dishes," she says. "*And* those jobs pay shit, and we wouldn't be able to take any days off for our feet to recover."

She's probably right. I bend to kiss her shins. I thought I'd feel guilty and awful stripping, but mostly I feel guilty and awful for not feeling guilty and awful enough. I feel relieved, bordering on proud. Proud of what I'm not doing—not on a plane heading back to Long Beach with my tail between my legs.

"The thing I'm having trouble with is what to say to Bubbe and Rachel. I can't tell them any of this," I say.

"Oh my god, Hannah! Of course you can't."

"I haven't talked to Rachel in forever, and with Bubbe, it's been almost a week and so much has happened. A week ago, we didn't have money or jobs or an apartment. But what can I tell her?"

Sam thinks for a moment.

"You told me it was better to lie to my mom than not contact her and make her worry we were dead in a ditch somewhere," she says, twisting a lock of hair around her finger, before lifting her eyes to find mine.

"That's true." The thought of making Bubbe worry we're dead in a ditch turns my stomach. I look over at the phone we bought at Fry's Electronics on Van Ness yesterday. It's plugged into the wall, and our line is supposed to be connected tomorrow.

"We'll call everyone tomorrow," I say. "We can tell them about the apartment, but we'll just say we're waitressing together at the same restaurant."

"Let's tell them we're working at Sparky's Diner," Sam says. "It's twenty-four hours, so at least we won't have to lie about why we're working so late."

I turn off the light, and Sam and I curl into our little

twin bed together. The streetlights are bright through the window, but I don't mind. I spoon her, tucking my hand under her breasts and kissing the back of her neck. I know I'm not supposed to feel lucky stripping and living in the Tenderloin, but right now I do. I can't help it. We have money for food and rent and a cute little place, and we have each other. I don't need anything else.

7

"Hannah?" Bubbe asks.

"Bubbe!" Hearing her voice immediately makes my eyes go soft and damp.

"Hannah, I've been worried sick! Everyone has been—your mother, Rachel, Sam's mother. You two have to contact *someone* every few days. We were about to call the police!"

Guilt swells in me. "I'm really sorry, Bubbe," I say. "For real I am. I just wanted to call when I had something good to report."

"Does this mean you have something good to report?" she asks.

"Yes! We have a really cute studio apartment above a donut shop, and we got jobs waitressing at a twenty-four-hour diner!" I say enthusiastically, but the lie feels thick in my throat. Lying to my mom would be fine. But how can I lie to Bubbe?

"Oh, Hannah, I knew you two could figure it out. You

are strong and you find a way. Whenever your mother says you'll be back within a month, you know what I say? I say Hannah is strong like her bubbe."

I feel myself beam at her praise. "I miss you so much, Bubbe. I don't really want to come back for the High Holidays but I want to see you so bad I just might."

"Don't worry about that now, shefele. You just put one foot in front of the other. We don't know where we will be then."

Bubbe and I talk for almost an hour. She keeps asking if I want her to call me back so my phone bill won't be too high, and I keep saying, *No, no. I make good tips, Bubbe.* Which is the truth. A truth I can be proud of. Before we get off the phone she asks, "Now can you ring your mother and Rachel as soon as we hang up?"

I think for a moment. I want to tell Bubbe what she wants to hear, and I want to talk to Rachel so bad, but I can't handle being berated by my mother.

"Hannah," Bubbe says, pausing, "Rachel needs her sister. You are somebody's daughter and you are somebody's sister."

"I'll call them soon," I offer. The thought of hurting Rachel hurts me.

"Tell me the truth, shefele. If you won't today, I'll have to call over there myself. It's not right to make them worry."

"Can you? And I'll do it soon?" I ask sheepishly.

I hear Bubbe clicking her tongue and I know by the sound she is shaking her head in disapproval. Why isn't it obvious to her? Rachel can fit herself to our mother like a spoon, but when you add me, you can't even close the drawer.

Sam and I are full of pride as we head downstairs to Happy Donuts to sign the lease. When we walk in, Mr. Patrick is at the counter catching up with Li Wei, but as soon as he hears the bells jingle, he turns to greet us, hands on his belly like a jolly mall Santa. We slide into a booth together and Sam launches into our lie.

"We got waitressing jobs, and the tips are pretty good, so we're doing just fine," Sam says while writing out *Sparky's Diner* under employment on the rental agreement. I slide Mr. Patrick an envelope thick with ones, fives, tens, and twenties.

"Honestly, I'm relieved. I was really hoping you'd pull this off because I sure didn't want to kick you out. My daughters, they're a lot older, but I still worry," he says. I watch him make seven stacks of bills, privately, behind the napkin dispenser. He turns to make sure nobody's watching and scoops up the whole row, tucking it back into the envelope, then inside his coat pocket. "You should move to a safer neighborhood soon. That's why I made it month to month. Even now, when my daughters are in their thirties, no way in hell I'll let them live here."

I know he's trying to tell us he loves them, but all I hear is an old man trying to dictate what his fully grown daughters can and can't do. Is love really love if you're squeezed in a tight fist? Maybe he doesn't know how it makes you twist and turn, desperate for a faraway place to call home. A place where love isn't a hook in the lip.

Sam and I take a few days off and explore the city. She wants to go back to Josie's Cabaret and Juice Joint and make friends with Pink-Haired Girl.

"She'll think we're so weird! We don't even know her!" I protest.

"Who cares!" Sam throws her hands up in exasperation.

But maybe Sam is right not to worry, because when we walk in, Pink-Haired Girl immediately gives us a "Hey! Long time no see!" and a big smile to boot. I wonder if she's actually happy to see us, or maybe just relieved to know we didn't get murdered sleeping in the van.

"We never introduced ourselves. I'm Sam and this is Hannah," Sam says, sticking her hand over the bar, offering a handshake like a businessman.

Pink-Haired Girl looks down at Sam's waiting hand and giggles, but then reaches for it and shakes it emphatically. Now they're both giggling at each other.

"I'm Molly."

"Like Molly Ringwald?" Sam asks.

"Like Molly Ringwald, the hottest actress of the eighties," she says, still shaking. "That's why I picked it."

"You picked your own name?" I ask from behind Sam. "What was your old name?"

"Not telling," Molly says with her eyes still on Sam.

"Not telling?" Sam asks.

Molly shakes her head slowly side to side and mouths the word *no* at Sam. I guess San Francisco is the place to pick a new name. And I guess this is the way girls flirt with girls here. I realize I'm frowning and turn toward the pastries in the glass case to readjust my face before they notice.

To my relief, Molly doesn't ask about our new jobs. She's too busy telling Sam all the cool stuff to do here. She pulls out a takeout menu, flips it over, and writes down more "dyke" and "queer" hangouts for us to check out. At the bottom, she writes *Molly* with a heart for an O and her phone number and then hands it to Sam. When we walk out, I elbow Sam and give a little glare.

"What?" Sam asks, feigning ignorance.

I lift my eyebrows.

"She wrote her number down for both of us!" Sam says, elbowing me back.

We head out on the treasure hunt Molly made for us immediately. First, we go to a café on Fourteenth Street called the Bearded Lady, which is brimming with the dykiest-looking dykes I have ever seen. The ones you can spot a mile away. They have shaved heads and combat boots and piercings and tattoos, and some wear slips like they're dresses while others wear leather pants and men's button-downs and beanies. I feel embarrassingly young. Nobody is particularly friendly to us except the girl behind the counter, who has the kindest smile, a septum piercing, and amber eyes like Sam's, which makes me immediately think she's cute. There are Bearded Lady sweatshirts for sale, and on the back, they say, *I may not go down in history but I'll go down on your sister.* I blush just reading it in my head. I wish I had the nerve to walk around wearing it. I imagine how horrifying it would be to my family, and Bubbe wouldn't even understand what it meant. To me it isn't the sex part that matters. It's the part where we laugh about how we're in a special club, one that the rest of the world could never understand, could never love, would never write about in their dumb books. But we know about us, and we can love us, and we will write about us, even if it's just in our journals or on the back of a sweatshirt. Maybe when you aren't alone in your queerness, queerness is thicker than water. I want to be a part of that "we" so badly I can hardly make eye contact with anyone in here. When the cute girl behind the counter asks how my day is going, I whisper, "Good," under my breath and walk away blushing. I don't understand how I can get myself to dance naked on a stage and then turn into the most nervous flustered weirdo around queer girls. It's almost like it's too real. So real I feel more naked than when I'm naked.

After we drink soy lattes and eat Tofu Pups at the Bearded Lady, we go in search of a bathhouse on Valencia tucked into the first floor of a Victorian. We struggle to find it at first, but we eventually do, approaching and knocking at a frosted glass door. Osento is a "women-only space," which I've only ever heard of in terms of schools, never businesses.

It has a large blue-tiled hot tub and a meditation room with a tiny hand-painted sign that reads *Hanky Panky Is Strictly Forbidden.* There's a dry sauna and a wet sauna and a cold plunge and an outdoor deck to lie naked in the sun smack in the middle of San Francisco. Between stripping and Osento, my discomfort being nude in front of people I don't know has been obliterated. I've lost the urge to turtle-curl forward and hide my breasts.

In the front entrance of Osento, there's a bulletin board with flyers for events, queer clubs, readings, art shows, and rooms for rent in "dyke houses." Warm and calm from the tubs, we pull on our socks and boots and scan the wall in silence. My eyes latch on to a flyer that reads *Sha'ar Zahav, San Francisco's Gay and Lesbian Synagogue.* I lean in to read the rest: *Where our lives and our love are celebrated. Come join us!* I think about the promise I made my mom. It's not the kind of synagogue she had in mind. I nudge Sam and point to it. She glances over for a second, offering a surprised expression, but continues perusing the board. It doesn't mean anything to her. But what does it even mean to me? I think I'm allergic to all synagogues now. It's not *just* about being gay. Stripping would be my new and improved shameful secret if I showed up to a gay synagogue. It's easier to just try to forget I'm Jewish.

"We should go to that," Sam says, pointing to a flyer that reads *Sister Spit has moved to the CoCo Club! Every Sunday. Doors open at 8.* I look up at the clock on the wall. It's seven fifteen.

"I don't even know what that is," I say.

"I don't either, but why do we have to know? It sounds cool and we should go. It's in forty-five minutes."

I look at Sam, her wet hair hanging around her pink cheeks.

"Maybe we could go next week?" I ask. "I feel so chill right now."

She rolls her eyes. "Why does chill mean we can't do anything?"

"It doesn't!" I protest. "It just feels overwhelming to go to queer stuff where we don't know anyone."

"We have to go places where we don't know anyone if we're ever going to meet people, Hannah."

I bump her shoulder with mine. "Hey," I say, "I *do* want to meet people, just not tonight."

Sam stands up. "Fine, let's go eat," she says.

I finish lacing my boots. I know she's right. But I'm too awkward around dykes to stand in a room full of them and be *chill.* I care too much. I want to belong *too* much. I want to belong *so* much, I end up not belonging at all.

When Friday rolls around, our pockets have shrunk and it's time to head back to the club. We get there early, at five p.m., planning on busting our buns until two a.m. to see how much we can make in one night. We say hi to the bouncer, Jimmy, and push through the curtain. When our eyes adjust to the dark, we see Mama Beth sitting in the audience. She's watching a girl we don't recognize dance onstage. The girl has long, stringy blond hair. She slithers around with droopy eyelids, long satin gloves pulled up to her biceps. Marla walks up and stands next to us, crossing her arms over her chest.

"Long gloves are a dead giveaway. She's hiding track marks," she whispers to us. "Mama Beth isn't going to hire her."

Suddenly my heart hurts watching her. She's fully nude now, spreading her legs wide, her ribs poking out as she leans her head back. Then she sinks against the pole, squeezing a breast in each hand.

Sam elbows me. "This is just like April at Pancho's Cantina. She's totally nodding off into her taco right now," she says with a giggle. I feel my face burn. I know I'm supposed to laugh at the double meaning of *taco,* but I can't. I won't.

"Sam, don't be a jerk," I whisper.

She looks at me like *What the fuck?* I turn away and head toward the dressing room, my heart pounding. I hear Marla ask, "What was that about?" behind me. I can't bear for April to be a joke we share. She's not a joke. She's my oldest friend, and guilt washes over me as I realize I've hardly thought about her since we arrived three weeks ago. I'm pushing my Vans into our locker when the girl with the long gloves pulls open the curtain and trots down the ramp. Our eyes catch. I feel mine well with tears and turn away.

"You okay?" she asks. I wipe my eyes and turn back to her. She's bent on one knee to unbuckle the strap of her heels, looking up at me with sleepy, kind eyes, waiting for an answer. I swallow and nod before I look away again. *See?* I want to yell at Sam. *She's a person!*

I can't stand her being written off like she's nothing. What if she needs this job to survive, just like us? And if Mama Beth won't hire her, will another club? And if not another club, where will she go? What will she do? I take off my sweatshirt and shove it in our locker. I need to get myself together to face the night ahead, and now it feels impossible. Why do I care so much about a girl I don't even know?

But it doesn't really matter why. I do. I can't help it. I care about a lot of things, even when I try not to.

It's four a.m. and I'm wide awake with Sam asleep next to me. The girl in long gloves was on my mind all night, and now I can't stop thinking about April. I'll call her tomorrow, I promise myself. My entire body aches. I cover my face with my hands in the dark and feel my heart crack open, spilling everywhere. I'm so mad at Sam, but I roll toward her anyway, bury my face in her hair, and weep as quietly as I can for April. Because I miss her. Because of the pills. Because we left her. Because I love her. I cry until my nose is stuffed and my eyes ache, until I'm numb enough to sleep.

In the morning when Sam goes down to get us coffee and bagels from the donut shop, I find my phone book and dial quickly before she comes back up.

"Hello?" I recognize April's foster mom's voice.

"Is April around?" I ask.

There's a pause. "She doesn't live here anymore. Can I ask who's calling?"

"It's Hannah. Where'd she go?"

"Hannah. I'm so glad you called. I've been waiting for you to call. Have you heard from her?"

I tell her I haven't. I can hear her breathing in the silence that follows.

"Oh, honey, this is so hard," she says quietly. "April's eighteen now, and unfortunately, well, for now at least, she doesn't want to follow our household rules. Unfortunately, she left and didn't tell us where she was going."

"Oh," I say, choking up.

"If she calls you, please let us know."

"She won't," I say. "I mean, she can't. She doesn't have my new number."

When I hang up the phone, I sit stunned, staring at the wall.

"Oh my god. April, where are you?" I ask out loud.

I imagine her strung out, homeless, walking the streets, dead. I imagine all the worst-case scenarios. But April was so much more than that. More than *what*? What does that even mean? Everyone strung out, homeless, walking the streets, dead, is so much more than *that*. The girl in long gloves who didn't get the job is more than *that*. And April was my friend. She had the best record collection. She knew about bands I'd never heard of, full of boys with Mohawks.

She was the only girl who could do a kickflip, a heel flip, and an ollie on her skateboard. She was the one who swam out too far from the shore in summer, forcing the lifeguards to stand on their tower, binoculars lifted to their eyes. She was wild and risky but also kind and tender and true. Always offering presents. Pins for our backpacks, stickers, lollipops, cigarettes. She disappeared down the beach, hurt and furious, and I never said goodbye. I was a coward. And now she's strung out, homeless, walking the streets, dead, and we left her in Long Beach to die alone.

Sam swings the door open, returning with bagels and coffee. She can tell something's up from my soggy eyes.

"What's wrong?" she asks. I think for a moment, looking away, wondering if I should tell her. I decide against it. She doesn't even care about April. She knows how important April is to me, and she still doesn't care.

"Nothing really, I'm just missing pieces of Long Beach today," I say.

The Cheese Parade keeps dishing out the dough, and I wonder if Sam will ever want to leave. Eventually I ask and Sam says she wants to stay, she's content sticking it out, "the pros *waaaaay* outweigh the cons," she explains. She can brush off the hard parts so easily. But the heavy stuff sticks to me like leeches. Sam is *good* at being insensitive, even as the bad stuff piles up. First there was the man who slid his thick hands down my back to jerk my butt back and forth on his lap. "But he stopped when you told him to," Sam pointed out. Then Reba chased a guy out, cussing and wielding her stiletto like an ax, after he rammed his fingers inside of her during a lap dance. Reba was so freaked, she didn't come back to work for a whole week, and even though Mama Beth handled it, clicked his picture while Jimmy dragged him out by the collar, the whole thing still left me shaking. Actually shaking, a tremble in my hand that wouldn't quit.

At work tonight I can't fake my way through it. I can barely put in the effort, and my tips are low to prove it. I'm forcing myself through my set onstage when I do a double take. There's a dyke in the audience. She's by herself, salt-and-pepper hair cut short, the sides shaved close to her head. She looks like she's in her late thirties, wearing a men's button-down, leaning back in her chair. I can see a roll of bills in her hand. She's the odd one out in a sea of men. Do they think she's a man? I feel myself redden. I smile at her as I slip my bra straps off my shoulders, watch her register the smile's for her, watch a grin widen on her face.

During my next song, she moves up to the stage and sits right in the front. The man next to her side-eyes her, before he moves his chair a couple feet farther away. She doesn't acknowledge him, the slight of his actions. She's watching me.

I feel shy pulling my clothes off in front of her. How does she see me? Men feel simple; their eyes pick out the parts they want, clips of a porn they'll take home to wank over later. She can't be simple like men. Or is it, she can't be simple to *me*? I angle away from her when I pull my G-string off, propping myself on my elbows so I can swing my legs wide open and closed. Jade taught me this is the most relaxing way to give the patrons what they want. Pussy from an I to a capital A and back again. She doesn't look down. She keeps her eyes fixed on my face.

At the end of my set, she leans forward and slides a twenty-dollar bill next to me on the stage. I've never been tipped more than a ten for dancing. I look at her and smile again, absorbing her features. Her eyes are wide and sit far apart. Her lips are pale, fine wrinkles extending from the corners of her mouth. I don't know if I think she's cute, she's too much older than me. And she doesn't have the kind of mouth I'd want to kiss. Not like I'd ever be kissing her. But I like her attention. I like the bubble of her gaze, even if I'm more naked inside of it. I like the way it scrubs the rest of the patrons from the club.

"I'm getting a lap dance out of her," I announce to the other girls as I thump down the ramp into the dressing room.

"*Her?*" Sam asks. Sam's sitting in a folding chair with her feet up on the counter eating fries out of a bag. "A woman?"

"There's a dyke out there who just tipped me a twenty," I say.

"Oooooh!" Sam sings. "Go get her!"

When I walk out of the dressing room, I spot her, but when she sees me coming, she stands, gesturing toward the back of the club. I guess I don't even have to ask her if she wants a lap dance. I pivot, and she follows me to the red-curtained booths.

She sits down on the bench and hands me a hundred-dollar bill.

"Do you want me to get you change?" I ask.

"No," she says. "I just want the best lap dance you've ever given." Her eyes gulp me in, and I feel shy again. Painfully shy. Dancing for a dyke is better, right? It feels safer, but it's also confusing. I don't know my part. I don't know my lines. The charade doesn't apply, so what do I work with? I take the bill, tucking it into the strap of my G-string, and spread my legs over her lap. I lean in and breathe in her ear while I unhook my bra. I put my hands on the wall behind her and lift up onto my knees, pressing my hips against her chest, pinning her with my whole weight. She takes one of my wrists in her grip. I don't know what she's doing and resist for a moment, but as she brings my hand to her face to press my palm against her cheek, I soften. I sit down on her lap. Her eyes are glassy.

"Are you crying?" I ask.

"Not exactly," she says. She laughs uncomfortably, turning away. "But I do feel like shit today." Another girl coughs in the curtained room next to me, code for *Stop talking so loud.*

"My mom died," she says.

I open my mouth, but I don't know what to say.

"But I'm fine," she adds, flashing a quick smile, like *No big deal, don't worry about it.* She's rubbing her jaw like she wants to suck all the words back in. I pull her close, wrap my arms around her back, and begin to move against her. I keep her close so she doesn't have to look me in the eye. When the song ends, I ask what I always ask.

"Do you want to stay for another?"

She holds up her roll of bills, eyes no longer glassy, a stride back in her voice. "I gotta save this for your stage tips," she says, winking at me.

On the way back to the dressing room, Sam meets me halfway and loops an arm around my shoulder.

"What was her deal?" she asks.

"She's sad. And she's kinda cheesy, she winked at me. But look what I got for one lap dance." I flash her the bill.

"Tell her to come back to see you tomorrow," she whispers before she slips away, heading in the direction of reliable Eric. I push through the dressing room door and feed the bill through the slats of our locker. Her mom died. But she's fine. I imagine my mom dying with a sudden thud, a brick striking the ground next to me. I flood with panic, then heartache, and have to lean against the lockers until the feeling freezes solid. It only takes a moment. I have too many old resentments to keep it warm for long, and now, too many secrets I'll have to keep forever.

8

I didn't have to ask her to come back, she shows up almost every night. Even on nights I'm not working. Jimmy keeps teasing, "Your girlfriend stopped by. 'Is Scarlet here? When is Scarlet coming back?'"

Her name is Chris. I learn more and more little by little. From the stage I frequently catch her swigging from a silver flask in the dark. During a lap dance one night, she tells me since her mom died, she's been on a bender, but then on another night, she backtracks and tells me it's really not that bad, she just likes to have a good time. She mentions an ex-girlfriend she recently broke up with, then a few days later lets it slip it was actually the other way around, her girlfriend broke up with her.

Tonight, when I get her in the back for a lap dance, she opens her palm to reveal a pill and asks, "Want a Vicodin?" I stare at it, a small white promise in the palm of her hand, telling me, *You could feel different, better than you do right now.* I think about taking it, imagining a looser and hotter version of myself emerging, better suited for approaching men in a strip club. But would Sam be able to tell I was on something? And what about Mama Beth? I decline it in the nicest way I can, stare at it pinned between her teeth before the flask returns and she disappears it with a gulp.

She tells me she's a train operator for BART. Sam and I hate BART. We took it only once, standing the whole ride, before swearing it off and returning to the streetcars and buses. It's like the New York subway system but worse because the trains don't come as often, and they're upholstered and carpeted. Like they're *trying* to spread bedbugs and head lice.

"We've got a strong union. I've been at the job for almost fifteen years, so I make a lot of money," she says during a lap dance.

I don't know how she wants me to respond. She's running her hands down from my shoulders over my breasts to the insides of my thighs. I know I'm not supposed to give extras. But it doesn't feel gross having her touch me like it would if she were one of the guys. Sometimes I'm nervous, but I'm never scared. And the more lap dances she gets, the more my nerves soften, the more my body loosens in her hands. I don't mind her touch; sometimes I even like it. Plus, she pays a hundred dollars a lap dance, which makes me feel like I should give her a little bit more.

Chris tells me she lives in a town house up in the fog of

Twin Peaks. She says since her breakup she's been bringing girls home from bars, pulling their panties off with her teeth, and never calling them again.

"Sometimes I'm an asshole," she whispers. There's a pause.

"Sometimes I'm an asshole too," I admit. I'm thinking about April when I say it. And Rachel waiting for a phone call that doesn't come. The song ends and I ask what I always ask. "Do you want to stay for another?"

"Isn't the old guy with the bowler hat waiting for you out there?"

"Yeah," I say, shrugging. "But if you kept me in here longer, maybe he'd lose interest and go away."

"Don't you want his money?" she asks, pushing my hair out of my eyes, a palm under my jaw.

I shrug. "What if I like your money better?" I ask, surprised by my own boldness.

I watch a slow grin spread across her face.

A few hours later, Sam and I are lying in our little twin bed. It feels so good to be behind a locked door, freshly showered and horizontal.

"I'm insanely tired," I say.

Sam rolls toward me to show me her sleepy eyes. I lift up her head and tuck a towel under it, sweeping her wet hair away from her face.

"I feel like the thrill of the money is wearing off," I start to say, then pause. "I mean, now that we have enough of it"—I smooth her eyebrow with my thumb—"I'm getting sick of talking to all these guys and pretending I like them. And I know that guy stopped when I told him to, but it still happened and it still bothers me. And then there's that whole thing with Reba." I pause. Sam looks up at me. "She got assaulted at work, and yeah, Mama Beth and Jimmy got rid of him, but she still got assaulted at work."

Sam leans in and kisses me, her lips motionless against mine while she thinks, before pulling back to say, "All of that *is* shitty. But nobody said shitty things aren't going to happen in a strip club. Overall, it's better than we thought it would be, but it's still going to have its crap, just like any other job."

I frown. "I feel like being assaulted at work is more than just run-of-the-mill work crap."

"Well, it should be, but it might not be," Sam says. "You remember when that kid at Long Beach Cinemas got punched? He got punched in the face because he wouldn't put more butter on some douche's popcorn? Think about how bad his hourly pay was."

"That guy got arrested," I point out. "Why didn't the guy who messed with Reba get arrested?"

"I can't imagine Mama Beth calling the cops. She doesn't trust them. Jimmy's her cop," Sam says. She leans in to kiss me again, but her mouth lands off-center as I open mine to respond.

"But isn't it weird that if we were in college, and a

professor walked up to me in class and shoved his fingers inside me, he'd be arrested, right? But it's just a regular old job risk in a strip club?"

"He'd only be arrested if he did it in the classroom. If it was in his office, it would be a 'he said, she said' situation, and we all know how that would go," Sam says.

"You're probably right." I sigh. "But don't you feel exhausted by the hustle?"

"Every job's a hustle, Hannah. This one just pays a lot more."

I stare at her. Sometimes it feels like we're built from different materials, like the houses in "The Three Little Pigs," hers made with bricks, mine made of straw. She props her head up on her fist.

"Maybe Chris can be your sugar daddy," she says, a smile creeping across her face.

I look at her, confused. "What do you mean? Like she takes me to Cancún? Like how Becca called Jamie her sugar mama?"

"No, like a real sugar daddy."

"Like, sex for money?" I ask.

Sam shrugs. "Yeah, like fake dating and you get paid."

"That's sex for money, Sam," I say, irritated.

"Okay, but why not?"

"I can't have sex for money! I can barely strip. Plus, Mama Beth would fire me."

"Mama Beth doesn't have to find out about it!"

I think about the rules Mama Beth spouted in the dressing room. How I already broke the no-touching rule with Chris.

"Wouldn't you feel weird if I slept with her?" I ask.

She pauses, stares at the ceiling, then looks at me. "It's work, right? Are you jealous when I go into a lap dance with some dude?" she asks.

"No. If anything I'm worried he's going to try and mess with you."

"Yeah, I don't worry about that with Chris. She's harmless. She looks like a sad little raccoon." Sam puts her paws up, widens her eyes, and pinches her lips tightly. I can't help but laugh. "Or maybe a cross between Pee-wee Herman and a sad racoon," she says.

"You're so mean, Sam!" I say, shoving her in the shoulder. "Her mom just died."

"I'm just kidding. Relax."

I sit up in bed to get her to stop joking around and really think about what she's suggesting. I need her to hear how it sounds. "You're saying, instead of moving from stripping to a normal job, I should go from stripping to prostitution?" It sounds next-level bonkers. The highest level of bonkers we could possibly go.

"Don't think about it like that," she says. "Think about if it would work for you. Chris obviously likes you a lot and then you'd only be hustling one person a night, and at least it would be someone who doesn't repulse you."

"She doesn't repulse me *yet*," I say. "But that might change if I had to sleep with her."

If she was paying me, I'd owe her sex, and owing someone sex seems like the fastest route to repulsion. And what would sleeping with her even look like? I've only slept with Todd and Sam. Todd didn't count, and Sam and I are always just making it up as we go. What if there are gay sex rules I don't even know about?

"You could just ask her," Sam says, pulling me by the elbow to get me to lie back down. "Ask her and suggest a really steep price, and then you're psyched if she says yes and relieved if she says no. You can't go wrong."

I hold the idea up. I hold it up like a sweater, wondering if it could fit, wondering if I could get away with it. It's a terrible idea. *And*, it's not a terrible idea. The reality might be easier than stripping, even if it sounds like a step lower, maybe even the lowest step a person could take. But things aren't always how they sound, how we were taught to see them. Stripping is still worth it, even if I don't want to do it anymore. We went from scraping the sides of a peanut butter jar and sleeping in Scooby, to having our own apartment and phone line, buying groceries made up of all the food groups, getting pricey takeout we'd never heard of before, going to the movies and getting Milk Duds and the biggest bags of popcorn, buying ourselves cute new outfits and really anything we want. I tell Sam no. No way. She says, "Just think about it." And I do. I always think about what Sam suggests. This one, I think about all the time.

In mid-August, when the East Coast has already slogged through its hottest weeks, San Francisco begins to flirt with real summer temperatures, offering a stretch of days in the eighties. By dusk the heat has usually dissipated, but tonight it lingers. I meet Chris at a bar in Chinatown called Red's Place. Red's lives up to its name. Both the outside and inside are painted red, and there are red stools, red booths, red T-shirts and hats with *RED'S PLACE* printed across them. Chris is already parked at the bar when I arrive, her face brightening as I walk toward her. I adjust my skirt. I'm wearing an outfit I wouldn't normally wear, a particularly girly one: a black pencil skirt and a low-cut maroon top with strings cinched up the middle. Sam helped me pick it out at Gadzooks in the Powell Street mall specifically for the occasion. She walked the aisles pulling out hangers and pressing them against me, searching for the right look for this type of "interview." Underneath the cinched shirt, I'm wearing the bra Chris called "cruel," a black sheer demi cup with a stupid amount of lace. Sam did my hair and makeup and coached me all afternoon. "Pretend I'm Chris and say it to me," she said as she swept up my lashes with mascara.

Chris doesn't know it yet, but we're here to negotiate. I slide onto the stool next to her.

"A gin and tonic for the lady," she tells the bartender.

I try not to visibly recoil. I hate tonic.

"How do you know I want a gin and tonic?" I ask, trying to sound flirtatious instead of irritated.

"You strike me as a gin and tonic kinda girl," she says, giving me a sly smile. What can I expect? She doesn't know me. None of this is me.

We talk for a while, or rather Chris talks. She tells me about running into her ex-girlfriend, how cold she was, then complains about a guy she works with who's been on the job half the time she has but loves to explain everything to her. "I'm like, *Man, I trained you.*" I nod and try to show interest, but I'm distracted. I'm trying to get down half the drink to work up the nerve. There's a lull in her monologue. She's staring at me. "I think I'm nervous," she says. I smile and take a sip. I don't tell her I'm nervous too.

Leaning in, I ask quietly, "Do you want to know what I'm wearing under here?" Men love cringey lines like these, lines that leave Sam and me rolling on the floor in stitches, but Chris seems to like them like men do.

She glances down at my body and then back up to my face.

"Of course I want to know what you're wearing under there," she whispers back.

"I'm wearing the black lace bra you love."

"Show me."

I lean forward. I don't know if she can see the bra, but she can see cleavage and looks thoroughly pleased. She tips her head up and kisses all five fingertips of her hand like an Italian chef. I laugh. I like being good Italian food.

Looking around, she spots an open booth, kicks her chin in its direction, suggesting we move somewhere more private.

Once settled in a corner, she rests an elbow on the table and a cheek on her palm. "So why'd you want to meet me here? I thought meeting customers was a stripper no-no." I guess she's not nervous anymore. She looks happy, but also droopy now, and I wonder if she's on something more than booze and lust.

"Have you ever hired an escort?" I ask, wincing at my directness.

She laughs, leaning back. "You mean a prostitute?" she asks.

I roll my eyes at her like she's funny. But the word *prostitute* has teeth, and I wonder if she intended to bite.

"No, I've never hired a prostitute, Scarlet," she says. I've offended her. I nod my head slowly and take another sip. She's staring at me. Her expression shifts; she's perplexed.

"I think," she says slowly, a revelation unfolding, "*you* want to sleep with me." I feel resistance rear. I want to take the question back, argue with her, tell her I absolutely don't, but that would defeat the whole purpose of the expedition. What if she's right? What if there *is* a small part of me that wants to sleep with her? Not her specifically, but maybe I want to sleep with a dykey-looking dyke, someone so completely different from Sam. Maybe I want to know what it would be like to sleep with someone *like* Chris.

Chris is now looking at me like I'm cake. And Chris

looks like she wants cake the way a kid wants cake, to take giant handfuls and squeeze, so cake ribbons shoot out from between her fingers. She wants to smash her face in cake and shovel it in her mouth with two open palms. I study her studying me. Maybe I want someone *like* Chris to look at me like I'm cake. Maybe I want a dyke, a boyish one, a cute and charming one, to look at me like I'm cake, then take me home and ruin me.

"You want to sleep with me, Scarlet," she says again, a smile taking shape on her face. It's not a question. She's saying it with certainty.

"Maybe," I say. I press my lips together, then add, "Can we leave it at—maybe I want to sleep with you?"

She laughs. "How much do you want?" she asks.

"How much do I want you?" I ask.

She tips her head back and laughs again, louder this time. "No, but maybe that's what I should be asking."

"Oh, oh, oh, how much *money* do I want," I say, blushing. I lean in to whisper, "I want twelve hundred dollars for a twelve-hour night, at least seven of those hours taken up with sleeping, and no more than two hours of sex."

I say it like a speech, ears burning. I say it just like Sam had me practice. "Try again," she'd said as she cinched up the strings on my shirt.

"Well, you've thought this through," Chris says, reaching a hand under the table to circle my knee with her thumb. Her other hand taps her wallet in her pocket. "Do you want me to pay you now or later?"

I swallow. We're talking about twelve hundred dollars. Twelve hundred dollars in one night. I tell her I need to call my roommate before we go to her house. I head to the pay phone outside.

"Hello?" Sam answers.

"Sammie!" I whisper. "She said yes to twelve hundred dollars! Can you believe that? I'm going back to her place with her, and I'll see you pretty early tomorrow morning. Wish me luck."

Sam is silent.

"Sam?" I ask. "You there?"

"Yeah, I'm just surprised actually, but that's amazing. Rolling in the dough!" She pauses. "But does it have to be tonight? Molly invited us to go to Junk. It's a queer club, and I really want to go."

I twist the cord and look out into the street.

"I feel like I already sealed the deal for tonight," I say. A man in an Oakland A's cap is jaywalking toward me. I look away when he tries to make eye contact. "But you should go with Molly. It'll be fun and you can tell me all about it. I'll go next time."

"Okay," she says quickly. "Love you. Be safe."

"Love you too. See you tomorrow."

She hangs up. I stand there for a moment. Why is she being weird? It feels like there's a screw tightening in my jaw. When I turn around, the same man is standing right in front of me looking me up and down.

"Baby, baby, baby," he sings, bobbing his head back and

forth, and then he whistles in my face. His breath smells like sugar and metal. Like canned corn.

"Fuck you," I say to the whistler as I dart around him and duck back into Red's.

He pops his head into the door and barks, "Bitch!" before disappearing. The whole bar turns to look at me.

"Do you want me to take care of that?" Chris asks.

"I don't need you to take care of it," I say, irritation prickling my skin. "I already took care of it, that's why he's calling me a bitch."

Chris puts her hands up as if to say, *I relent*, and smiles. I take one last sip of my drink while she stands up and unclips the keys from her belt loop. Dread lands itself in my stomach with a thud. *You can do this, right? Maybe?* I've signed up for sex I don't even know how to have. I don't even know what sex is. I only know Sam, our bodies together in our twin bed; mouths and hands, our hips grinding, moving in and out of each other, in and out of sex, no beginning or end. The sweet daze of sex with Sam. *Sam.* My dread has a side dish of jealousy. I wonder if Sam has a crush on Molly. I'm pretty sure Molly has a crush on Sam. Suddenly I'm certain of it.

Chris unlocks the door to her town house, gestures me inside, and I'm surprised by how nice it is. There's a spacious open-concept living and dining room with tall windows on the far side displaying a twinkling view of downtown. Chris sees me eyeing the staircase and explains the bedroom and second bathroom are up there.

"You have two bathrooms for one person?" I ask.

"It's how I really impress the ladies," she says. I pop her in the stomach with the back of my hand and she pretends to double over.

The living space has a gray L-shaped sectional covered in pillows, an empty coffee table, and a big TV on a stand. There isn't much in here and I wonder if she just moved in, or if her ex moved out and took everything with her. I follow Chris into the kitchen, watch her face light up in the open fridge while I slide onto a stool at the counter. She stacks Chinese food boxes in her arms, closing the door with her knee.

"Do you want a Vicodin and some Chinese food?" she asks, dropping the boxes on the counter in front of me and reaching for an orange pill bottle on top of the fridge.

"How do you get those?" I ask, watching her unscrew the cap.

"They were my mom's."

"You took them?"

"After she died." She pops two in her mouth, swallowing them down without water. "What's with the interrogation?" she teases.

She shakes another pill into her palm and holds it out for me. Here we are again, and I should say no again, but I'm nervous, and I desperately want to feel different, better. I think of April, how desperate she was to feel different, better.

I think of Sam. Sam whom I pinky-promised no drugs, never again. But Sam isn't here, she's not signed up to do this. She's at a queer club with Molly.

I take the pill from Chris's hand. She pours me a glass of water, and I swallow it quickly before I can think more about it. She's microwaving a plate of fried rice, telling me I need to eat so I don't get nauseated.

Within an hour, I'm loopy and squishy and warm and I've made it upstairs to lie across her bed. Vicodin is the opposite of coke, but they have one thing in common: I feel better in every way. Maybe even good. Chris has a king-sized bed with a fluffy comforter that smells faintly of bleach like the white sheets in a fancy hotel. It feels ten times the size of our tiny twin back at the apartment. Chris stands at the edge of the bed holding my foot against her chest and rubbing it. I sit up a little to pull my shirt over my head before falling back again. I wonder if she wants me to keep on the bra she likes. But it's too tight on me, and I'm too melty and shapeless for such shaped things right now. I lift myself up again, pull off my bra, and flop back down.

"We should get this off you too," she says, attempting to pull the skirt by the hem, but it won't budge.

"You have to unzip the secret zipper here," I tell her, patting the top of the skirt. We both laugh as Chris crawls up the bed straddling me to get to the zipper. She finds it, pulls it down, and as she yanks off my skirt, she bites my lower belly gently, the way a puppy might. Then she stands up again to toss my skirt on a chair in the far corner.

I thought I'd still feel nervous, but my nerves have been soaked in the melt of a mild high. Instead, I feel something else. Something I didn't expect to.

"Chris," I say, trying to figure out how to say it.

"Yes, Scarlet?" she says back softly.

"I want you to come here and fuck me." My face goes hot. I said it because I know it's what she wants to hear, but maybe the Vicodin's making me want it too, whatever *it* is.

Chris is looking at me with tender eyes. She pulls her belt off and tosses it, leaving the rest of her clothes on. I feel the pressure of her weight as she climbs on top of me. I know I don't like her like that, but my body seems to; the weight of her feels good and one of my hands finds the other across her back. I'm made of pudding. I ooze under her, and she moves her legs between mine and turns my face with her hands, kissing my cheek first and then my neck slowly. My body hums. I've lost my bones. She stops for a moment and brushes the hair from my forehead, trying to look me in the eyes, but my eyes are too mushy for that.

"I'll be right back," she says as she climbs off me. "I'm going to go put a dick on."

"What?" I ask.

"I'll be right back," she says again.

But I heard her the first time, and my anxiety rushes in again. I was worried about something like this. I have no clue what I'm doing. What if she's like Todd, and I die a little just wanting it to end?

She comes back and slides into bed, and I purposely

avert my eyes. I don't want to see what she is or isn't wearing. I can feel that she's topless now, her skin warm on mine.

"I won't kiss you if you don't want me to," she says.

I don't want her to. I press my cheek against hers, and she curves her face into the crook of my neck, her teeth grazing me. She's gentle, but I can hear it in her breath. I can tell she wants to put me in a vise grip, make a mess of me. I wrap my arms around her. The way she wants me makes me want her, and I hold her tighter. She's spreading my legs, rolling them open with her own, and I'm worried she's going to fumble around and it will hurt. But I don't have to worry for long. She pushes inside of me slowly, easily, rolling my legs wider as she does. She bites down harder on my neck. I don't want to like it as much as I do.

A couple of hours later we're sitting on the couch watching a *90210* rerun on channel 20. When I moved a foot away from her to lean my elbow on the armrest, Chris scooted in, closing the gap. The high is over, and what remains has curled into a hard lump in my stomach. I can feel her looking at me, but I don't turn toward her. I'm queasy, and I just want to be done. What kind of prostitute sleeps over and has to do a whole twelve hours? How did Sam come up with that and why did I listen? Chris's fingers slide along my arm and curl around my thumb. I glance at her as I shift myself out of her grip.

"Are you trying to hold my hand?" I ask. I want to take

my words back the minute they escape from my lips. "Sorry," I add. "I'm just really tired."

A wave of hurt washes over her face. I *am* an asshole. But just as quickly as it arrived, the hurt drains and is replaced by a cold smirk. "You can fuck for money, but you can't hold my hand?" she asks, narrowing her eyes. She's an asshole too. A total asshole.

I can feel the heat rising in my cheeks. I want to shove her in the chest, grab my stuff, and run out into the dark, into the cool night air, but I turn back to the TV, and the burning in my face starts to dissipate. Dylan's father just died, his yacht exploded. I saw this episode when it first came out. Sam, April, and I were eating donut holes on my couch, a Wednesday night, our freshman year. A lifetime ago. Thousands of miles away.

In the morning I wake up to Chris handing me a cup of coffee. The sunlight is shining through the sheer curtains and I rub my eyes, then sit up to take the mug as she fixes the pillows behind my back.

From her dresser drawer she pulls out a thick roll of money. I watch as she counts out twelve hundred dollars all in one-hundred-dollar bills. Why does she have so much cash if she works for BART? I wonder if she lied and she's actually a drug dealer. It would explain almost everything. She holds the roll up to show me and tucks it in with my clothes on the chair, before she sits on the bed to face me.

Does she think it was worth it? I'm trying to think of something to say, but she beats me to it.

"My mom would have thought you had a sweet smile. That would have been the thing she said if she had met you," Chris says.

I fight to keep a bewildered expression from forming on my face. The thought of meeting her mom, of her imagining our meeting, none of it makes sense. I take a sip of coffee.

"Your mom knew you were gay?" I ask, removing myself from the scene she set.

"Have you looked at me lately?" She laughs. "I'm doing a terrible job of hiding it."

"So she met your ex-girlfriend?" I ask.

She smiles. "She met every girlfriend I ever had. Is that surprising?"

I watch her rub her knuckles. I want to ask how her mom died. And when. And where. But I can see her eyes getting glassy again.

"You would have definitely introduced her to your escort?" I ask, lifting my eyebrows.

"No." She shakes her head and grins. "Nope. Not when you say it like that."

Is there any other way to say it?

"Can we try this again next Saturday?" she asks. "I'm sorry I said that thing I said . . . last night. I just reacted, without thinking first. Maybe I like you a little *too* much."

What does she like? The bits I've let slip? The banter? The clothes, the makeup, put on like a life jacket?

Next week, another twelve hundred dollars. I need this. I can do this, I can pretend, for now at least. I reach for her forearm. "I'll be here next Saturday, and you can hold my hand if we watch TV next time." Then I lean in and kiss her on the neck.

When I get back to the apartment, Sam is still asleep, and I head straight for the shower. I want to be brand-new. I take the bar of soap to every inch of me. It's not that I feel dirty, I just don't want to get Chris on Sam. It's like being at a potluck and watching the juice from the brisket soak into the cake on your plate.

After I get out, I wrap myself in a towel and crawl into bed with Sam, kissing her awake. I want to remind her that I love her and I'm still the one.

"How was it?" she asks. "Were you good at faking an orgasm?"

"I was good at everything," I say.

Sam smiles with her eyes still closed. I bite her ear. I can't bear to tell her I didn't fake it. It happened without my even trying.

9

On Sunday Sam and I wander into Thrift Town, a secondhand store so massive it's two stories high and takes up half a city block. We buy up all the big-haired heavy metal band T-shirts: Poison, Mötley Crüe, Twisted Sister. We score psychedelic vintage bedsheets with yellow sunflowers the size of umbrellas, matching *#1 Dad* and *#1 Mom* coffee mugs, and a gallon Ziploc bag full of plastic neon bangle bracelets. Then we walk up to Leather Tongue Video, our loot heavy on my back. Leather Tongue has a photo booth that prints mini sticker pictures. Sam grabs me by the back of the head and kisses me right in time for the flash. We pick up coffee at Muddy Waters and stick one of our pictures to the counter and another on the mirror in the bathroom. Then we head up to Dolores Park, leaving stickers on parking meters and phone booths and one on the window of the 500 Club. "Can you imagine if we put these all over Long Beach?" Sam says. "Like in Moshe's Deli and Glatt's and Rudy's Wash N Fold?"

I take her hand, grateful to be here.

We lie down in Dolores Park. Sam uses my backpack as a pillow, and I snuggle in the crook of her arm. My arm across her warm stomach, the feel of it rising with each breath, the sun on our skin; we're lizards on our very own rock. Looking around, I wonder if it's safe to lie like this in public, but no one seems to be staring or even noticing us at all.

"I wish you were out with Molly and me last night," Sam says. "Her roommate, Luz, didn't want to go, so I got to use her ID, which is way less stressful than trying to transfer a wrist stamp. I don't look anything like her, but the girl working the door just waved me in. It was so cool. All queer people, like, it was packed, and there were so many cute girls."

"So many cute girls?" I ask, squeezing her. "Were you like flirt flirt flirty flirt?"

"Of course I was! I knew you wouldn't care!" she says, laughing.

It would be cooler not to care. I'm glad she thinks I don't, even though I do. Especially if "cute girls" means Molly.

Across the park, I'm watching two girls talking near the bathroom, and then one leans in and starts kissing the other.

"Oh my god, Sam, look," I say, trying to inconspicuously point with my elbow in their direction.

"Aw, cute!" Sam says.

"I've never seen two girls kissing in real life before," I say, mesmerized.

"See? That's why you should come out to the clubs with us! You're missing out on seeing all the girls kissing."

My eyes are locked on them. I can't look away.

"Do you think it would be fun if we made out with other people?" Sam asks.

I look up at her. "Why are you asking that? Do you want to?"

Sam shrugs and shields her eyes from the sun.

"Well, do you?" I ask again.

"Kind of. It's not that big of a stretch with us stripping, and now that you're working for Chris—"

I feel myself stiffen. She was the one who said it was different. It was work and work was different.

"—I mean, we're young and this city is full of cute girls, and Molly and her friends were talking about how monogamy is a tool of the patriarchy."

"What? What does that even mean?" I ask.

Sam laughs. "Forget it. Just come out with me! Next Saturday! See all the cute girls for yourself, pleeeease?"

I curl deeper into her and squeeze her waist tight. "You're mine," I growl, and then I bite her cheek, feel her grin with my teeth. "But I can't go out next Saturday. Chris asked if I'd work for her again."

I pull back to look at her and see she's dropped her grin.

"You said yes?"

"Yeah, I thought that's what we decided. It's so much money and now I don't have to go back to the club anytime soon."

She stares at me blankly. "I guess that's good," she says. "So, when are you going to tell me more about sex with Chris?"

"What else do you want to know about it?" I ask, caught off guard by the question.

"Everything!"

"Why?" I try to pull her even closer, moving my head to her chest, dodging her gaze.

"What do you mean? Why would I not? We talk about all the weirdos in the club. Why wouldn't I want to hear about actual sex with an actual dyke?"

It feels different from talking about the weirdos in the club. And then there's the Vicodin, the broken promise—I want to sweep it out of my mind, tell myself it never happened.

"Okay," I say. "I mean, I didn't know what I was doing but I didn't really have to because she was the doer."

"I kind of assumed that." Sam laughs. "What did she do?"

I feel my face get hot. She pulls back, getting a good look at me.

"Oh my god. You're blushing, Hannah!" She sits up, unsettling me from her chest. "Why are you blushing? What did she do?"

"She put on a dick," I whisper, squinting as I brace for her response.

Sam's eyes turn to saucers. She gasps and covers her mouth, but the giggles spill out. My face is on fire and now I can't stop giggling either.

"Do you think all the really gay-looking ones do that?" she asks.

"How am I supposed to know, Sam! I'm not an expert on the really gay-looking ones!"

"So then did you just act like Julia Roberts in *Pretty Woman*? Like lay back on the piano and—"

Sam flops back, throws her legs up in the air, and moans.

"Stop it!" I yell, my eyes darting around while I wrestle her legs down. Now my face is on fire for a whole new reason.

Sam cackles and rolls side to side in the grass. "I'm never dating anyone I have to have straight sex with!"

"How is it straight sex if there isn't a man involved?" I ask.

Sam doesn't answer, she ends her giggles with a sigh, then quiets. I look away, quieting too. Down the hill, the kissing girls have disappeared into the bathroom, and now I'm wondering what they're doing in there. Probably not having straight sex. A man with a Popsicle cart walks the paved path through the grass, bells jingling. It wasn't straight sex because Chris isn't a man. But she isn't exactly a woman either. What is she? Both? Neither?

"Look," Sam says, pointing down the hill. Close to Dolores Street someone has strung a tightrope between two palm trees, held taut a couple of feet above the grass. People take turns trying to walk across it, but nobody seems to be able to stay on. They try and try again, laughing as they fall.

"What if you start liking Chris?" Sam asks. At first she looks curious, but I watch the corners of her mouth sink with unease.

I wrap my arms around her and pull her back down to lie on my backpack. "Sam, there's no way I'm going to like Chris. I'm eighteen, and I'm pretty sure she's in her late thirties, and she's not my type. And you're the one who wants to make out with all the cute girls in this city. It isn't me!" I laugh. But I'm not laughing on the inside. I'm unnerved, anxious. And Sam must be too, because she doesn't laugh with me. She rolls herself out of my reach.

For the next couple weeks, Sam works at the Cheese Parade on Thursdays and Fridays and goes out on the town with Molly on Saturdays while I'm with Chris.

"Saturday is the only day I can work for Chris!" I complain. "She works like sixty hours a week. If you really want me to go out with you and Molly, can't you plan something on a different day?"

Sam rolls her eyes. "Molly works Fridays, Sundays, and Mondays at Josie's, and the best club nights are always on Saturdays. It's not like you want to go out anyways. Every time I ask you, you're too tired, or you say you don't have anything cute to wear. It's fine, so just forget about it."

I look out our window and rub the back of my neck. I could argue, but I don't have the energy.

Later, I call Bubbe and she asks how Sam and I are doing as roommates. I let out a groan.

"Are you two quarreling?" she asks.

"I don't know what we're doing," I say.

"Young women quarrel like lovers!" Bubbe chuckles. I feel my breath catch in my throat. "Silly girls," she continues. "But you'll work it out! Az men muz, ken men, no?"

"What does that mean again?"

"'If you have to, you can,'" Bubbe says. "And so you will."

I wonder if Sam knows we have to work it out.

I have my Sam problems at home, and then when I'm with Chris I'm still uneasy, guarded when she wants to sit close on the couch, stare into my eyes, and talk. I can't relax anywhere.

I start my nights with Chris waiting for her to offer a pill or a drink or a bump of coke. Waiting to feel different, better. I take whatever she offers and decide I'll never tell Sam.

"Who are you, Scarlet?" Chris asks, her eyes thirsty. She passes me her flask.

"Who do you want me to be?" I vamp, taking another swig. It's a ridiculous response, straight out of a bad movie. But it's true. The question *is* the answer.

The strange thing: despite my overall discomfort around her, when she puts me in a cab in the mornings, I think about the sex and liquefy. I can't reconcile the urge to quit while I'm ahead with the wants of my body. She doesn't know me, but she knows sex. And I want to know everything she knows. I want to know what the girls kissing in the park know, the dykes at the Bearded Lady, the couple with the shaved heads we saw walking the Castro the day we arrived.

Sam and I get along best on weekdays when we wander. We go to thrift stores and come home with vintage kitchenware, stiff floral swimsuits from the fifties, beaten-up tennis rackets. We go shopping at the Powell Street mall, sit in dark movie theaters in the middle of the day, eat Thai food from take-out boxes at night. We live. But we don't live enough for Sam. She picks up flyers for queer clubs and poetry slams and performance art and leaves them all over the apartment. Sam's wrong about me, I *do* want to go out. I want to meet queer people. Queer people our age, with their cute clothes and their Manic Panic hair. Queer people I can barely look at, my eyes dropping to my feet when they pass me on the street. I want their world so badly that when Sam passes me a flyer, I flood with anxiety, my pulse tapping in my ears. The real me isn't cool or hot. I can't fake at life more than I'm already faking. The flyers become fallen leaves, the dates pass, and they collect in a pile under the bed where I've kicked them.

On the last Saturday in August, I wake up feeling like I might have a yeast infection. I've only had one once, in high school, so I'm unsure at first, but Dr. Sammie confirms it for me and goes out to Walgreens to get me the seven-day cream I'm too embarrassed to buy myself.

"Ugh, what am I going to tell Chris about tonight?" I ask when she returns. "I guess I could tell her I have a migraine or something. Maybe just a headache?"

"Why don't you just tell her the truth?" Sam asks. "I'm sure she's had a yeast infection at some point in her life. She'd be happy you were being real with her."

I consider this. "You're probably right."

"Call her right now," Sam says.

For some reason, I don't want to call Chris in front of Sam. But why? I pick up the phone and dial.

"Hello?" Chris answers.

"Hey, it's Scarlet," I say.

I'm watching Sam watch me. I try to wave her eyes away, but she gives me the *What?!* look and keeps watching.

"I knew it was going to be you, even before I picked up," Chris says. She wants to flirt. But I can't flirt with Sam staring at me.

"Chris," I start. But then I pause. Sam covers her mouth with both hands. "I don't think I can have sex tonight," I say. Sam looks like she's about to lose it.

"That's okay," Chris says. "Can I ask why?"

"Because I have a yeast infection, and I'm super uncomfortable, and now I have to use this gross cream for seven days."

Sam flops on the bed and holds a pillow over her head, burying her laughter.

Chris chuckles too, and then goes quiet. Maybe I've permanently broken the spell I have on her.

"That's okay," she says. "I've been wanting to take you on a real out-of-the-house date anyway, but would you drop your price by a couple hundred? I have to keep racking up the overtime so I don't go broke over here."

I think for a moment. Is she doing all that overtime for me? This is the first time she's said anything about going broke, and it makes me feel bad. Guilty bad. But I don't want to do it unless it's a lot of money. And plus, a real out-of-the-house date doesn't make any sense. Wasn't sex the premise of the whole arrangement?

"I can drop it to one thousand," I say, "but are you sure you still want to?"

"Yeah, I want to take you on a daytime date. Can I pick you up outside of Red's in an hour?"

"An hour from *now*?" I ask.

"Yeah, an hour from now."

I hesitate. "Okay," I say.

I hang up the phone and hold it down firmly on the receiver. Oh god, what have I done? A daytime no-sex date is problematic in so many ways. It will be all talking. Talking and talking and talking. I flop back on the bed and put my hands over my face.

"It's not gonna be *that* bad," Sam says.

"That's what you think," I say. "You don't have to do it."

She scootches closer to lie beside me, resting a hand on my chest.

"You don't have to do it either, Hannah," she says, her voice softer. "You could call her back and say you changed your mind. You don't have to do anything with her."

I uncover my face to look at her. It should be easier, not harder. But when Chris wants to talk instead of fuck, I feel like a snail with no shell, nothing to hide under. Sam is better equipped for this line of work. She's charismatic and unperturbed and thick-skinned. She's actually better equipped for everything.

"I can do it," I say. I pull myself up and head to the shower.

It's eleven a.m. I'm standing outside Red's, shivering, my back against the locked door. It's foggy and cold today, when yesterday was clear, with a high in the seventies. I couldn't make Northern California weather up if I tried.

Chris pulls up in a red convertible, the top up, her elbow hanging from an open window.

"What the heck is this?" I ask, amused.

"I borrowed it from my buddy," she says.

"I don't know what kind of buddies you have," I say, shaking my head.

I get in and she pulls my hand to her mouth to kiss the back of it like a suitor at a ball. It's a silly move, kind of sweet, and a laugh escapes me. "Where are we going?" I ask.

"You'll see," she says.

I was sure I'd feel tense trapped in a car with Chris, taken god knows where, with nothing offered to loosen me up. But as we head through the streets, climbing over giant hills into neighborhoods I've never seen, I feel my trepidation shedding. I'm a snake molting skin, layer after layer, one after the other. The heater is on, so I'm not freezing anymore, and Chris is letting some quiet in, not blabbering a monologue at me like usual. We head onto the Golden Gate Bridge. I can't believe I haven't driven over the Golden Gate Bridge yet. The color is vermilion against the gray. I look up through the windshield, but the bridge towers disappear into fog, and when I look down, the water is veiled in mist, barely visible. We're barreling through a cloud. We cross into the rolling hills of Marin, where we're swallowed by a tunnel, the arch painted with a rainbow. And when we come out the other side, we're blasted into clear blue skies and sunshine. Just like that. Light bouncing everywhere, miles of golden rolling hills. I look at Chris. She's been watching me take it all in, a soft joy on her face. She drives without saying a word. I don't mind this. She rests her hand on my thigh, and I move mine to the back of her neck, turning my head toward the window to watch the houses drop away, the clean hills speckle with trees, then cows, then sheep. It's a flip-book going on and on and on. She keeps her hand on my thigh. I keep mine on her neck. I know what it means to her. It means something to me too. I don't need to have feelings for her to have this. She doesn't have to really know me for us to have this moment: it's just something sweet. It can be simple, like toast.

Chris takes me for coffee and scones at a charming little bakery in Petaluma on the first floor of a yellow Victorian. Then out a winding road to a hike around the perimeter of Tomales Bay that leads to the sand dunes of Dillon Beach. As it gets dark, we head to a restaurant in Olema called the Farm House, for which we are woefully underdressed. At a white-clothed table, after a glass of wine, Chris tells me her mom loved this place. I study her face, wondering if she wants me to ask about her mother, what she was like. Instead, I fumble and ask when she died.

"A year and a half ago now," she answers, setting her elbows on the table and weaving her fingers together. She rests her chin on her knuckles.

"Oh," I say. I take another sip of wine. "For some reason I thought it was right before we met."

"I wake up and it always feels like yesterday," she says.

"You were really close, right?" I ask. "That probably makes it feel brand-new for a long time."

She rubs her jaw with her hand.

"I have a lot of regret."

Her eyes dampen and I wonder if I should do a U-turn, veer her away from the topic.

"I wanted to get my shit together before she died," she says. She scratches the back of her neck. I watch tears pool, threatening to spill.

"You have your shit together," I say. "You own a town house in San Francisco, and you have a union job with health benefits and big money. You *clearly* have your shit together."

She stares at me, opens her mouth to speak, but pauses.

"I don't know how you can think that," she says.

The waiter interrupts, arriving with two plates across one arm, and sets them in front of us. Chris looks up at him and smiles. I look at my plate: a few slices of steak on a nest of shredded brussels sprouts, and three small potatoes. Chris jokes the portions here are too big for her. The waiter feigns amusement. When he leaves, Chris launches us back into safer territory. She tells me about camping. The gear you've got to get. The trip she took with all her gear and her ex-girlfriend to the Yuba River. "Clear water. Clean air. Nothing like it," she says.

As we drive back across the Golden Gate, she keeps up the chatter. I want to promise her I won't ask about her mom again so she can relax. But instead, I half listen and let my eyes ramble the darkening landscape. If she needs to talk, she can talk all she wants. I don't mind. Today she introduced me to an entirely different California. A California with eucalyptus trees and bay trees and giant redwoods.

A rocky coastline, dunes tufted with long grass, meandering country roads. There are endless possibilities of what California can look like. Maybe endless possibilities of who I can be in it.

When I get home, I find the apartment dark, Sam already out for the night.

10

On Monday the weather flips again like a switch. Wicked hot. Manic, there's no other way to explain it. Sam and I take a bag of frozen grapes and two tattered beach chairs we found on the street up to the roof. It's four floors up and the last set of stairs ends at a heavy door with a construction paper sign that reads *NO TRESPASSING* and below it *PELIGRO! NO TRASPASAR!* written in Sharpie. Sam pushes it open, and we're blinded by light, our eyes pinching.

"Whoa!" Sam says. "I can't believe we've never come up here before!"

We can see San Francisco in all directions from this vantage point. The high-rises tightening in toward downtown, Potrero Hill, Sutro Tower like a pitchfork stuck in the middle of Twin Peaks. As I step closer to the edge, I see why we were warned PELIGRO! It's flat. No rail. Nothing to obstruct the view, nothing to keep us safe.

We take off our shorts and sit in our underwear and T-shirts. I pull my knees to my chest, my toes skimming the metal edge of the folding chair, and I line them up with Twin Peaks to pinch Sutro Tower between them when I close one eye. We pass the bag of grapes back and forth in silence.

"Are you ever gonna call Rachel back?" Sam asks.

I groan and drop my head.

"She's already left two messages. Are you just going to ignore her forever?"

It's actually three, but I don't correct her. Rachel is pissed. Rightfully. Her voice on the answering machine is demanding at first, before it inevitably trembles and cracks. I have to bury my head under a pillow to listen.

"I'm just scared my mom's going to answer," I say. "And then if I do get to talk to Rachel, what do I even tell her?"

"Tell her we have an apartment and jobs. Tell her whatever you tell Bubbe."

I don't respond. I bite a frozen grape in half.

"Hannah," Sam says quietly.

"What?"

She's silent. I lift my head to look at her.

"What?" I ask again.

She chews. Swallows. "I don't want you to work for Chris anymore."

"Why?" I ask, confused.

"I just don't like it. I want you to come back to the Cheese Parade with me."

I study her face, trying to read her motivations.

"But it was your idea," I say. "And I couldn't handle the club. That's the whole reason you came up with it."

"I know, but now I don't want you sleeping with her anymore, okay?"

She pushes a grape into her mouth and hands me the bag. "Are you jealous or something?"

"Maybe a little, but mostly, it's not fair you're having sex with someone else, when I'm not allowed to. You're the only girl I've ever slept with, and you're, like, deep in dyke sex ed with Chris."

"What? I'm *working* for Chris! It doesn't count like that. I wouldn't sleep with her in real life, and you're the one who said it was work and that makes it different!"

"Well, I changed my mind. I'm allowed to change my mind. And Molly agrees. She thinks it's not fair too."

I feel my body stiffen and drop the bag of grapes to the ground. "Why are you talking to Molly about me?"

"She's my friend."

"Sam, it's illegal! You can't go around telling people, and Molly doesn't even know me!" I feel a hot panic rising, burning my throat, my eyes aching with it. "Have you told anyone else?"

She doesn't say anything.

"Who else did you tell?!"

"I told Jade," she says, shamefaced. "But she promised she wouldn't tell Mama Beth. She said lots of girls do it. She's not judging you. Molly isn't either. She just thinks we should stop calling ourselves monogamous when we're obviously not."

"You can tell Molly it's work, just like stripping is work. I've never even let Chris kiss me! Not even once, Sam." I'm furious, my hands shaking with it. "Sam, *all* of this, the Chez Paree, Chris, *you* came up with all of it. You're so full of great ideas, and I'm the sucker who goes along with whatever stupid shit you come up with. If you want to sleep with other girls, just say it. Don't use Chris as an excuse, and don't talk about me behind my back when you know I've told nobody. I *can't* tell anybody. We left Long Beach because we were sick of secrets, but now we've just got new crap to hide." Sam doesn't respond; she puts her feet on the seat, hugs her legs against her chest, and drops her head onto her knees. "Stripping is fine for you," I continue, "but I'm not you. We're not the same." I shade my eyes from the sun. I want her to pick up her head and look at me, to see that I mean it. "I will *never* go back to stripping."

She lifts her head and glares at me. "So, what are you going to do when you're done with Chris? Huh? Try and find a job at a shitty gas station again? You still don't have any experience, for any job," she scoffs.

She's right. There's no reason to think finding a job will be any easier now. It's not like we can put stripping on a résumé.

"I don't know what I'll do, but I'm telling you I'm not done with Chris. And I'm not going back to stripping."

"That's what I'm worried about, Hannah," she says,

squeezing her arms tighter around her folded legs. "You feel like such a faker with the guys at the club, but you don't feel like a faker with Chris because there's a little piece of you that likes her. *That's* why you're not done with her."

I want to shove her chair over. Tell her I hate her. But what if she's right? How can I know how wrong the Chris situation is for me, the drugs, the unsettled feelings, and still cling to what it offers?

"I can't tell if you're jealous or if you're trying to open up our relationship. What are you trying to do right now?"

"I'm trying to tell you, I don't want to be with you if you're going to keep working for her," she says.

"Seriously, Sam?" I ask. "This is the first time you're telling me you don't want me to do it, and you're already threatening to break up?"

I get up and yank my shorts back on. For a moment Sam looks like she wants to take it back, before her expression turns cold and sullen and her head drops back to her knees.

"You sound crazy right now. You think you have me on a leash, and I'll just do whatever you say!" I yell. "Well, I'm not going to do what you say this time!"

I head for the door and swing it wide so it slams with a bang. I hear Sam's voice shouting after me as I tap down the dark stairwell flight by flight, nearly knocking into an older man in a bathrobe. I run past him, past our apartment door, down the last flight of stairs, and then burst from the gate. Workers are setting up scaffolding on our building and they stop to watch me stalk by. I'm clearly pissed, my eyes wet and red. I cross the tracks on Powell, past a line of tourists waiting to ride the cable car, then go down Market Street to Third. Crossing over the Mission Creek Channel, I head out, out, out. Out to where the vacant industrial buildings shadow the sidewalks. It's desolate, an occasional homeless person passing with a cart. I want to be alone. I want the ocean. I want an expanse of cold nothingness to wade into. At Pierpoint Lane, I take a left and head toward the bay, walking until I can't get any closer. A loading dock, poking its metal finger into the water, is barred by a chain-link fence in front of me. I look around and still see nobody. Threading my fingers through the links in the fence, I hoist myself up, flip a leg over the top, and startle a few pigeons when I land in a squat on the other side. I walk out to the end of the dock, the hot wind whipping my hair.

I need just one person to know me all the way, to know every unsavory detail and love me anyway. Just one. Love me anyway. Sam's as close as I've ever gotten, and her allegiance is slipping. So slowly I didn't know I was losing it, how alone I've become.

If I could tell Bubbe any of this, I know what she would say. If I weren't selling sex and totally gay, if it were something tolerable like I'd flunked calculus or I wanted to be a poet, she would say: *Bubbeleh, whatever reassurance you want, you give that to yourself first. That's your job, what you do for yourself.* I try to say it to myself now, but it falls flat. It falls right into the water, sinking out of view. I want to fall and sink with it.

It takes me twice as long to walk back now that I've lost the heat of my anger, sweated it out, and gone numb. I'm tired, hungry, and thirsty. When I get back to the apartment building, I see what I think is a teenage boy talking to one of the guys who was setting up the scaffolding. They're pointing up to the highest level, but as I get closer, I realize the teenage boy is a dyke, maybe midtwenties. She looks like River Phoenix. His hair. His eyes and lips. I feel my hands get sweaty. I wipe my nose and push my hair out of my face. I know I look like shit, but I want to look like the best shit this shit can look like when I walk by her, in case she notices me. But she doesn't. I'm invisible. I pass and unlock the gate.

When I get back inside, the studio is dark, our seventies sunflower sheets hanging over the windows like curtains. My eyes take a moment to adjust.

"I had to cover them. They were setting up scaffolding and suddenly a bunch of dudes were looking in on me," Sam says, sitting on the edge of the bed to lace up her boots. She won't look up at me. She's freshly showered and dressed up cute, wet hair falling over her eyes, and my heart leans toward her in my chest. I love her. I can't help it. I don't want to fight with her.

"I'm going out with Molly and her friends, and if we stay out super late, I might just crash on Molly's couch," she says. Just hearing Molly's name again stings. She doesn't seem angry anymore, but she doesn't invite me, and she's never crashed at Molly's before. I sit down next to her. I don't want her to leave mad. What if she never comes back? I lean in and kiss her cheek. She turns toward me, softening, and brushes my hair behind my ear.

"Remember the first time you kissed me?" I ask.

"The ChapStick trick," she says, offering a melancholy half smile.

"Remember the quarries?" I ask. I want to take her hand, rewind, drag her back in time and try again.

"I want to figure this out," I say. "Maybe it's a hurdle, but it doesn't need to be a breakup."

Sam nods but looks unconvinced. "There's other stuff too, Hannah, but yeah, we can try," she says, sighing. "Let's just talk about it later."

She gets up but turns back to kiss me. Only a quick kiss, hardly more than a peck. It's a foot wedged in a door right as it's closing, holding it open a crack, for just a moment longer. I want to ask her about the other stuff, but she's already grabbed her bag. The door closes behind her. I sit for a moment, rubbing her mint ChapStick between my lips. Then I kick off my shoes and lie back on the bed. We still have a chance. Tomorrow I'll go out looking for a regular job. I'll keep applying until I get one. That was the plan all along anyway. I'll go back to the old plan, and maybe Sam will be happy again.

Sam is gone all night, and I can't sleep. I imagine her in a club with Molly, making out with cute girls and then each other. A fist tightens deep inside of my chest. In the morning, I wake up alone and picture Sam on Molly's couch, and then worse, in Molly's bed, and then worse, naked.

After a shower, I blow-dry my hair, creating a mountain of frizz, then flat-iron it, flipping up the ends. I carve a side part and comb it into position with my fingers, assessing in the mirror. Not terrible. As close to looking professional as I can get. I put on one of Sam's sweaters, black jeans, and the vintage black cowboy boots I picked up at Thrift Town, and try to ready myself for a day of filling out job applications.

When I step out of the gate, I see River Phoenix again. She's wearing paint-splattered coveralls and an orange beanie. She must be a painter. I feel a familiar wave of anxiety wash over me, the urge to drop my head and scuttle off like a hermit crab, but I breathe and force myself to stay. Looking up, I see several other women high on the scaffolding. It's a crew of women painters. *Only in San Francisco,* I think, beaming. When I pass River Phoenix, I make myself smile, and to my surprise, she smiles back. Her grin is heart-meltingly cute. She's got thick unplucked eyebrows and black lashes. As I walk down Ellis Street, then over to Union Square, I imagine being cake for River Phoenix. Let my mind run wild with the stories I make up.

When I find myself on the north end of Union Square, I stand under the pillared statue, watching rich people go in and out of Tiffany & Co. In front of the store, there's a hot dog stand with an attached red and yellow umbrella hanging over it. It reminds me of the boardwalk in Long Beach, and smells like it too. *I could be a hot dog vendor,* I think. *I could do that.* But then a Help Wanted sign catches my eye in the window of a café a couple doors down.

I cross the street, breaking through the steady current of pedestrians to get to the shop's door, and step inside. It isn't a fancy place, just like how I'm not a fancy person, so maybe we're a good match. A family of flies buzzes a tight circle in the middle of the room, and the pastries are all individually wrapped in plastic. The guy behind the counter is in his fifties, and I make the assumption he's the owner, or at least the manager.

"I saw your sign and I'm interested in working here."

"Okay," he says, reaching under the counter, "here's an application to fill out."

Ugh, the dreaded application. He hands me a pen along with it. At least I have an address and a phone number now.

"Can you tell me what the starting rate is?" I ask as I write the letters of my name, each in its own little square.

"Minimum wage," he says, lifting the tip jar to wipe the counter beneath it.

"What's minimum wage these days?" I ask.

"Four twenty-five," he says.

"Four twenty-five?" I ask. "An hour?"

He looks at me like I'm an idiot. "What else would it be?"

I hardly paid attention to my hourly wage when I worked

at Rudy's Wash N Fold. I sit down at a table, flip the application over, and write on the back:

$$\begin{array}{r} 4.25 \\ \underline{\text{x}\quad 8} \\ 34 \end{array}$$

That's thirty-four bucks before taxes, for the entire day. I wonder if anyone has figured out how to live on so little in San Francisco without food stamps, without sleeping next to the fountain at Civic Center. I make that in less than thirty minutes with Chris. I made more than that in one topless lap dance at the Cheese Parade. Holy shit. In the land of shitty options, I'm lucky.

I don't want to work forty hours a week in a fly-filled café, wrapping muffins in plastic, and still be broke. I want time. I want days to walk around and cash in my pocket. And maybe that kind of freedom is worth a few shitty nights each month.

The most valuable asset I have right now is this eighteen-year-old body. What the hell is wrong with this whole picture? Everything. Or maybe nothing. I'm not sure. Custodians, carpenters, coal miners, chiropractors—so many people use their bodies to make money. But Sam and I, and Jade and Monique and Marla and Reba and all the rest, we're invisible by design. Nobody's mother is bragging to her friends at synagogue, *Well, my daughter is a very success-*

ful prostitute. But I'm so free! I want to argue. *Show me my better option!*

I look out through the window of the café, at the flurry of people rushing in every direction. *Show me my better option!* I want to scream. But watching them, I see. They're frazzled, and I'm frei. Maybe not the version Bubbe wanted for me, but frei.

"I'm frei," I say to myself out loud, and saying it changes me, momentarily at least, pops a parachute over my head right when I'm falling so fast.

I get up and walk out, down to the pay phone on the corner. The receiver is greasy, so I wrap my job application around it and hold it away from my face. I call Chris and leave her a message. I tell her I want to go on another date, day or night, whenever she does.

"Anytime," I say.

11

I call Bubbe while Sam's out thrifting on Haight Street with her new friends. Of course she didn't invite me, even though thrifting is *our* thing.

"Sam and I can't stop fighting, and I don't even know why," I complain. We've been at each other's throats for days, unable to get through a conversation without setting each other off.

"What are you two bickering about now?" she asks.

I think for a minute about how to say it without saying it. On the surface, it's about Chris, and how she wants me to give the Chez Paree one more chance, and why she never invites me out with Molly and her friends. But I keep thinking about what she said: *There's other stuff too.* She hasn't told me what the *other stuff* is, and I've been too afraid to ask.

I let out a long sigh. "Literally everything. Everything and nothing. It's like we're spiraling downward. Like down a drain."

"Hmmm," she says. "You are very good friends, and good friends are to support each other, not pull each other down with nonsense. If you make an effort to stop the nonsense, she will follow suit. Somebody has to lead the way, so why not you?"

"Sam wants to control me, control what I do, and I just want to control how she feels," I say. I know how absurd it sounds. Bubbe clears her throat.

"Hannah," she says.

"Yeah?"

"I've been meaning to tell you." She pauses, clears her throat again. "I'm going to come out to see you."

"What?!"

"I'm coming to see you—"

"Have you ever even been on a flight that long?"

"I've thought a lot about it," she says, "and I really haven't traveled in my life, so when you were on your way to California, I thought, *Why shouldn't* I *be on my way to California?* And when we were on the phone you promised you'd take me somewhere, and I thought, *Why not now? What's stopping me? I'm a tough lady, I like adventure.*"

I *did* promise. My eyes dart around the mess of the room, two pairs of stilettos leaning against the wall, dirty G-strings looped on the closet doorknob, then out the window, the sound of the chaos in the streets below, deafening now, and not a single tree in sight. I can't imagine Bubbe here.

"Where are you going to stay? Our apartment is tiny and there are too many stairs," I say.

"I'll stay at a hotel by the airport. It will only be a few days." She pauses. "Hannah, I'm going to think you don't want me to come if you keep on with all that. Your mother is very worried about this plan, but she's also worried about you. She hasn't spoken to her daughter for almost three months. It's difficult to accept you have no intention of calling her. That's a difficult thing for me to accept as well. Your mother is *my* daughter."

I go heavy with guilt, slumping with the weight of it.

"But she knows we're a good team," she continues. "This visit could be very good for us. For both of us."

I *don't* want her to come here. I can't be Bubbe's Hannah here. It would be impossible. Not in Scarlet's city, not with Sam halfway out the door. I hardly exist. And if I do exist, how will I avoid being seen? My heart thumps in my ears.

"Of course I'm excited," I lie. "When are you coming?"

"After the High Holidays of course. Late October? I'll come from a Thursday to a Sunday, not too long, but long enough to spend a nice Shabbos with you."

On Saturday Sam is furious when I leave to meet up with Chris. I keep asking her what she expects me to do for work if I won't go back to stripping, and every time I say I won't go back she throws a fit, begging me to give it another chance. She tells me she needs me for the creepy walk home.

"You have the pepper spray!" I argue. "And I can meet you there and walk you home!" With that problem solved she changes her approach. Now she needs me back at the club for the comradery.

"Everything is better when we do it together!"

"*Everything?*" I implore. "Like hanging out with Molly?"

We go in circles. I have to get out of the apartment. I can't fix this. I wash off my tear-melted eye makeup, squeeze in some drops of Visine, reapply my mascara, and leave without saying goodbye. I'm already thirty minutes late.

Red's has become our regular meeting spot, and when I get there, Chris is at the bar with a beer bottle in her hand, an empty one in front of her.

"I almost thought I was getting stood up!" she laughs, pulling out the barstool next to her. She pushes a drink in front of me. "I got you this," she says. "Gin and tonic."

"I'm sorry I'm late. I totally lost track of time," I lie. I sit down and look at my drink. I'm still pretending I like gin and tonic. Still pretending I like Chris. All week I was fighting with Sam for *this.* My heart sinks and I try to remember how I felt at the minimum-wage café. *I'm free, I'm free, I'm free,* I say to myself. But it doesn't work this time.

Chris launches into a never-ending rant about work. They're making her train another guy who pretends to know everything already, and I'm trying to say comforting things while throwing a pity party for myself. I keep hearing myself say, "Wow, that sucks," while I fake listen, stare at my hand on her knee.

"I have an idea," she says.

"What?"

"Let's go back to my place and do mushrooms and order takeout."

"I've never—" I start, but then I stop myself. Maybe I shouldn't tell her.

"You've never done mushrooms before?" She acts shocked. "They're so fun. You'll love 'em."

I think for a second, which is exactly one second too long. I could cry right now. I could explode into a million tears. I swallow twice and stand up, look away so she can't see it in my eyes. *Get your shit together. Get your head back in the game.*

"Okay, I'm in," I say, turning back to her. "Can we go now?"

When we get to her town house, she pulls a jar from the freezer and uncaps it. I look in and see what looks like shriveled-up moldy mushrooms. It looks like something a person shouldn't ingest.

"You do so many different drugs," I realize out loud. "You're not just into one thing." I bring the jar to my nose and take a whiff. It smells like the arcade on the boardwalk in Long Beach, the one I dragged Todd from by his wrist a million years ago.

"I'm kind of a Renaissance man," she says. "I like to keep you on your toes."

We order pizza, and when it arrives, she puts chopped-up bits of moldy mushroom all over my slice and hands it to me. Then she puts in a VHS of *Ferris Bueller's Day Off* and we watch it while we eat.

The mushrooms hit me like a ton of bricks halfway through the movie. I realize it when I get up to pee. I practically swim to the bathroom. I feel like a fish in an aquarium. All the objects in the room have been placed here to entertain me. They're all fake. Fake towels on a rack, fake magazines by a fake toilet. Even the toilet paper roll is a prop, the way it unfurls like a cartoon ribbon when I bat it. How many nights have I spent swimming doltish circles without realizing?

It's the mushrooms, I tell myself. I need to keep a firm grip on reality. But the thought leaves me uneasy, and when I get back to the couch, I tell Chris I want to go upstairs and lie down. Now climbing the stairs is impossible. They seem to be moving down like an escalator, and it takes forever to get to the top.

In the bedroom, the carpet rolls like an ocean under my feet. Sensing Chris behind me, I turn, unsteady. She walks to me, and we stand face-to-face, her flesh warping, rippling in piggish-pink waves as she speaks. It should be disturbing, but I find myself fascinated instead.

"Are you tripping?" she asks. But before I can answer she says, "Tim-berrrrrr," and pushes me onto the bed.

I fall for an inordinate amount of time, and even after

I've landed, I still continue to fall. The shove was obnoxious and not funny, but now that I'm horizontal I don't care. I'm better this way. Chris wanders around lighting candles in tall glasses, and the flames burst open slits of light on the walls; I bet I could push my finger into one of them, split the tear wider, and enter another world made of pure gold.

My eyes drift closed, pinching out the flames around me. Now I'm a giant submarine, sinking down. It doesn't matter what she's doing, what either one of us is saying to the other, I keep descending. I feel her weight on top of me, which only drops me lower, faster. I must be in the ground now, under the dirt, under the city. Slowly, my eyes begin to see again, even though I can't tell if they're open. Colors and shapes collide and flash, but if I try to focus on any of them, they disappear and another shape appears, lights up and dances to draw my attention. And then farther back, somewhere beneath sight or above it, everything goes white. Blinding white. Out of this whiteness, images form. I see the front of an aluminum boat. It's rocking on water and the light that reflects fractures into large triangles of glass that float away in every direction. Is the rocking motion coming from Chris fucking me or from the boat? The question wanders off without an answer. The light bounces off the water and the aluminum, and everything flashes and blinds. I extend my hands toward the edge of the boat, fingers spread wide, and feel the hot metal. I grip it firmly. It *is* real. I *am* in a boat.

It must be a small boat. Bare feet wet in a puddle at the bottom, warm from the sun, and now I can see behind me without turning at all. Bubbe is here. I see my bubbe, her face weathered and dark and strong. The sight of her, her eyes gleaming at me, her hands with a firm grasp of the oars, moves me. I'm so happy. She lifts the oars, dripping with water, then leans forward and dips them down again. It's her rowing that's making the motion, not Chris. Now I'm certain of it, even if I can feel Chris inside of me. I see my Bubbe's arms, her shoulders, solid with muscle. I know it's just us. And I can see both of us, how the sun has turned our olive skin dark, how deliberate and strong we are today, and then my eyes find her soft weathered ones, her lids, heavy and kind, her crow's-feet stretching all the way to her hairline.

She knows. She knows everything, and she isn't mad. She knows what I'm doing with Chris at this very moment but her knowing is inconsequential. It's already loose, floating downstream, getting smaller and smaller in the distance without us. She looks at me, floods me with soft love. She loves me anyway. She lifts the oars, they drip, then she dips them down to pull again. Lift. Drip. Dip. Lift. Drip. Dip.

I must have fallen asleep. I wake up naked with Chris naked next to me in her bed. It's 3:47 a.m. I had sex with her. Or rather she had sex with me. If a tree falls in the forest and nobody is there to hear it, does it make a sound? Why is sound the pivotal factor? Unrooted, roots exposed, lying on the forest floor. I must have fallen in silence. I can't remember how it went. All I know is I awoke untethered.

When I wake for the second time it's 6:45 a.m. and I hear Chris in the shower. Did she know how hard I was tripping last night? Why would I take a psychedelic for the first time on a night I was working for Chris? She was paying me for sex after all. What did I expect? But why would she give me a psychedelic for the first time and assume the same transaction applied? I reach down and touch myself. I'm a little bit sore, gooey with lube. Why do I need to know what happened anyway? It happened, so what. A lump swells in my throat.

Getting up, I throw my clothes on, push my feet into my boots, shove my arms into the sleeves of my jacket, and yell, "Chris, I've got to go! I'll talk to you later!" I jog down the stairs and out the door, walking in quick strides the whole way home. I keep feeling like someone's following me, keep looking over my shoulder, but no one's there, and I pass no one on the street for blocks. Maybe I'm nobody. Nobody passing no one. The birds are trying to tell me what this is. They swoop in unison and then splay out in every direction across the gray. Disintegration. Should I blame Chris or myself? I hate both of us.

When I get home, Sam is gone. I find a note on my pillow:

Hannah,

I'll be back in a few days. I'm going to sleep on Molly's couch because I'm sick of fighting. We need a break. Maybe we can talk on Wednesday or something.

—Sam

I don't need a break. I need Sam. Groaning, I kick off my boots, pull off my shirt and pants, and get into bed, pulling the blankets up to my neck. I need Sam. But I can't tell Sam what happened without telling her about the drugs. If I had kept my promise, or if I had shut the whole thing down like she wanted, I wouldn't be sitting here moping about having had sex I didn't know I was having. I need to hear Sam's voice. I need her arms around me, the way you need someone to pull you injured from a car wreck. But she's not coming. Nobody's coming.

"Fuck you, Sam!" I scream out loud, ripping the note in pieces, dropping them to the floor, and then I erupt in a million tears. I sob my way to the shower, wailing for a good half hour in there. I weep while making myself a PB&J, my eyes too blurry to see what I'm doing. Back in bed, I bawl some more, take a bite of my sandwich before tossing it back on the plate. I hold a pillow over my face and wail as loud as I hurt.

Once I've gone numb and quiet, I call Bubbe, but she doesn't answer. I wish I could call Rachel. I consider it for a brief moment, brim with panic, and toss it aside. I wish I could call April. I would do anything to hear April's voice.

I have no one to call. I don't know what to do with myself, and I find myself wanting to call Chris, unsure of what I would say.

A doorbell. My head pops up. Is it ours? Do we even have a doorbell? I've never heard it before, and for a moment I have no idea what to do. It rings again. I grab a T-shirt from the floor, rub the tears off my face with it, throw it on, and tuck my hair behind my ears, before pulling back the makeshift curtain and yanking up the window sash. Leaning my head out, I give a tentative, "Hello?"

Two girls about my age step into view and look up at me. Two dykes. Both with short hair. One is wearing a jean vest covered in patches over a T-shirt, the other is in leather shorts and Doc Martens. Both of their faces glint with piercings.

"Oh, is Sam around?" one of them asks.

"No," I answer, "she's not here right now." I pause, unsure what to say. "Do you want me to tell her—"

"Nah," the other one says. "We'll go see if she's at Molly's."

I watch them turn the corner under the Happy Donuts sign before I pull my head back inside and yank the window closed. I fall back onto the bed and stare at the wall.

Today is the worst. I cover my face with my hands and groan again, even louder this time, until it turns into a roar. I could go to the corner store and buy a bottle of whiskey to spend the day with. But whiskey isn't enough. I want Vicodin, and the only way to get Vicodin is to call Chris. I think about rifling through the pill bottles that live on top of her fridge. And then I think about her mom, all the pain pills she needed before she died, all the pain pills Chris needed after she died. I think about Chris and all her drugs, her flask always tucked into her coat pocket. And then April with her pills wrapped in tinfoil pops into my head, how she slumped against me at Pancho's Cantina, temporarily freed from the burden of herself.

None of it's for fun. People pretend it's for fun, but it's not. I know now. I need to tell April I get it now. April, wherever she is.

How can I do this god-awful day? Sit inside it, desperate and hungry for a way out?

I know what Bubbe would say. She would look at me with her gray eyes, put her hand on my cheek, and say, "Shefele, it *is*, nu? So let it be."

I roll on my side and let new tears soak into the sheets. Softer ones. I unclench my jaw and loosen my throat. I have to let today be what it is. The absolute worst. I'll sulk and pick up takeout and watch shit TV. But tomorrow will be a new day. Maybe tomorrow River Phoenix will be on the scaffolding outside my window when I pull the curtain open. She'll smile at me. I'll smile back. Unlikely, but maybe.

After River Phoenix and I press our lips and hands to the glass, I'll take myself out to Muddy Waters and Osento and Thrift Town and Valencia Pizza and Pasta with this big roll of cash. Maybe I'll meet people. Maybe I'll make my own friends.

When I wake up the next morning, River Phoenix isn't outside my window. I get out of bed right away before I can think too much, get dressed as cute as I can for my date with myself. Once cute, I pull the sheets down from the window in case she shows, while I eat a bowl of Mini-Wheats. No luck, no River. I need to head out before the apartment sucks me into a melancholy vortex.

I jog down the stairs, push through the gate, and find River Phoenix standing at the curb in front of me smoking a cigarette.

I'm starstruck. My heart races and my hands sweat.

River Phoenix smiles at me and I try to smile back, casually. Nonchalantly. No biggie. Not like a girl with sweaty palms. She's wearing Levi's, a paint-splattered hoodie, and the same orange beanie, her messy hair sticking out at the bottom about an inch. I close the gate with my back and lean against it, rifle through my bag pretending to look for something.

Sam would just walk up and talk to her, so why can't I? *Do it. Do it. Do it.* I swallow, and force myself in her direction.

"Hey," I say, approaching.

"Hi," River Phoenix says. Her eyes are lighter in color up close, gooey like honey.

"I was wondering how long it takes to paint an apartment building this size," I say, and then I cringe at asking such a mediocre question.

"We'll have the scaffolding down in a couple of weeks. Are you sick of us hanging outside your window already?" she asks.

"No, I don't mind, just curious. I always wondered what it would be like to climb scaffolding that high and paint." I wince. I'm terrible at this.

"Have you painted before?" River Phoenix asks.

"I mean, I've helped with interiors," I lie, "but it's the scaffolding that's the exciting part."

She gives me a wide smile that makes my heart jangle like a tambourine. "I'd let you climb it right now if it wasn't a liability issue for my boss. But we're always looking for painters if you really want to find out. We don't pay bad either."

"Seriously?" I ask. "What if I'm terrible at it?"

"It isn't rocket science," she says, laughing as she pulls a card out of her back pocket and hands it to me. "I'm sure you could learn. But yeah, I guess you'd get fired if you were *really* terrible at it."

I look down at the card in my hand.

Barnum and Babes Painting Company
Interior, Exterior, Residential, and Commercial
Billie Rodriguez, Crew Leader

"No joke, I'm going to call you," I say. "I'm Hannah, by the way."

Another painter approaches. She looks like she's a natural redhead, freckled with two long braids hanging from under an SF Giants hat.

"Billie," River Phoenix says as she stretches out her hand to shake mine. "And this is Heather." I take Billie's hand and then nod at Heather. Billie's grip is strong and warm and sends a rush up my arm.

"Got it. I've been calling you River Phoenix in my head," I say, surprising myself with my honesty.

"Oh my god," Heather laughs, turning to Billie. "I promise you, you don't look like River Phoenix." She turns back to me. "Don't give her a big head!"

Billie looks down at her feet. I can see she's blushing.

Sam would have said the River Phoenix comment and then teased her when she blushed, but I'm pretty sure that would be too much too soon. I slide her card into my bag, thank her, and walk away. But I feel her behind me as I go, feel the hand that shook hers glowing in my pocket.

The next couple of days are surreal. Time drags, starts, and stalls without Sam at my side. The neighbors above are arguing daily now. Nobody cute appears like an apparition in the frame of the window. What did Sam and I do together that made the hours move? I call Bubbe, bored, leave a message, then wait a whole day for her to call back.

"Where were you?" I ask.

"Wherever I was!" she chides. "Are you keeping tabs on your bubbe now?"

I try to get out of the house and wander, but even while my legs take me striding through the city, I'm stuck in one place.

On Wednesday I'm in bed reading *People* magazine and eating Twizzlers for lunch, hoping Sam will call to talk like she said she would. Madonna is super pregnant even though she's almost forty. It's amazing someone was able to write four whole pages on the subject. Midway through the article, I hear a key in the lock and my heart starts to thump. Sam appears in the doorway. She drops a big green duffel bag I've never seen before by her feet. She's wearing a cropped tank top with an oversized flannel I don't recognize over it, a black ribbon as a choker. She looks sheepish and tired, but the sight of her changes me. My cards get shuffled and then fall to the ground face up.

"Sammie," I say, but I can't find anything more to add.

We look at each other. I can see someone all over her, a fleck of glitter on her neck, her eyebrows plucked thinner.

"I'm still upset," she says, dropping her eyes. "I just want to get some stuff. Please don't say anything, and don't ask me anything. I don't want to talk right now."

She's totally sleeping with Molly. Or maybe it's one of the dykes who stopped by. Or maybe it's both of the dykes who stopped by *and* Molly. Maybe all her problems with me were a way out, a way to blame me, so she could move on unscathed by guilt. I want to scream at her, yell at her, fight.

"Okay," I say, my eyes welling instead.

But after a moment of standing by the door, she moves toward me, pushing my shoulders to lay me back on the bed. She climbs on top of me and rests her head on my chest. She can feel me thumping in there, my heart gives me away. I brush her hair from her face and wipe her wet eyelashes.

"Han-nah," she whines.

"What's going on?" I ask quietly. "Will you *please* talk to me?"

She doesn't say anything.

"Tell me, Sammie," I plead. I feel like a kid. I want to hold her and yell *MINE! MINE! MINE!* over and over again. But before I can say anything more, my face is in her hands and her mouth is hot all over mine, and my chest physically hurts, the hurt rippling through the rest of my body like rings from a rock thrown in a lake. I love her. She holds my face with one hand while she kisses me, reaches for my shirt with the other, trying to pull it off, over my head.

"What are you doing?" I ask, pulling it back down. She sits up, straddling me, hands moving to my waist.

"I don't know," she says.

"You can't just show up and try to have sex with me after being gone for days without even talking."

She shifts her hands to her legs, balling them up on her thighs.

She's silent. I should tell her to get off me. But I don't want her to leave again. I want her to stay, and I want everything to be simple. But we aren't in high school anymore. We aren't innocent or shy, or at the tipping point of falling in love. We aren't in the dark in Long Beach finding each other for the first time.

"Why don't you want to talk?" I ask. She shrugs. I know why. Suddenly I'm itchy with irritation. "I always think of you as the gutsy one," I say, "like you're more capable than me, and you can handle more than me, but that's not true, Sam. You want to fit in wherever you go, and you do, but you can't handle the real stuff." I watch her expression stiffen. She climbs off, stands up.

"That's not what's happening, Hannah. I just need a minute. I'm just not ready to talk yet," she says. I study her eyes, which are unwilling to hold mine for more than a few seconds at a time. She's going to believe whatever she decides to believe. "If I don't want to talk, I should go, right?" she asks.

I nod, even though it's not what I want. I want her to beg and plead. I want her to apologize over and over again and hold me around the waist, sobbing. But she doesn't. She just looks at me like I broke her, while she breaks us.

She wanders around throwing her stuff in the green duffel bag in silence. When she's done, she doesn't look at me or say goodbye. She opens the door and shuts it behind her.

I stare at the closed door. I imagine Sam descending the stairs, the metal gate clanking behind her. I imagine her turning the corner around Happy Donuts and disappearing out of sight. I feel the distance widening between us and my mind moves back to the quarries. We were so fresh from home. I had pulled myself out of the water onto a warm dry rock. I lay belly down and watched Sam swimming away from me about forty feet out. Her hair was dry and frizzy on top and then clumped into wet columns. As she swam away the back of her head bobbed side to side and made me laugh out loud. I felt lit up like a sparkler. I held my thumb up extended in front of me and compared the size of her head to the size of my thumbnail. *I can do it again*, I think to myself. I can love her while she swims away from me. I unclench my jaw, soften my fists, and open my hands. I let my tears roll loose into my ears and listen to the sound of my breath.

12

On Rosh Hashanah I wake up alone and stare out the window. "L'shanah tovah," I say to myself. I pick up Billie's card from the windowsill and read it for the hundredth time. I really want to call today. It's the start of a new year. A new year in which I can call cute people who offer me painting jobs. "L'shanah tovah," I say to the card, and to Billie, wherever she is right now. I don't have apples or honey and suddenly I worry I won't have a sweet New Year without them. I'll have to go out walking to Rainbow Grocery later today. But I know even with apples and honey, it won't feel like Rosh Hashanah. I miss Bubbe, and I want Rachel. I want the sound of the shofar, and maybe even my mom stressing over the state of the kugel. I want the smell of Long Beach. I want to sour my face in the direction of the stuffy ironed clothes laid out on my bed for me to wear. I want to be dragged to shul against my will, complaining the whole way to Rachel in a whisper. How can I miss twisting inside such a tight space? Maybe a loose space is just as much trouble. I'm shapeless, an entirely different problem.

When I call Bubbe she doesn't answer. I leave a message: "L'shanah tovah, Bubbe! I love you! I can't believe I get to see you so soon." I hang up and stare at the phone.

Bubbe will be out to visit me in a little over a month. What do I have to show for all my efforts? Some stilettos. A roll of cash. An "efficiency studio" in the Tenderloin. What will I say when she asks where Sam is?

I should call Chris and make plans for our next date. I need the cash for Bubbe's visit. For rent. For life. But we haven't talked since the mushrooms night. And I don't want to talk to her about it anyway. What would I do? Tell her how I feel? We aren't in a relationship. It's only about whether I can handle working for her again, and I have to be able to handle it. For a little while longer at least. I pick up the phone and dial.

"Hello?" Chris answers.

"Hey, Chris, it's Hannah—I mean—" The words come out of my mouth like a burp I wasn't expecting. My head drops and I squeeze my temples.

"I knew you'd slip one day! *Hannah.* That's a nice name. It actually fits you so much better than Scarlet. Scarlet is so . . . it's so trying too hard. You aren't like that," she says.

I must be good at pretending I'm not trying too hard. I prickle at her glee.

"Somebody else made up the name Scarlet for me, so maybe that's why it doesn't fit," I say.

"I'm pretty sure someone else made up the name Hannah for you too," she says, "but it sure fits a lot better."

"So do you want to plan a date?" I ask. It comes out cold and impatient, and I will myself to back down. Zip on Scarlet like too-tight jeans.

"I actually wanted to talk to you about something," she says, and then she pauses for so long I wonder if we've been disconnected.

"Hello?" I ask.

"I'm here," she says, but she sounds uncertain, her voice muted. "I don't know how to start."

I wait, then open my mouth, then close it, afraid to ask why.

"Well, first, I guess, I keep thinking about our last night together," she says.

My face goes hot.

"We were having sex, and I didn't realize how hard you were tripping until later. I mean, I was tripping hard too, and then after the fact I just, I felt like shit." I twist up my face and close my eyes. "You're a lot younger than me," she continues. I try to remember how old I told her I was. "And sometimes I feel really guilty about giving you drugs on a regular basis. You think I have my shit together, but I don't. Can't you see I'm a mess? I'm a mess. I told my mom I'd get sober before she died. That was a year and a half ago now and look at me. That's not an excuse, I should have asked you. And then when I realized how hard you were tripping . . . and I'm the one who fed you a bunch of mushrooms. You're only like twenty-two? I'm almost forty. It's pathetic. I don't have any excuses anymore, but every time I try to get sober—"

"Chris," I interrupt. "Will you stop for a sec?" I try to pull my thoughts together, but I can't find the words. For the first time, I wish I could show her how I really feel. I wish she could see how my breath gets stuck at my neck when I think about it. "I don't think you intended to hurt me," I start. "I *know* you didn't mean to." I pause; *How do I explain?* "But what if you still did?" I pause again. Swallow. "I can't do drugs with you anymore. I just can't."

I listen to her sniffle. Picture her wet face turned to the ceiling, a hand rubbing her jaw, elbows propped on her knees. I don't hate her. And I didn't know her regret could change the shape of what I feel. File the sharp edges a little smoother. But it does.

"I'm really sorry. I won't offer you drugs anymore, and I'll try not to drink . . . I'll try not to drink as much in front of you. I'm really sorry and I don't ever want to hurt you again."

I open my mouth to tell her it's okay but think better of it.

"I want to get sober, and it's like I can't. I never even last a day," she says. "And hiring you as an escort was fun and hot in the beginning, but I never planned for it to go on this long."

I bite the side of my cheek and stay quiet.

"You don't have to answer this if you don't want to," she says, "but if you do, I want you to be honest."

I pause, feeling apprehensive, but say, "Okay?"

"I was just wondering . . . how do you feel about me?"

I take a deep breath. How do I feel about her? I feel everything. Anger. Irritation. Dread. Lust. But also disgust. I don't like her like that. But a part of me *does* care about her. Though I know I don't trust her. I'm free. I'm trapped. I'm losing Sam and I want to blame her.

It's quiet before I answer. "I feel complicated about you."

"Okay," she says slowly. "Do you ever consider dating me for real?"

I look out the window. She doesn't know she's work. I don't want to be asked to work for free, and I don't want to be forced to hurt her with my answer.

"No," I say, cringing as I say it. "I don't for a lot of reasons, and if you knew more about me, you wouldn't want me either."

"I feel like I do know you. I mean, we have a connection, right? I don't know you entirely, but I know enough to feel like I'm falling—"

"Chris, you don't," I interrupt, frustrated. "How could you? Strippers and escorts are paid to be who you want them to be, not who they are. This isn't me."

She's quiet.

"And I'm not twenty-two," I add.

A silence widens between us before she asks, "How old are you?"

"Eighteen," I say, letting the truth out like an animal

from a cage, unsure what it might do. "I graduated high school in June."

I listen to her breath catch. Then go quiet. Registering. "Oh my god," she says. Another pause. "Oh my god," she says again. "Why'd you tell me—" But she answers her own question before she's finished asking it. "Could it get any clearer I'm supposed to stop seeing you and get sober?" She sounds exasperated. Sick of herself.

It may be clear to her, clear to me too, that I need it to end, but I feel a yank of desperation. I'm scared to lose the money before I have anything lined up.

"Can we do one more night?" I ask tentatively. "So we can say goodbye?"

When I get off the phone I pull the covers over my head. It still smells like Sam under here. I sigh, toss them off, and get up. While I'm brushing my teeth in the mirror, making instant coffee, pouring a bowl of Mini-Wheats, my mind works the conversation with Chris like dough. Tomorrow is my last night with her. No sex, no drugs, we agreed. Just one last date to say goodbye. My last big chunk of money, followed by nothing if I don't hurry up and do something about it. And still, I'm relieved it'll be over. I lift the cereal bowl to drink the leftover milk. I need to call Billie and nail down this painting gig. And I have to do it without Sam here egging me on, dialing the number for me.

I drop the bowl in the sink and reach for Billie's card again.

"Barnum and Babes painting company, interior, exterior, residential, and commercial. Billie Rodriguez, crew leader," I read out loud. I put my hand on the phone and feel a shot of nerves run up my arm. How will I make sentences with her? *Do it,* I tell myself. *Just do it.* I pick up the receiver and dial. It rings and I gulp. It rings again and I gulp again. When it rings a third time, I realize it's eleven a.m. and she's probably working. Her answering machine picks up and I warm at the sound of her voice.

"Hi, River Phoenix, this is Hannah. I met you outside my apartment building on Ellis Street the other day, and if the offer still stands, I'd love a trial day painting." I leave my number and hang up with a zing. *Done!* I pace the room, grinning, shaking my hands loose at the wrists until my breath moves easily again.

In the evening, I come home with a bag of groceries and try Bubbe again while I slice apples and drizzle honey from a bear-shaped bottle. She answers this time. I fill a shot glass with grape juice for the prayer, and we toast to the New Year, lifting our glasses, hers to the west, mine to the east. We talk about her childhood, growing up in the tenement buildings and how much her father loved her and how he sold bananas from a cart and what it was like to have a limp in school and the way the other kids stood still to stare as she walked by. She tells me about her first job, selling candy at the Yiddish theater, a tray slung from her neck, how her father fashioned a belt to secure it well so she could use her arm crutches. The candy sellers had to sneak in and out of a tiny door under the stage to refill their trays. "I was so short, I didn't have to duck!" she tells me. We laugh so hard, tears pop out of my eyes.

Before we get off the phone she asks, "Bubbeleh, have you and Sam made any new friends in San Francisco?" I press my cheek into my palm. Chris, Marla, Jade, Mama Beth, Mr. Patrick. I haven't made any friends at all. I've only lost Sam.

"Working on it," I say. "But I've got my bubbe coming to visit me. I'm super excited for that."

"I'm looking forward to it too," she says. "And remember, wonderful friends don't just fall out of the sky. You go out, you find the gems, and then you hold on to them."

April. Her name slams into me like a car I didn't see coming.

The next morning, I wake to the phone ringing. It's bright out, and I reach to answer it as I glance at the alarm and see it's already ten a.m. My guess is it's Chris calling to say something about our date, hopefully not canceling after mulling over my age all night.

I clear my throat. "Hello?"

"Is this Hannah?" the voice on the line asks. I sit up. It isn't Chris.

"Yeah, this is Hannah," I answer.

"Hey! It's Billie." There's a pause while I pull myself together, long enough for her to think she needs to jog my memory. "The painter, the one that hangs outside your window. You left me a message yesterday . . ."

"Yes! Yes!" I say. "I'm just—well, I just woke up and I haven't had coffee, so, you know." I sound flustered, comical, I want to crawl under the bed and hide. "I thought I should give it a go, you know, see if painting is the next thing for me." I pin my bottom lip between my teeth to force myself to stop talking.

"So, what kind of work are you doing now?" she asks.

"Um, just boring stuff, I've worked at a wash and fold, stuff like that," I say, pinching my eyes shut as hard as I can. I'm doing a terrible, terrible job.

"All right," she says with a laugh. "Well, does Monday work for you?"

"Yes! Monday definitely works for me."

"Cool, so we start at twelve dollars an hour. We'll pay you under the table for the trial day, and I'm going to put you on Heather's crew. She's running a team up in Noe Valley doing the interior of a Victorian on Fountain Street. She'll teach you. Heather's a really good teacher. We always start new people with her, the basics—sanding, prepping, priming—and we'll just play it by ear, see if you like it. Does that work?"

My heart sinks a bit—she's not going to train me herself. My fantasy of spending an entire day with her is squashed. But if she wanted to, she could, right? Maybe River Phoenix doesn't have a crush on me.

"Great. Perfect," I say, jotting down the address and Heather's number. It *is* great and perfect, even if I don't get to work with her. It's a job, and I need a job desperately.

I get off the phone and do the math of twelve dollars an hour. Under the table it comes out to ninety-six bucks a day. It's a wage I would have been psyched about in the past, and it's so much better than minimum wage. It's enough to get by, I tell myself, and I guess I have to readjust, settle into the world of just getting by.

For our last night together, Chris wants to meet at a restaurant instead of our usual, Red's. Tú Lan on Sixth Street. It's a Vietnamese place, so tiny you're basically seated in the kitchen, so when you leave, your hair and clothes smell like garlic frying in oil, lemongrass, and fish sauce.

I arrive before her, grab a table, and open a plastic-covered menu the size of a newspaper with pictures of each dish.

"Hello, beautiful Hannah."

I look up and see Chris pulling out the chair across from me, taking her jean jacket off and sliding it over the back of her seat before she sits down. The sound of my real name coming from her mouth is strange but not terrible. I'm surprised to feel neutral, even okay. Maybe because it's our last night, no drugs, no expectation of sex.

"I was getting ready, and I was thinking, *What's this going to be like?*" Chris says, laughing nervously. "Usually by this time in the day I've downed a flask. So, I'm way behind."

"Really?" I ask, surprised. "I mean, I know you drink, but I guess I have no idea how much."

Chris rubs the sides of her face, and I can see her hands are shaking. "I actually feel like shit. I think I'm having alcohol withdrawals," she says. Looking at her closely, I can see a slight sheen of sweat on her forehead. I reach for her hand, hold it in mine, and find it clammy. She's trembling.

"That's scary. Do you have to go to the ER or see a doctor for alcohol withdrawals? I don't know much about them."

"No, I've been through this before. I'm just going to have one beer. It'll be enough to get rid of the shakes."

"Okay," I say, unsure of what else to add. "I'm getting the chicken vermicelli. Are you going to be able to eat?"

Chris flips open the menu, and I watch it quiver in her hands. "Um, I'm just going to get an appetizer. I'll get the barbecue pork salad. Will you eat some of it?"

"Well, probably not. I have an aversion to pork," I say, which is actually true. I break my chopsticks apart. It's our last night. What does it matter? "I have an aversion to pork because I'm Jewish and I wasn't raised with it, and pigs feel dirty to me. It's a hard thing to shake."

"You're Jewish?" Chris asks. "No way."

"Is that a good 'no way'? Or a bad 'no way'?" I ask with trepidation.

"It's just funny because I've been trying to figure out

what you are since we met. I mean, I knew you were *something*, and I just came up with all kinds of wrong answers and never thought Jewish."

"If I'm something, does that make you nothing?" I ask, but she's too busy talking to register my question.

"I was like, *She's Greek. She's Iranian. She's Italian. No, she's Egyptian. No, she's Turkish.* I basically circled around and around and never landed on it." She spins a shaky finger in the air and pins it to the table. She means no harm, but it feels like being pinned in the chest, and I fight the urge to push my chair back and stand. Instead, I shake my head, as if to disagree, with what I'm not sure.

The waiter arrives with a notepad.

"I'm going to have two Heinekens and the barbecue chicken salad," Chris says, and then to me, "I'm not going to eat pork in front of you. I don't want you to think I'm dirty in *that* way." She chuckles.

I hate this conversation. I shouldn't get personal on the last night. She's paying Scarlet to say goodbye. *Just be Scarlet.*

We sit in silence, and I press Chris's hands flat against the table to stop the shaking. It's futile. Her entire system is agitated. She can't be calmed. I'm relieved when her two beers arrive and she chugs half of one, tipping it high to take a long guzzle.

"Why is that so good?" she asks when she puts it down.

"Do you want to tell me how much you actually drink and use drugs?" I ask. I'm curious.

Chris stares at me. Blank.

"You know what's funny?" she asks. "I don't think I've ever answered that question honestly. I didn't want my mom to worry when she was sick. And my ex-girlfriend was always trying to figure it out and control it, so I worked really hard to hide it."

Our food arrives, greener than green. Vermicelli noodles, cilantro, pickled daikon and carrots, a quarter of a miniature lime on the side. I look up at Chris, who still looks sweaty but now a little green as well.

"I can't eat any of this," she says. "Sorry, I thought I could, but now that it's here, I can't." She picks up her second beer and nurses it. "Maybe today isn't the day I'm supposed to stop drinking. I have to go to work early in the morning. I'm assuming you're not sleeping over, right?"

"Oh, I assumed I was. I mean, no sex, no drugs, but still a date?" I ask. I need the money, and I'm afraid I won't get it if I don't spend the night. But does she even want me to? I hate how it feels to ask for something neither of us can get behind anymore.

"Oh, yeah, okay," she says, but she looks unsure. "You can sleep in and let yourself out. I have to cover an early shift."

Chris orders a third beer while I work on both plates. I slip up again, saying too much, telling her about April, how she was the only one I knew in high school who was stuck on pills, that I don't know where she is, and how guilty I feel for leaving her behind.

"I wanted to ask her to move out here with us, my roommate and me," I clarify. "I thought a different place, a change of scenery, would be better for her, but I knew my roommate would have none of that, so I never asked."

Chris laughs. "God, I wish it worked like that."

She tells me she lost two friends to black tar heroin last year, that it's the only drug she won't touch.

By the time Chris and I are walking out, the sun is gone, the remains glowing pink at the bottom of the sky. The color has returned to her cheeks. She's stopped shaking. She isn't clammy and agitated anymore. We walk up Market Street, both of us with our hands stuffed in our pockets.

"So, are you going to answer my question?" I ask.

"What question?"

"How much do you really drink and use drugs?" I ask again. I don't know why I want to know so bad, but I do.

"I told you, I can't answer it honestly," she says. "Not because I think you'll never see me again if you knew. I know you'll never see me again. I just can't. I can't tally it up even for myself because it'll make me want to die."

"Let's stay away from wanting to die," I say, threading my arm through hers. I want to argue with her about the never-see-her-again part, but she's probably right. I lean in and kiss her on the cheek instead.

As we lie in her bed face-to-face, I listen to her recount each time she tried to get sober, standing up and falling, then standing up again, only to take three steps forward and fall. She tells me how good she is at staying 100 percent functional on the job while drinking and using 100 percent of the time. "Everyone told my mom, 'You have to let Chris hit rock bottom.' But I don't hit rock bottom. I just hover," she says, showing me with her hands, fluttering her fingers like the wings of a moth. I think of April, hovering through our senior year. I think of my own mother, five thousand miles away, however misguided, praying I'll hit rock bottom, fall flat on my face, and return home, more malleable this time.

Chris runs her thumb from my hairline down the edge of my jaw to my chin. I watch her lips quiver. She presses them together. I'm confused by my own feelings. New feelings, ones I didn't expect, surfacing. My heart hurts for her, for her mother, for my own mother, for my father, for Rachel, for April, for Sam, for all the ways we lose each other, for all the ways we get lost. Despite everything that has passed between us, I want to pull her closer, for just this one moment. It's our last, so what does it matter?

"Chris," I say.

"Yeah?"

"Do you want to kiss me?"

She shakes her head. "I don't want to, if you don't want me to."

"I want you to," I say. "To say goodbye. A goodbye kiss."

Chris looks at me, questioning. I feel like crying. She can tell. I watch her expression soften as she returns her thumb to my chin and leans in, pulling down gently so my lips part. She kisses me slowly, her tongue soft. I draw her closer by the shoulders, but she pulls away.

"What?" I ask quietly.

Her eyes pool with tears now, then they spill across her face. "Turn around," she says, her lips shaking. "I'll spoon you."

In the morning when I wake up, she's gone. The light is coming through the windows in sharp bright angles. I listen to the sound of crows in the trees outside. I've never been alone here. Sitting on the edge of the bed to get my boots on, I find the roll of cash Chris left me with a note wrapped around it. I put the money in my pocket and unroll the note.

Hannah,

You are beautiful and I am so in love with you. I'm in love with your kind heart, your big smile, your beautiful eyes . . .

You told me I couldn't know you because you're paid to be what I want you to be. It makes sense and it broke my heart. In some other universe we're the same age, and I'm sober, and maybe, if I'm lucky, you'll show me exactly who you are. And then, I'll show you I can love that exact you. I hope you find someone who appreciates you fully, if you haven't found them already.

Love, Chris

When I arrive home, I pull an empty aluminum can out of the recycling, roll Chris's note up thin as a cigarette, and slide it in, put the can in the closet. I can't throw it away, and I can't read it again. Reading it once was once too many. It's all I want, all I've ever wanted, to be known, and loved anyway. But not by Chris. It can't be Chris. I can't love her, and I can't trust her. But I can't hate her either.

The answering machine light is blinking. I push play and hear a throat clear. I know it's Sam before she even speaks.

Hannah, I'm really sorry. I don't know what I'm doing, I just miss you a ton and want to talk. Her voice sounds weak; she pauses, clears her throat again. *But like, I feel like if we talk, we'll just fight, you know what I mean? I don't want to fight anymore. I guess if you want to call me back, call me back. I miss you even if everything's all fucked up between us.*

I rub my temples with both hands. I could call her and tell her I'm done with Chris and starting a regular job soon. But I know it's not enough. It was never about Chris.

13

With Chris, Sam, and the Chez Paree all out of the picture, my body is a closed door, mine and mine alone. I test it out by scratching a heart into the skin above my left breast with a safety pin. Blood crumbs the surface when it dries. When I go out to pick up Thai food, my T-shirt chafes against it and it stings, but not in a bad way. A reminder that it's here. That I'm here.

In the evening before my trial painting shift, I try on my clothes like I'm preparing for the first day of middle school. Levi's with a tear across one knee. The tattered Twisted Sister T-shirt Sam and I thrifted. Sam's worn-out black hoodie with a rip in the neck. I put it on and look in the mirror. Tear the rip an inch wider. Then line my eyes in kohl, smudging them with my pinkies. Tousle my hair upside down, pull the sleeves of Sam's sweatshirt over my hands, and stand back to get a good look. I hear Sam's voice in my head: *Yessssss, hot in a dirtbag way,* she says, and I feel satisfied. I strip down, wash my makeup off in the shower, and get to bed.

My alarm goes off at six thirty a.m. I haven't woken up to an alarm since my last day of high school, and the sound knocks my body upright in bed. Crossing an arm over my naked chest, I pull open the makeshift curtain to peer through the scaffolding into the street below. By eight a.m. Billie will be here with her crew, and I'll be way up in Noe Valley with Heather's crew. My stomach is full of acid, or butterflies, I can't tell which. How many new people will I have to meet today? I feel like a hermit crab expected to take off my shell and head to a party. I could get crushed. I could literally die. Heather's crew is nameless, faceless, and somehow I'm already desperate for every last one of them to like me.

After I get dressed, I check my teeth in the mirror and scan my nose for blackheads before I lean in for eyeliner. On my way out the door, I stuff a ChapStick and a twenty in my pocket, then head down to grab coffee and a donut from Li Wei. Heather told me the bus number, the one that could take me all the way to the top of Noe Valley, but I forgot it, so I opt for a streetcar.

The J Church takes me from the chaos of Civic Center through a tunnel, into the light of upper Market Street, then the train climbs up Church Street on the far side of Dolores Park. The park is misted over and nearly empty. A lone man chucks a neon tennis ball, his terrier shooting after it. I get off at Twenty-Fourth and Church at the lower end of Noe Valley and pull my hoodie over my head.

Noe Valley is wholesome and bland, blunt in its contrast to the Tenderloin; it reeks of money. The storefronts—a baby clothes place, a natural foods grocery, an orthopedic shoe store, nail salon after nail salon—are all shuttered at this hour, except the glowing coffee shops.

Walking block after block, I eventually find Fountain Street at the tippy top of the hill, cutting into Twenty-Fourth Street when it can't stand to get any steeper. When I turn onto it, I know immediately I'm in the right place. Among the fancy new cars are several old trucks, and a motorcycle parked on the sidewalk. Heather and three other painters stand in front of a two-story Victorian. I need to catch my breath, but it won't be caught. I wipe my face on my sleeve, my sweaty palms on my pants, and clear my throat as I approach.

"Hi," I announce myself, fluttering a timid wave close to my face, before tucking my hands in my back pockets.

"Hey, Hannah," Heather says, pulling me into the circle by my shoulder. "Guys, this is Hannah. She lives down at the apartment building we're painting on Ellis. She's doing a trial with us today. Hannah, this is Tamika." Tamika reaches out her hand to shake mine. She's tall and cute, the sides of her head shaved, short dreads on top pulled into a bundle. When she smiles, deep dimples appear in the center of each of her cheeks.

"Little Danny," Heather says, pointing to a short waifish boy in a cropped T-shirt, eyebrows plucked to pencil lines, a dust of glitter sparkling his face. I stare, my eyes moving down to his belly button piercing, up to the light brown waves sweeping his shoulders. He looks like Kate Moss.

"Little Danny?" I ask, making sure I heard it right.

"Yesss," Little Danny says. "Are we okay?"

"Oh yeah," I say. "I just—" They're all looking at me, waiting. "For some reason I thought you only hired female painters," I laugh.

Tamika throws an arm around Little Danny. "He's way more of a lady than the rest of us."

"Yeah, Tamika's dick is like ten times the size of mine," Little Danny says.

"Fact," Tamika agrees.

My face goes hot. I open my mouth to speak, let it hang there, trying to come up with something to say. But before I can, Heather jumps back in. "And this is Anna G. You have to say 'Anna G.' because we know way too many Annas to just call her Anna."

Anna G. smiles at me. It's a big warm smile with a head-tip of pity. She has long black hair and eyeliner that reminds me of April. I think she's gorgeous right off the bat.

"Come on," Little Danny says, hooking his arm in mine as we head up the cement stairs leading to the house. He pats my forearm, as if to say, *There, there, child.* But it's a sweet pat, a pat forgiving my awkward arrival. Behind us, Tamika teases Anna G. for the glass jar of wheatgrass she's carrying. "Don't sneak up on me with your green teeth smelling like cow farts," Tamika says.

"Shut the fuck up!" Anna G. cackles.

Heather unlocks the door to the house and lets us in. It's completely empty in here. An empty beautiful old Victorian with high ceilings, perched at the top of a hill, views in every direction. The floors are protected with paper and covered in paint scrapings and footprints.

"Hannah, you're going to be with me today, priming the kitchen," Heather says. I follow her toward the back end of the first floor as the others peel off into different rooms. The kitchen is large and airy, wood cabinets covered in plastic, only the walls exposed.

She explains they prepped Friday, so it's time to prime. I'll be prepping and priming for the first couple months on the job, then we'll talk painting. She pins a giant bucket between her feet and holds up a tool, a five-in-one, she explains, before she uses it to pry the top off the bucket.

"So where are you from and when did you get here?" she asks, filling a tray with a smooth pour of white primer.

"Oh, um, my friend and I just got here in the beginning of July. We drove out from New York. Long Beach, New York," I say.

"Can I ask you how old you are?"

"I'm really, really young," I say.

"Nothing wrong with being young! You don't want to tell me?"

"I'm eighteen."

"Holy crap! That is young. I thought you were more like twenty-one or twenty-two." She holds up a fluffy yellow tube. "This is a new nap," she explains, shoving it onto a metal roller.

"How old are you?" I ask.

"I'm twenty-five, but the age range is wide with us. We've got everything from twenty to forty-five working here, and now apparently eighteen."

"How old is Billie?" I ask.

"Why are you asking?" Heather smirks, lifting her eyes toward me.

"Just curious," I say, but I feel my ears begin to burn.

"She's only twenty-three, but she's a total go-getter. She practically runs this company while the owner sits on her butt."

Heather explains how to properly soak a nap, rolling off the excess paint at the steep end of the tray. She glides it up and down and side to side, then hands it to me. I roll it in the primer again, make a drippy mess on the wall next to her perfect work. I turn to her, frowning. She shakes her head and we both laugh.

"You just need to do it—you have to learn this stuff by doing it," she says, heading out into the dining room. "Go ahead, just do your best."

By the time I'm on my second wall, I've started to figure it out and relax into the sound of the sticky roller, the sweeping motion in my body, the way it feels to be alone in this kitchen.

Heather comes back after an hour or so, pulling her beanie off and tossing it on the counter.

"Much better," she says, inspecting my work. "See? You're already getting faster and cleaner."

I stand back, eyeing it with her. Not bad.

"Pretty soon we're going to break for lunch," she says. "I'm picking up coffee for everyone. You wanna come?"

Heather shows me how to soak my nap and cover my primer tray so it doesn't dry out, and then I walk around taking coffee orders. When I get to Tamika she grins when she sees me. "You look like someone did some eighties splatter-paint art with a toothbrush on your face."

"I do?" I ask, grinning back at her.

"Go look in the bathroom mirror."

I turn down the hall into the bathroom and see my face.

"I totally do!" I yell back at her.

I look like shit, hair frizzed with sweat, paint splatter all over my face and neck. Good shit. Strong shit. Shit that doesn't have to get pretty to get paid.

Heather and I head out to her truck. A boxy Toyota four-by-four, white with mustard and brown stripes running down either side. The doors squeak as we open them, and the interior smells like cigarette butts, despite the tree-shaped air freshener hanging from the rearview mirror. The truck is a stick shift and Heather maneuvers it up and down the hills like a pro.

"So have you gone out much since you got here?" she asks.

"Not really," I say. "I mean, I've explored—like I've walked around a lot and I've been to the Bearded Lady and to Osento—but I haven't gone out to any clubs or bars or anything."

"Have you made any friends?" she asks.

"I haven't met any other dykes," I say, trying to let it slide easily off my tongue.

"So. You're a dyke, eh?"

"Apparently that's what I'm called out here," I say. She laughs. It feels good to make her laugh.

"But are you a femme dyke?" she asks. "Eh? Or a butch dyke? Or a sister-side-by-side?"

"There are subcategories?!" I drop my face in my hands and listen to her chuckle.

"I think you're going to be psyched when you start going out and meeting people. Queers come from all over to live here, we're like an enormous freaky dysfunctional family. A better version of that."

Heather parks on Twenty-Fourth Street and we jaywalk over to a café called Spinelli's, where she introduces me to a barista named Dusty with maple eyes and short hair slicked shiny with pomade. Dusty takes the scrap of paper with everyone's order and works through it while they talk about her new Honda motorcycle and how it's going on the dating front since her breakup a few months ago.

Back in the truck, I ask Heather how she knows Dusty while we groan up the hill in first.

"I forget how we actually met, but she's great. She's in this collective of photographers called Point Blank. They set up shows in parking lots and project slides onto the sides of buildings."

I'm watching the sun flash off the rounded windows of the Victorians as we chug by. "I want to go to a slideshow in a parking lot," I say.

"You should come next time! And then you can get sucked into the gay vortex, and about two seconds later you'll know almost every dyke in this city. And then you'll be like, *Why is my ex-girlfriend dating my best friend's ex-girlfriend?*" She pauses to laugh at her own joke. "You'll get so sick of how interconnected everything is."

I turn to her. "I can't imagine knowing every dyke in this city," I say, skeptical. "I've never been part of any scene, I'm too . . ."

"Queer?" she asks. "You were probably just too queer."

I consider this, quiet for a moment.

"Was that it?" I ask.

"I swear to god, in whatever way you think you are fundamentally different, you're going to meet at least ten people here even freakier in that particular way."

Back at the house, we find Little Danny, Anna G., and Tamika on the front porch pulling tortilla chips from a big bag and dipping them in something pink.

"What's that?" I ask, gesturing to the pink stuff with my chin as we hand out coffees.

"It's pink lunch! You should have some," says Little Danny.

"It's this dip made out of cashews and pimentos," Anna G. says. "If you ever had a thing for nacho cheese sauce, you'll like it."

Sitting cross-legged between Anna G. and Tamika, I try it. It's weird and gelatinous, but also so good.

"Billie just stopped by to see how it's going," Tamika says to Heather. "I told her you two were out getting your nails done, totally slacking."

Heather laughs, but the thought of Tamika making the joke, saying my name out loud to Billie, makes me want to hide under a rock.

"She wants us to meet up with the other crew at Zeitgeist for beers after work."

"What's Zeitgeist?" I ask.

"It's that bar with the big outdoor area, on Duboce and Valencia. We probably go once a week. You've never been?" Tamika asks.

"I've never been anywhere," I say.

"Hannah is eighteen," Heather says.

"Oooooooh!" Little Danny sings. "I'm not the baby anymore! Okay, now I forgive you for being a big-meanie lesbian separatist."

"I'm not a—" I pause, turn to Heather. "Wait, what's a lesbian separatist?" I ask.

"Don't tell her!" Little Danny begs. "She's a virgin!"

"Okay, I obviously know what a virgin is, and I'm not a virgin," I say. I beam when they laugh. I feel it in my insides. I feel carbonated, fizzy with it.

Anna G. asks if everyone can make it to Zeitgeist after work, her eyes on me when she asks. I tell them I don't have a fake ID, but they tell me not to worry. Nobody works the door at five.

"You just head to the back, and I'll bring you a beer," Heather says.

The rest of the afternoon moves quickly, and all I can think about is having a beer in the presence of my crush. That part sounds so exciting. But the part where I'm filthy, my armpits sharp and musky when I tip my nose in them to check, that part's not as fun to think about.

Around four thirty Heather walks me through the cleanup. Before we leave, I head into the bathroom to wash my face, soap my pits in the sink, put on ChapStick, and mess with my hair a bit. Little Danny pops his head in.

"Can I come in and primp with you?" he asks.

"Of course," I say. He pulls mascara from his back pocket and pumps the wand in the tube. I feel shy, watching him lean in and sweep his lashes skyward with the brush, his mouth open in an O. When he's done, he looks at me in the mirror.

"Do you want me to put some on you?" he asks.

"Sure," I say, surprised at the offer. Then surprised how he holds my face, my jaw cradled in his hand, telling me to look down and then up, just like Sam used to do.

"Gooorgeous," he sings to me when he's done. We both turn back to the mirror to look. "Your eyelashes are crazy long!" he says.

After locking up the house, Heather drives Little Danny and me in her truck to Zeitgeist. Little Danny sits in the middle straddling the shift and we all giggle every time Heather changes gears.

"Too rough!" he yells when Heather jerks the shift into reverse to parallel park.

As we head into Zeitgeist, I do as I'm told. File in with the rest of the crew, then peel off with Anna G. toward the open doors that lead to the patio.

The patio is big and enclosed on all sides. A dozen picnic tables are sprinkled with people, and there's a shell of an old pickup truck against the brick wall on the far end. It's probably from the forties, the hood open and plants overflowing from inside. Immediately I spot Billie standing next to the truck. She shoots us a broad smile and waves in our direction as she walks over, one hand holding a beer, the other moving to her pocket. I feel my heartbeat ramp up to a thump, hear it beating in my ears. Anna G. heads over to greet the rest of the crew sitting around a table, but I'm stuck in place watching Billie approach. The excitement I feel is bordering on queasy and faint.

"Hannah!" she says. "How was today?"

I tell her it was fun, that everyone was super nice, that I know she was told I was slacking with Heather, getting my nails done, but I can prove I wasn't. I hold out my hands to show her, but my fingers are trembling, so I pull them away quickly. "For the first fifteen minutes priming *was* rocket science," I go on, "but then I got the hang of it, so you don't need to fire me. Not yet at least." She looks into my eyes, her mouth shifting; she's holding back a grin. I wonder if she saw my hands shaking, if it's obvious why.

Heather approaches, hands me a beer, and tells Billie I did great before she heads to the table.

"I can get you on a crew three or four days a week for now, if you want the work," Billie offers. I tell her I'd love that, and then we stand in silence for too long. Shifting back and forth, heel to heel, I try to come up with something funny and smart to say.

"Heather tells me you're one of the younger ones, but you basically run the company?"

Not funny or smart. Billie chuckles her way to a sigh, looking down at her feet.

"That's a slight exaggeration," she says. "But I was raised Jehovah's Witness, and the work ethic is the only part I'm trying to hold on to."

I rack my brain, but I can't come up with anything about Jehovah's Witnesses. "So, you're not a Jehovah's Witness anymore?"

She cocks her head. I feel a wave of embarrassment wash over me.

"You can't be queer *and* be a Jehovah's Witness." She explains, "I mean, you can be a closeted one." She shifts her beer from one hand to the other, then back again. "I left."

"Oh," I say, not sure how to respond. "I guess I don't really know a thing about Jehovah's Witnesses. So are they known for their work ethic?"

"You have to go door-to-door saving souls, and I took the job really seriously."

"Whoa," I say. "That *does* sound like it requires a strong work ethic."

"Especially for a seven-year-old. Little ironed dress with puff sleeves." She gestures to her shoulders. "Braids so tight your scalp hurts. I really put my heart into the job."

I try to picture Billie's eyes, her dark thick lashes, on a perfectly dressed little girl. "Were you *so* cute? Did you convert everyone right off the bat?" I ask.

She tips her head back and laughs. "I probably never converted anyone. But people don't close the door on seven-year-olds, so I sure thought I did."

It's quiet for a moment while I consider how much to say. I want to tell her I get it. I know about dress codes, and the fear of God, and breaking your own mother's heart, taking away the you she believed you'd become. But I haven't met any Jews here, and Chris's response in finding out what kind of "something" I was left me uneasy. I don't want to be something else to Billie. "I'm Jewish," I start slowly, trying to gauge her reaction. "My mom became Orthodox when I was a little too old to get on board, so I'm the disappointing, not-particularly-committed, constantly-questioning-everything kind. I would have definitely been on your conversion list."

She looks into my eyes again, a tenderness moving the path of her gaze. "Jews love it when Jehovah's Witnesses come around trying to convert them, right?" she asks. "That's their favorite?"

"My mom would have been the first adult to slam the door on you if you'd come to our house. Even at seven, in your pretty dress with your perfect braids."

"Billie!" we hear a voice call out. We turn. Tamika's calling from the picnic table, her hand cupped around her mouth. "Stop flirting! Bring Hannah over so she can meet your crew."

Billie ignores the comment. "Come," she says, a slight blush in her cheeks. We walk over together. They open up a seat for me, and Heather pours me another beer from a giant pitcher. The two crews are loud. Raucous. Tamika and Anna G.'s banter gets theatrical and crude. A girl across from them laughs so hard into her folded arms, someone asks if she's crying. When she pops her head up she says no, with tears all over her face. "It's going to be okay. I promise," Little Danny says to her, leaning his head on her shoulder. After his second beer, he lies across four laps to nap. "I woke up too early, okay?" he whines when Tamika tells him he's being a princess.

The sun starts to set, and people trickle out. I might be imagining it, but I swear I keep catching Billie looking at me. Or at least I enjoy the fantasy that she is, the thrill it sends through me. At some point Billie gets up, takes a last swig of her beer, and announces her departure. She goes around hugging some of the crew, patting others on the shoulder, and when she gets to me, I stand up when I see she's leaning in to hug me. We have an awkward moment where I'm half up and half down in my seat.

"How about I just stand up all the way?" I ask. Billie straightens up and waits for me to stand.

"Ah, now it's less weird." Billie laughs. And then she wraps her arms around my waist, and I wrap my arms around her shoulders, and she hugs me, her chest against my chest. It's a quick hug, but it reverberates. I love her body, her height, the smell of her.

That evening, I walk the whole way from Zeitgeist to the apartment, tipsy on beer and the cool evening air. Tipsy on queers like me, on Billie's sweet smile, her sweet eyes, the ghost of the hug she left on me. I beam block after block. I would break into a skip if the streets weren't so busy. Instead, I walk with the lightest body I've had in a long time, maybe since I was a child, flying over the sprinklers, Bubbe slapping her thigh, my joy her joy. My freedom hers too.

I work with Barnum and Babes three more days in September, then twelve in October. Regardless of whether or not I work with her on that day, Heather invites me out to Zeitgeist every Friday. Both of the crews go out, and I put extra effort into dressing up cute because I know Billie will be there. Billie and I don't dare try to hug again. Instead, we bump shoulders, pat each other on the back, pull each other in for a sideways hug, or opt for exchanging grins while raising our pint glasses. I learn she shares a two-bedroom flat on South Van Ness with Tamika. That she doesn't have a girlfriend. That she's thinking about getting a dog and visits animal shelters on the weekends. On Friday nights I come home intoxicated by her, heart palpitating, my mind replaying every word, every glance, every touch of the hand.

14

Today Bubbe arrives. I had to take off a day of work and tell the crew I'd miss Zeitgeist tomorrow. *Bubbe.* Her presence here is so implausible I have to recite *Today, today, today,* to make it real.

I head out on my journey to get Scooby from Ocean Beach, where we've had her parked, Sam and I shifting her position in the streets every two weeks so she wouldn't get towed, until Sam bailed and it was just me doing it. I catch the N Judah at Civic Center with a Discman and the PJ Harvey CD I bought at Tower Records when money was falling out of my ears. Even in late October, it's still warm on the east side of the city. The ginkgo, with its flaming yellow leaves, offers the only signal we've turned the page to fall.

As the N Judah clacks westward, the train and the sidewalks outside begin to empty. The train stops when Judah

Street meets the Great Highway along Ocean Beach, and the driver calls out, "End of the line!" to no one but me.

Stepping off the train into a gust of wind, I see the water across the highway with its white frothy waves smacking at the sand. It feels about twenty degrees colder out here. There are only a few people walking the beach, their hair blowing away from the ocean, shoulders lifted from the cold, hands planted in pockets. I wait for the light, then cross the highway, walk down to the water, and pull my shoes off to feel the coarse sand. PJ Harvey is still wailing in my ears when the icy water rolls over my ankles, the cold knifing into my calves.

When my teeth start clanking around in my mouth, I head back to dry land to wrangle my socks back on damp feet. I can't believe Bubbe is on a plane right now moving toward me in the sky. I've never been so nervous to see her, but never so excited either. She's up there, aimed at me. Bubbe in the sky with diamonds.

I find Scooby covered in dirt. We haven't washed her since rolling through a free car wash in Nebraska. Inside, belongings mixed with rubbish are heaped in the passenger seat and footwell. I drive to the gas station to clear the mess, wash the windows, and fill the tank. In the process I find four of Sam's spearmint ChapSticks. I uncap and smell each one before I toss them into the trash.

By the time I'm done cleaning, gassing, driving to the airport, parking, finding the right terminal, and getting through security, I arrive later than I planned, right as the plane is deboarding. I watch a steady stream of people come off the jet bridge. They float past me on the way to baggage claim while I crane my neck to look around them. I'm trying to see as far back as I can. After the flow of passengers has dropped to a trickle, I see a flight attendant pushing a wheelchair, and I can tell it's her by her orb of gray curls and square shoulders and the arm crutches pinned between her knees. My heart leaps up into my throat, which is suddenly raw and tight. It's her. I wave wildly, almost frantically, my arm swinging high and wide over my head, my other hand balled up tight around the van keys. I immediately register the moment she sees me. Her face lights up and her shoulders lift. She leans back and says something to the woman pushing the chair, and I imagine her words, *That's my granddaughter,* and then we're grinning at each other like buffoons as the distance between us closes. As soon as she's within reach, I'm bent over her, holding on to her, hugging her too tight. *My bubbe, my bubbe.* She takes my cheek with one hand and kisses the other over and over. She smells like Dove soap, like home, and I can't help but tear up at the feel of her.

"Shayna punim, shayna punim," she says to me. I step back to take her in. We look into each other's wet eyes and laugh. I'm not sure what's so funny, but clearly we're both in on the joke. She's so beautiful to me. Her smile and her eyes are so bright. Her skin is dark and warm and crumpled all over. She has heavy jowls and eye bags, and I have never seen anyone more lovely in my entire life.

Bubbe thanks the flight attendant, and the moment she's out of earshot says, "That flight was very long! Next time I'm going to wear a diaper, so I don't have to get up to use the restroom so many times."

"Yeah, right!" I say as I step behind her wheelchair and roll her to baggage claim. "There is no way you're going to wear diapers until you absolutely have to wear diapers."

"I'm going to roll my wheelchair into the snow with a bottle of brandy when it's time for diapers," she says.

"Well then, I'll have to keep you here, where it never snows!"

"Did you know they don't serve meals on airplanes anymore? Just snack boxes. They used to serve hot meals with real silverware. Air travel used to be a very high-class experience, but now they just hand you a box of snacks like you're a child." She turns, trying to look back at me. "Come here, let me see that punim again."

I stop and step in front of her.

"Now we're officially blocking traffic, Bubbe."

"Ikh hob dikh lib, mayn zisinke," she says as she pats my cheeks again, this time with both hands.

When we get to baggage claim, I realize we're up for a tricky task. I'm not sure how to roll a big suitcase and push a wheelchair at the same time. We end up parking her outside of Arrivals, where I deliver her bag to her, then I get

Scooby from the parking lot to pick her up. When I pull around, I spot her leaning from her chair using one crutch as a tool to retrieve the other, which has fallen to the ground. I hop out to help.

After I get her suitcase and crutches in the back, I realize getting her in and out of the van will be another tricky task we'll have to tackle all weekend. She's only four feet eleven and you have to step up a full foot and a half to the doorframe to get yourself in.

I get back in the van and pull it as close to the curb as I can, then get out again to help. We both seem to want to tell the other how it should be done. After a few fumbling attempts, I realize there's only one way to go about this.

"New plan, Bubbe," I say as I widen my stance and bend my knees to anchor myself. "Put your arms around my neck."

"Do you think you're Popeye, Hannah? You can't lift me straight up into the air. You think you've joined the circus?" she asks.

We both start laughing.

"But I'm strong, Bubbe!" I say. "Circus strong!" I squat lower and wrap my arms under her butt.

"You can't get my big tuchus up there!" she says, gripping her arms around my neck.

Weaving my fingers together firmly under her, I squat even lower and hoist, lifting from my legs the way Heather taught me to carry buckets of primer. She lets out a little scream as I get her high enough to shove her butt onto the seat, but not without knocking her head against the top of the doorframe first.

"Ouch!"

"Sorry, Bubbe! I guess I'm *too* strong!"

She smiles and rubs her head. "That's a very rough way to handle your poor old grandmother."

"You can't park here!" we hear someone shout.

I turn to see the parking enforcement guy barking as he tromps toward us.

I help Bubbe turn her knees forward and scoot back into the seat.

"You can't park here!" he barks again, coming around the passenger side of the vehicle. His face is red and little specks of spit fly out with each word.

"I'm trying to get my grandmother up into this seat!" I yell back as I close her door and fold up her wheelchair.

"You still can't park here," he says again, a little quieter this time, knocking on the hood of the van with his knuckles. I load her wheelchair into the trunk and climb into the driver's seat.

"God, what an asshole," I say as I slam the driver's-side door shut.

"Watch your language, bubbeleh," she says. "He doesn't know any better."

I buckle up and turn the key in the ignition. "You always make excuses for jerks, Bubbe. You deserve to have help getting in the van without being yelled at."

"What I deserve has nothing to do with it," she says. "He

may be an asshole or a schmuck or whatever term you prefer to use, but he certainly isn't enjoying life as much as I am."

I turn, grinning. "You just said *asshole*, I've never heard you say a bad word ever."

"Asshole, bitch, fuck, fuck, motherfucker," she says, gesturing with open arms for each one.

"AHHH! Bubbe! My ears!"

"I'm in California now! I can use all of the rude language I want; nobody thinks I'm frum in California," she says.

"Nobody thinks you're frum in Long Beach either, Bubbe."

"You know, you used to be a little frum maidel when you were very young," she says.

"I'm practically a shiksa now, Bubbe."

"You are not, silly girl. You can't escape yourself that easily. You are just frei. There are lots of frei Jews in America and it's only the frum ones who whisper about them," she says, rolling down the window. She pushes her hand out into the cool fall air, opening and closing it in the wind.

The Rosemont Lodge is on El Camino Real in San Bruno, a busy four-lane road that runs from San Francisco endlessly south, a conveyor belt of strip malls and autobody shops. I picked it because they had plenty of ADA-compliant rooms and a heated indoor pool with a ramp. We pull into the roundabout, and I turn off the van.

"Looks all right so far," she says, lifting her chin to see over the dash.

Once we're parked, I pull the wheelchair out of the van and unfold it. This time we do our maneuver in reverse, a far easier feat. Bubbe turns her legs toward me and dangles them, and I pull her off the seat in a big hug to lower her to the ground. When she's settled in the chair, I hand Bubbe her purse. She opens it and pulls out a white hair pick and her coral Maybelline lipstick.

"Here," she says, handing them to me, "pick out my curls and put this on me."

"Are you getting fancy for the check-in person?" I ask as I slide the pick against her scalp, fluffing the roots and leaving the curls intact.

"Just a little," she says, tilting her chin up for the lipstick. When I'm done, she presses her lips together. "Nu?" she says. "Let's go."

Bubbe's room is on the first floor adjacent to the indoor pool. It smells like cleaning supplies, and the floral bedspread matches the drapes, which match the upholstery on the two chairs at the round pine table. Next to the table is a sliding glass door that leads out to a small, enclosed patio.

"Not too chintzy, you picked well," Bubbe says as I push her wheelchair inside.

"This place is kind of weird-fancy," I say, looking around. It looks like it stalled out in the early eighties, forever stuck in a pastel floral prom dress.

"I think it's quite nice," she says. "And I've been living very frugally my whole life, so I'm going to spoil myself rotten with the time I have left."

Bubbe directs me as I unpack her suitcase into the dresser drawers, set out her toiletries at the back of the bathroom sink, and put her shampoo and bar of soap on the bench in the shower. When we're done, she gets herself onto the bed and lies back with a sigh.

"I'm exhausted," she says. I plop down next to her, and she takes my hand, patting the top of it with her other. I roll toward her.

"Bubbe, I'm so happy you came to see me," I tell her. "I really am."

She turns to me and smiles. "Well, what are we going to do with our precious time together, bubbeleh?"

"Tomorrow I want to take you on an epic adventure across the Golden Gate Bridge to see some beautiful views and go out for an early dinner at a restaurant I like up there."

"Will we celebrate Shabbos at a restaurant?" she asks.

I feel ashamed that I didn't think about Shabbos at all. "How would we do it?" I ask.

"All we need is a bit of challah, some red wine, and the candles on the table. Is it a restaurant that would have red wine and candles on the table?" she asks.

"Yes, and I can pick up some challah from Rainbow Grocery. It's nothing like your challah but it will do. Is that okay with you? To do Shabbos at a restaurant? Nothing will be kosher."

"Since when do I keep kosher?" she asks, lifting an eyebrow. "Shefele, I hope you know there are a million and one ways to be Jewish. Don't let anyone fool you into thinking otherwise." She squeezes my hand and gives it two more pats before letting go to shift her weight and roll toward me. "My energy has been a little bit lower recently. Does this epic adventure have a lot of walking?" she asks.

"It doesn't have to," I answer.

"Then it sounds lovely, my dear."

When I get back home in the evening, I sit next to the phone with Molly's number in my hand, trying to get up enough nerve. I can't believe I have to call Molly's to talk to Sam. But Sam and Bubbe love each other. They always have, and I can't bear to keep them apart just because I'm pissed at Sam.

"Hello?" someone answers. I pause for a moment, anxious it's Molly, and contemplate hanging up, before deciding against it.

"Hi, I'm wondering if Sam is around? This is Hannah."

"Hannah who?"

I'm thrown by the response. Not Molly, so it must be her roommate, Luz. But was I never mentioned to her? Was I intentionally scrubbed from Sam's stories? I don't know what to say.

"She isn't here right now."

"Can you give her a message from me?"

"Sure."

"Can you tell her my grandmother's in town, and she should call me if she wants to see her?"

"Okay, anything else?"

"Tell her she's late on rent," I add.

In the morning, I knock on Bubbe's door. She doesn't answer, so I head to the lobby to see if she's eating her Continental breakfast. There's a basket of fruit, a bowl of ice filled with small cups of yogurt, and a platter of muffins spread out on a long wooden table. Quite Continental. Nobody's in here, not even the receptionist. When I don't find Bubbe in the lobby, I head to the pool and find her alone doing laps. The indoor pool is in a large, steamy tiled hall with windows looking out into the parking lot. There are white plastic chaise longues set around it on the concrete. I lay myself down in one and watch her swim.

"I couldn't find you and I was starting to get worried," I say.

She's doing the breaststroke in her floral bathing suit, a swim cap with a strap pulled tight under her chin.

"This is a wonderful pool, very warm," she says. "You should come in."

I take off my boots and socks, roll my jeans up to my knees, and sit on the edge, dropping my legs into the water. It's warm like a bath.

"I want to hear all about the life you are making for

yourself here," Bubbe says, swimming toward me with her head above the water.

"Oh, totally. I'll take you to some great places I've been to," I say.

"That sounds like fun, but I want to know about *you*, my dear. I want to know what you and Sam are up to and how it's going and what you see in your future here."

I look away. My mouth goes dry. There's nowhere to begin and so little I can actually say to her.

"Okay, Bubbe, but can we just have fun for today?"

She stands in the water with her hands on her hips and cocks her head, eyeing me.

"I take it that talking about it is not fun?" she asks.

I shrug.

"Well, let's go have fun then," Bubbe says as she heads for the ramp, a hand on each rail to guide her out.

As we fly across the Golden Gate Bridge, Bubbe is just as thrilled as I was when I first saw it. This time there isn't fog and it's even more magnificent from our vantage point sitting high in the van. There's a confetti of white sailboats on the water, Alcatraz with its yellowing barracks moody in the center, and to our left, a clear view of the craggy wide mouth of cliffs, open to the Pacific Ocean. I watch Bubbe's eyes widen, how she sits tall looking left, then right, then left again.

I take her to the bakery in Petaluma, to Tomales Bay,

and to the Point Reyes seashore. Then to a bench overlooking Chimney Rock, where we sit bundled together in our coats, our hair blowing back behind us, while she tells me stories about my toddler years, how she snuck me candy and sips of coffee full of cream and sugar when my mother wasn't looking.

We arrive at the Farm House restaurant in Olema right as the sun is falling low in the sky. I can tell Bubbe is spent by the sheer effort it takes for her to climb the three stairs to the entrance with her arm crutches. I pull the door open for her and she steps in.

"This is quite nice," she says as the warmth and the smell of fresh bread hit us. "Did you and Sam come here just the two of you?"

"I came with another friend," I lie.

"Well, now I know you have made another friend. I've gotten a pinch of information out of you!" she says, pinching the back of my arm.

The host seats us at a table by the window overlooking the back garden.

"Bubbe, dinner's on me tonight," I say, handing her a menu.

"This is too pricey for you, no?" Bubbe asks.

"It's okay, Bubbe. I planned ahead. I really want to do something special for you on this visit."

The waitress sets down a dish of olive oil with chopped herbs and warm bread wrapped in a white cloth.

"We're going to have a beautiful Shabbat dinner in your

restaurant, my granddaughter and I," Bubbe explains to the waitress. "Would you bring us two glasses of the house red and some matches? We would like to blow out this candle and relight it." She points to the tea light sitting low in an amber glass.

"Oh, okay," the waitress says. But I can tell she has no idea what Bubbe is talking about. When she walks away, I slip the challah into the bread basket and cover it with the cloth. The waitress returns with two glasses of wine and a utility lighter with a heavy orange handle and a long wand.

"We don't have matches, just this," she says, lifting it from her tray. "Is this okay?"

"It will have to do," Bubbe answers. "Thank you, my dear." As soon as the waitress leaves, Bubbe leans in toward me. "What kind of restaurant doesn't have matches?!" She clicks her tongue in disapproval. I blow out our candle.

"Would you like to do it?" Bubbe asks.

I shake my head. "I like watching you do it, Bubbe," I say.

"I don't know how to use that ridiculous lighter. How about you get it lit and I say the prayers?"

Using two thumbs to overpower an insistent child lock, I click the lighter into action, a perfect tear-shaped flame blossoming at the tip. I light the candle and watch as Bubbe moves her hands in circles three times over the flame, then brings her palms to her face and begins the prayer. "Baruch atah Adonai . . ."

Her voice is raspy, melodic, familiar. I watch her jowls tremble under her hands. I turn around and see the waitress at the bar watching Bubbe. She looks down when I catch her eyes, but I can't care about the staring. I turn back to Bubbe and stare too. Is there anything more beautiful in the world? After the lighting of the candles, she recites the Kiddush for the wine and the Hamotzi, the blessing over the bread.

When she's done, she smiles warmly at me. "It speaks to you even when you wish it wouldn't, doesn't it, bubbeleh?"

"Only when you do it, Bubbe. Only when you do it at a restaurant with a ridiculous lighter and a tea light."

She chuckles and pats the top of my hand. "You can't escape yourself that easily."

I can't help but laugh. "You already said that, Bubbe."

"I'm an old lady! I have every excuse to repeat myself, nu?"

Bubbe opens her bag and pulls out an orange pill bottle, uncaps it, and puts two pills on the table next to her water glass.

"What's that?" I ask.

"Oy. It's a long story that I'll tell you tomorrow, but the short of it is, I'm having trouble digesting fat now, so I have to take this before I eat a meal. Anything delicious like this," she says, gesturing to the dish of olive oil.

"What is it?" I ask.

"It's called Zenpep. It helps me break down the fat, I guess. The doctor explained it to me, but the appointment was too long, so I just said, 'All right already! Tell me what to take and when to take it and I'll do it.'"

"Why are you having trouble digesting fat?" I ask. "What's wrong with you?"

She reaches across the table and pats my hand again. "Remember you told me you just wanted to have fun today? No difficult conversations?" she says. "I was planning on respecting that request."

"I meant I didn't want to say anything about myself."

"You think I enjoy difficult conversations? We either have them or we don't."

"Okay, Bubbe, okay. Just tell me," I say.

"Oy," she says again, leaning back and pulling her napkin into her lap. "Listen, I'm going to tell you something, but I want you to know I'm okay with it." I nod, gesturing for her to start, and brace myself, hands balled in my lap.

"So, a few weeks after you left, your mother asked me if I was losing weight and I said I didn't think so, but that night I got on the scale and found I had lost about eight pounds, without even trying or noticing, which is a lot when you're only four feet eleven." She takes a sip of water. My eyes gulp at her, her upper arms, the slack in her face. I see it so abruptly, it takes my breath. "I had been having some stomach problems." She leans in to whisper, "Some issues with diarrhea at times, and a little bit of back pain and a little bit of stomach pain, and I wondered if it was connected, so I went to the doctor. He asked me a lot of questions and did some blood tests and then a stool test. So the blood tests came back, and they were showing some issues."

"What do you mean, 'some issues'?" I ask.

"Well, at first it sounded like my liver was having some troubles, and they knew this from the blood tests. Then they did more blood tests and sent me for a scan to see inside and they saw something they didn't like."

"What do you mean? What did they see?" I ask, suddenly hot all over.

"Well, they saw a mass in my pancreas, or on my pancreas, and they saw—"

"*Mass?* Like cancer? Just say what you mean, Bubbe," I say, trying to keep my voice from rising.

Bubbe cocks her head and looks at me. "Oy, shefele, this is not going to be easy for you, but I want you to know I'm okay."

"Cancer?" I ask again.

She nods.

"But you're going to be okay?" I can hear my pitch jump, desperate.

"I said I'm okay with it."

"So you *aren't* going to be okay?" I ask, too loud this time.

"Listen, I'm okay even if I won't be okay," she says. "They are telling me I have pancreatic cancer, but it's not just in my pancreas. It's outside of my pancreas, but I'm lucky that I'm not feeling very sick yet. I need these pills with food, and sometimes I take a pill if I'm queasy, and I take a pain pill at night so I can sleep with my aches, and I'm tired, but I can still take care of myself and it was very important to me to come see you. So here I am."

"Bubbe," I say, my throat tight. "Mom and Rachel know?"

"They know. They take me to all of these appointments. I found out it was cancer shortly before I told you I was coming. They knew I wanted to tell you myself. Your mother argued about that. She wanted to prepare you because she knew this would hurt very much for you, and she loves you even if she doesn't always get it right. But you don't call when they're home, and you don't answer your phone, so she couldn't have told you anyway. And Rachel, Rachel needs her sister. It has been very hurtful, Hannah."

Guilt fills me. I bloat with it, my throat knotting it in like a balloon.

"But they'll give you chemo, right? So you'll live longer? You're such a fighter. I know you're going to fight like hell, Bubbe, right?" I ask.

"Listen, I'm in my eighties now. Even if I was younger, the chemotherapy would only offer a few more months. And would they be a good few months? That's not what we fight for. I fought like hell for a good life, and I've had a wonderful life, Hannah. I really have."

"But how long do they think you have without chemo?" I ask. Hot tears tip over and run down my face, dripping onto my forearms. Our waitress arrives suddenly to take our order and I shield myself with the menu. I think if I speak, I will choke and cry out loud. Bubbe glances at me and then lowers her reading glasses onto her nose.

"We are both going to have the salmon dish, and after

that you can bring us one crème brûlée to share, and two decaf coffees," she says, folding up the menu. "Thank you very much, my dear."

As soon as the waitress leaves, I ask again, my voice cracking this time, "How long did they tell you without chemo?"

"Nobody knows the answer to that, Hannah," she says. "They tell you based on averages, but that doesn't tell me how long *I'll* be around. They made that very clear. There are people who die quickly and people that live a long time. I'm not interested in guessing. You know the saying 'Mensch tracht un Gott lacht'? We must accept there is no answer to how long."

"I can't believe in a God that laughs at basic plans like being alive another year. I won't believe in that kind of God!"

"Whether you believe in God or not has no bearing on his plans."

"But how long did the doctors say you had?" I ask again.

"The doctors are not God, even though they might think they are—"

"Just tell me, Bubbe!"

"I don't know. Three months? Six months? Nine months?" she says. "The impression that your mother and I got is that with or without treatment, I probably won't be around next fall."

"Bubbe," I say, my voice weak and shaky. I feel like I got the wind knocked out of me, and I cover my face with my hands. "I want you to get chemo because I need you."

She reaches for me, puts a hand over mine, trying to peer at me through the spaces between my fingers. Her eyes are wet too.

"You will always have me," she says. "When you are my age, you will still have me. We are two peas in a pod, no? I'm part of you. I'm inside of you. Unfortunately for you, you won't be able to shake me."

I put my hands down. "How do you die when you die of pancreatic cancer?" I ask.

"Well, I don't plan on going out slowly, but if I did, I was told I'd die of liver failure. I already have a spot on my liver, but eventually the cancer spreads all over your liver so your liver goes kaput."

"How are you going out if you don't go out slowly?" I ask.

"I haven't quite figured that out. Maybe you could come home when I'm close, buy me a bottle of brandy, and wheel me out into the snow?" She chuckles.

"That's not even funny, Bubbe," I say.

"I might just try to take all of the nausea medicine and the pain pills and maybe this Zenpep stuff, all at once."

"Please don't do that, Bubbe," I say.

"I can always stop eating and drinking, but I'd rather just die in my sleep."

"Bubbe," I plead. "I literally just found all of this out, I'm not ready to brainstorm how you should die."

"I'm sorry, I'm sorry. It's on my mind but it isn't right to burden you with it. I just don't want to become incapable and confused and I certainly don't want to suffer. They helped me fill out some forms saying I didn't want CPR, or a tube . . . a breathing tube, if I remember correctly. I don't want any tubes."

"Bubbe," I whisper. I can't stop the tears. She blurs in front of me.

"Shefele, I know how much you love me, and I know I can't ask you to help me die, but I need you to know that's what I want. In a perfect world, I want you to help me die. I just want to be clear, so if there's ever a question, you understand. And the last thing I want is to lie around soiling my sheets. So if anyone is trying to keep me alive when I'm a bedridden vegetable, you can remind them, *She signed the papers!* What I want is to enjoy my time with you and the rest of the family and my friends and c'est la vie."

"Nobody around you feels like c'est la vie!"

"Fortunately for me, I still have the wherewithal to tell everyone what I want. Hopefully they will listen."

"How are Mom and Rachel doing with this?"

"Can you guess how your mother is doing?"

"I'm guessing she's trying to bully you into doing chemo or trying to get the doctors to convince you?"

Bubbe laughs and nods. "And Rachel?" she asks.

"Rachel is trying to be strong and positive? Like telling you some people cure themselves with prayer and some kind of special diet?"

"See?" she says. "They're inside of you too, even if you won't speak to them, they're in you."

"It's not that I won't speak to them, I just—I don't want

to fight with Mom. And at this point I feel so bad about Rachel, I can't get myself to call. She hates me right now. The last message she left was all yelling."

"What is hate between two sisters, eh? It's hurt, Hannah, it's the heart hurting."

Our dinner arrives, salmon with roasted potatoes and rosemary, and a stack of shiny asparagus drenched in olive oil, a lemon wedge on the side. I'm nauseated. Bubbe takes another pill and starts cutting small bites of her salmon.

"All right, now it's your turn," she says.

"What do you mean?" I ask.

"I mean it's time to talk to me. Whatever is eating you up, tell me what it is."

I take a bite of potato, try to get it down my throat, and wipe my nose on my napkin.

"What are you so afraid of?" she asks, shrugging her knife and fork in the air.

"I'm afraid of upsetting you and causing a rift between us when I don't know how long I have you. I need you, Bubbe," I say, the words bringing tears back to my eyes. I can't tell her anything. I can't tell her about stripping and Chris and drugs. Could I tell her about Sam? Could I tell her I'm gay?

"What if I promise you, whatever it is and whatever I feel, I won't push you away or become angry with you," she says.

I take a bite of salmon and force it down with water. Bubbe places her knife and fork on either side of her plate and leans in toward me.

"Are you pregnant?" she whispers. "Sometimes young women find themselves pregnant and very afraid."

"No! Bubbe, I'm not pregnant," I say, laughing, and then I pause, considering what the admission might cost against the weight of the secret, the distance it will dial between us. I lean in. "I'm gay," I say, articulating so she can hear me clearly.

"You're what?"

"Gay. You know what gay is, right, Bubbe? I'm gay, okay? Sam and I were together and—" I stumble. "Well, I'm not sure what we are now. We aren't really talking." I look up into her eyes. I'm trying to gauge her reaction, but I can't. We're on some new planet with pancreatic cancer; shouldn't gay be small potatoes?

"You feel you have fallen in love with Sam?" she asks.

"I fell in love with Sam in high school, but I'm not talking about Sam. I'm gay with or without her. I'm just all the way gay. I just am, Bubbe."

Her brow furrows, and I can see the worry in her eyes, worry I've burdened her with. I look down and pick at a stalk of asparagus with my fork.

"Bubbeleh, I felt very close to my girlfriends when I was young, and you might be confusing the feeling of closeness with—"

"Bubbe, please. I'm not."

"Have you tried to date any young men since you've been in San Francisco?"

"Bubbe, you promised, you can't push me away. You can't try to convince me—"

"Okay, okay," she says, her hands lifting toward me.

"I knew it would be a bad idea to tell you, I don't want to stress you out, and you can't tell Mom—she'll lose her mind." I feel myself breaking into a sweat.

"Hannah, give me a moment to process what you're saying. It's a lot to process." She pushes her plate away and takes another sip of water. "If you're really gay you won't have children," she whispers.

"You don't know that, Bubbe."

"Do you know gay people with children?" she asks, her hands up as she shrugs.

"I don't know any, but I'm sure they exist."

"The only homosexual person I've known was the waiter that used to work at Moshe's Deli, and, well, there's that singer, what's his name? The short guy with the glasses."

"The short guy with the glasses?"

"The one with big glasses like Sally Jessy Raphael." She holds her palms up to her temples to show me how big.

"Are you talking about Elton John?" I laugh.

"Yes! Like I said, the short guy with the big glasses," she says with a chuckle.

"Bubbe. Somebody who's four feet eleven can't really call Elton John 'the short guy,' and I don't think he counts as someone we know."

"Narishkeit! I will count him," she says, swatting my

objection away and smiling. I smile back at her, but as her eyes hold me, I feel ashamed and look down at my food again.

"Shefele," she says. I can't help but squirm in her gaze. What does she see now that she knows? "Shefele, I don't love you any less, I'm just worried," she whispers, reaching her hand out to pat mine again. "I faced so much discrimination and hardship and I don't want you to face it too. I want you to enjoy having children if you want them."

I lift my eyes. "Your worry doesn't do me any good. Does it help you when someone says something like 'Poor her, she faces a lot of discrimination, I worry a lot about her'? Does that help?"

She looks focused and seems to consider what I've said. "No." She shakes her head. "It makes me want to show them how capable I am and how beautiful my life is."

"Well, I hope I feel like that at some point, but right now your worry just feels bad."

I pull my hand from hers and push her dinner back in front of her. She picks up her fork and takes another small bite of salmon. I want her to eat, but I can't seem to get anything down myself. She looks up at me and gestures with her fork.

"Listen. I'm sticking to my word. I'm not angry, I'm not pushing you away. I want every moment I can have with you before I go. But I *am* afraid for you," she says, leaning in, "and I will try to work on my fear. But here is what I want: I want you to work on your fear about my death. It's coming whether you're kicking and screaming or not."

I look into her eyes. I can do that for her, can't I?

"I will try to work on my fear," I say, gulping on my own words.

"We'll both be working on our fear," she says, resting a hand on my forearm.

On the drive back to the hotel, she falls asleep, and I'm flooded with grief. Floored by it. My throat keeps squeezing shut like a sea anemone every time I imagine losing her, then it opens tentatively when my mind wanders, only to squeeze shut again when the thought rushes back.

When we get to her room, I help her get ready for bed. I hang up her coat and place her shoes neatly at the foot of the bed the way she likes, then help her change into her nightgown. I watch her put on her reading glasses to sort through a large Ziploc bag of prescription bottles, reading the label of each one.

"Bubbe, can I stay here with you tonight?" I ask.

"Of course, my dear. There's certainly enough room in this king-sized bed for the two of us."

I close myself in the bathroom, stick a wad of her toothpaste in my mouth, swish it around, and catch my reflection in the mirror. I look exactly how I feel, eyes red and swollen, skin pale, wrecked, incapable of this. I can't do it. I have to look away before I fall into sobbing again.

Crawling into bed next to her, I find her already asleep, lying on her back, her mouth open, a hand on her chest.

What if she dies in her sleep tonight and I wake up next to her body? I can hear her breathing. Thank god. Her breathing is loud, on the edge of a snore, and I'm grateful for the sound. The sound of still living, of air in motion, moving in, moving out.

15

I sleep terribly. I'm in and out of dreams where I've lost Bubbe momentarily, like losing a child in a grocery store, and I run down the aisles screaming, *Bubbe! Bubbe! Bubbe!* But I'm the child. I look down at my feet and see I have Salt Water sandals on, and when I look up, I'm eye level with the hips and hands of strangers and can't find the eyes that know me and love me, that I know and love. Then I dream she told my mother I'm gay, and Mom tells me I'm not to come home again. Not ever. But I'm in Long Beach when she tells me, so I decide to walk to Bubbe's house, but I can't find it. The streets keep changing, they are familiar and then they are not, and so I remain always almost there. Almost.

After the sky has cracked into early dawn, I finally fall into a deep sleep. When I wake up, Bubbe is gone. She must be at her Continental breakfast or in the pool swimming. I lie in bed awash in panic again. I promised Bubbe I would work on my fear, and she promised me the same. It feels unfair. Gay is different than dying of pancreatic cancer. This morning I'm mad. I'm insulted and defiant at the comparison.

I hear a key in the door, and she appears, a bag hanging off the handle of one of her crutches.

"I snatched a few extra yogurts and another muffin when no one was looking," she says. Seeing her, I can only feel love.

"Breaking the law, Bubbe!" I say as I sit up in bed. She hands me the bag.

"I want to go to your restaurant today," she says.

"My restaurant?" I ask.

"Yes, the restaurant where you and Sam have been working."

I feel my face flush and look down into her bag at two little yogurts and a blueberry muffin. Lying over the phone was easier than lying to her face.

"I lost that job, Bubbe," I say.

She cocks her head and frowns.

"But I have a new job painting."

"Did they fire you? Did you work hard and do your very best?" she asks.

"They didn't fire me. I don't like hustling for tips and having to be super nice even if someone is kind of jerky," I say, the truth feeling like solid ground to stand on.

Bubbe chuckles. "That's any job, bubbeleh. You're going to have to do some version of that charade wherever you go and whatever you do. It doesn't matter if you are president of the United States of America or a school custodian."

"I know, Bubbe," I say, peeling the paper off the blueberry muffin. "That's what Sam was always telling me too."

"So, what's this new job?" she asks.

"Painting houses."

"Women can get hired to do that kind of work?" she asks.

"Of course, Bubbe. We aren't in the dark ages anymore," I say. I don't mention a woman needs to start her own painting company to make it happen, and Bubbe seems pleased with this news that's not actually news. It makes me want to offer her more good news about the world outside of Long Beach, more of San Francisco, more new experiences. "What if I take you for Indian ice cream, and then we go up to Twin Peaks with your wheelchair to see the view."

"Indian ice cream? What is that, curry flavor?" Bubbe asks.

"No, Bubbe!" I say, laughing. She's the most hilarious when she doesn't intend to be. "You'll love it, I promise."

I take Bubbe to Bombay Bazar and Ice Cream on Valencia Street, a grocery store thick with the smell of spices and incense. There are shiny bangle bracelets in rows at the counter, labeled with a handwritten sign that reads *Five for a dollar.* I buy ten, sliding five on my wrist and five on hers.

"There," I say, "twins."

She jingles her wrist at me. "We'll fool everyone with these," she says, grinning.

I push her wheelchair through the arched doorway connecting the grocery store to the ice cream parlor next door. She sits up straight and then leans forward to see through the glass, reading the flavors out loud. All of them. The woman behind the counter looks thoroughly amused. Bubbe's East Coast Yiddish accent sounds heavier, foreign, way out here in California. Bubbe orders rose, I order cardamom, and we head outside to eat. Parking her wheelchair next to me, I look around, nervous, imagining running into someone I know. One of the painters, or maybe a girl from the club; how Bubbe would look at them, what she might see.

She pops two Zenpep before she pinches the ice cream with her lips tentatively. "This is delicious, Hannah. It tastes like perfume, but I mean that in a wonderful way."

"That's exactly what I thought when I first had it," I say.

"I love being with you here, and when I go home, every time I smell a rose, I will think of having this here with you."

"I want to go home with you, Bubbe," I say between bites.

"Why would you do that?" she asks, looking up at me.

"I need to spend all my time with you now."

"Bubbeleh, I want you to come home for Hanukkah and Chinese food on Christmas, but the greatest gift you can give me is to move forward with your life. I don't need you to see me lying in bed moaning. I don't even want to see it myself."

"How do I move forward with my life," I ask, my voice cracking, "when you're going to die, and I love you so much?" My eyes well and I look around. Whether I know them or not, there are too many people on Valencia to openly sob. I need to keep it in.

"Az me muz, ken men."

"But I can't!" I cry, unable to contain it, tears spilling down my face.

"Shefele, it's a gift you will give me," she says, resting a hand on my hip. "Give it to me like a gift. Work hard. Make friends. Enjoy this beautiful city. You have so much more freedom than I did at your age. I want you to make the most of it."

"Bubbe, if I was dying you wouldn't just go on with your life like nothing was happening."

"That's different," she says, shaking her head.

"It's not different. It's not different to me!" I wail, my eyes blurring. "I'm going to miss you, and I'm going to worry about you all the time between now and Hanukkah."

"Well then, let's talk every day," she says. "It's going to make me sicker faster with everyone standing over me fretting."

"Fine," I say, wiping my face with my sleeve. "I don't want to argue with you, so fine for now." I look at her ice cream. It's hardly been touched, pink running down the back of her hand.

"I can't finish this," she says. "It's delicious, but it's not sitting well with me."

After ice cream, I drive Bubbe up to Twin Peaks and push her from one end of the lookout to the other and back again. I point out Market Street, Potrero Hill, Bernal Hill, and Coit Tower, but I can tell her energy is fading. It's only two o'clock and she's exhausted by the time I lift her by the butt into the passenger seat.

"Do you want to go back to the hotel, Bubbe?" I ask.

"I don't *want* to need a rest," she says, looking out the window, "but I do."

As we head back to the Rosemont Lodge, she falls asleep. A nap is no longer a nap. Each time she doesn't finish a meal, I take it as a sign we are one step closer. How can I send her home on an airplane and just stay in San Francisco like nothing has changed?

When we get to the hotel, I wake her up and help her inside. I help her onto the bed, take her shoes off, and lie next to her as she falls asleep again. As I listen to her breathing, it starts to rain. At first, it's so light I'm not sure what the sound is, then there's a heavy patter rapping at the glass. Grief and rain belong together; the sound of it soothes me.

Right around dinnertime, she wakes. I pull back the curtains so she can see the large puddles forming on the patio. We lie in bed in silence, listening, watching the raindrops tap and roll down the glass.

"Will you help me bathe and pack up for the flight tomorrow?"

I nod.

I set up the bathroom, help her out of her clothes, and get her seated on the shower bench. She gestures for me to pass her the handheld showerhead. Now I can see clearly the weight she has lost in her arms and legs, her flesh hanging slack from her bones, but her belly is still heavy, and her breasts graze her thighs when she leans forward to wet her back. She straightens up as I rub shampoo between my palms, then she tips her head back into my hands, and I work it into her scalp with my fingertips.

Washing her hair brings back the flood of tears. This is her human body, naked on a shower bench. It is incapable of lasting forever, even if I tend to it with more diligence, with more devotion. How many times can I overflow with tears before I run out of water? I'm at the very beginning of this grief, but is grief bottomless?

She sits on the bench holding the showerhead, letting the water run over her neck and chest while I soap up a washcloth and scrub her back. Tipping her head and closing her eyes, she rinses her hair, then leans forward to rinse the soap from her back. I squat down to wash her feet, taking each in my hands.

Lifting my chin with one hand, she asks, "Are you crying again?"

I nod.

"I hope you're crying for yourself and not me. I'm going to be fine. You shouldn't worry about me."

"I *am* crying for myself," I tell her. "I need you."

"You have me. You must remind yourself, Hannah. My

father is still inside of me," she says. "I still hear his voice advising me. I'm certain you've already heard my voice inside you. It will only get worse." She chuckles. "You will be so sick of me telling you what to do."

"I do hear your voice when I'm not with you, Bubbe. But I need to hear your voice in real life too. What if you just tried the chemo? Maybe—"

"Listen," she interrupts, "when we're afraid, we try to grip even tighter. I'm afraid for you, but squeezing you tighter won't make your life any easier. Gripping me tighter won't make my death any easier." She aims the water at each of her small feet, wiggling her toes as she rinses them. "Yesterday after you told me you were gay, I tried to figure out what made me so worried. I know I'm worried that people will be unkind to you and might even try to hurt you. But the worry is because I want you to have a good life. I want you to be happy. Hannah," she says, looking down at me, "are you happy?"

I think for a moment.

"No," I say. "I'm not happy. But it's not because I'm gay, not directly because I'm gay. I feel like I don't know what I'm doing. I don't know what I want, and I don't know how to make decisions, and I'm scared of everything. You never seem like you don't know what you're doing. I think you're so brave, Bubbe."

"I'm brave because I've always had to be; that doesn't mean I know what I'm doing. I've certainly never died before, and my father isn't here to tell me how it's done. But bravery is a muscle, Hannah," she says, gesturing for me to turn off the water and hand her a towel. "Stronger every time you use it. You are brave too, shefele. You've always been brave. Certainly braver than you can see right now. When you're older you will look back at this time in your life, and then you will be able to see yourself very clearly. You will say, *How on earth did I get all that chutzpah?*"

It's still dark in the morning when I help her dress, buttoning the sleeves of her white blouse and pulling her coat up onto her shoulders. I push her folded wheelchair and drag her suitcase while she walks to the van with her crutches. The morning light is creeping in now. The air is cold, the windshield covered in dew, the ground still wet from last night's rain.

Our ride to the airport is only ten minutes, and it goes by too fast. I try to tell her how much I love her, but she seems distracted, worried about getting to her flight on time, so she asks me to drop her curbside and ask for assistance. After I get her out of the car and in her wheelchair, her suitcase and crutches beside her, I flag someone down. Before I can tell her again that I need her, that I love her, that I can't live without her, she is kissing my cheeks, and the airport attendant rolls her away.

"Bubbe, call me when you get home!" I yell after her, but she can't hear me, she's already gone.

I get back in the van and turn the engine on. Again, the

floodgates open, but this time I let myself wail; I roar with it, my face contorting. Wiping my nose on my sleeve, I realize it's the same sleeve I've been sopping up tears and snot with all weekend. I'm disgustingly dirty. I've been so preoccupied with Bubbe, I've barely noticed the unbrushed teeth, the dirty underwear I've been wearing for days, the skunky smell of my armpits. Now I'm supposed to go home, shower, and return to my life like nothing has changed.

The scaffolding is gone from the apartment when I get back, and the building looks pristine. Nothing like the grungy dark hallways it holds inside. When I walk into the apartment, it feels foreign. Who was it that lived here before Bubbe was going to die? I pull off the makeshift curtain and let the light in. The answering machine is blinking. I press play and lie down on the bed.

Hannah, it's Sam, I can't wait to see Bubbe, and I have rent money for you. I can hang out today or tomorrow, either one, and I'm ready to talk with you alone once Bubbe is gone. I love you. You're my family. Okay, call me back at Molly's. Love you, bye.

I stayed with Bubbe all weekend and forgot I'd invited Sam. Hearing her voice brings me back to tears.

Hi, Hannah. It's Billie.

The tears stop and my eyes go wide. I sit up all the way. Hearing Billie's voice sends a buzzy zap up my neck.

I'm just calling because . . . I missed you at Zeitgeist on Fri-

day, we all missed you, and I was just calling to see if you wanted to go to Luna Sea this coming Friday with me, to see my friend's one-woman show. We can swing by Zeitgeist first if you want. The show should be fun, she's funny . . . If nothing else we can practice hugging goodbye, get over the hump so we can try again. We could choreograph it. Count it out in steps so we get it right . . . um. Okay, bye.

Was she asking me out on a date? She wasn't *not* asking me out on a date. Why did it have to be so ambiguous? I squeeze my fists and rapid-fire pummel the pillow.

Hannah? . . . I miss you so much.

I freeze.

I guess this is also Sam's number. Miss you too, Sammie. It's April, by the way. Hannah, I got your number from your mom. I ran into her. She's super bitter about you FYI, just be prepared. I heard you're not calling her at all. Anyway . . . I miss you a lot, like I said before. I have my own little apartment, but I don't have a phone yet, so I'm just going to try to call you again later. I'm doing really well now, and I have exciting news to tell you. At least I think it's exciting, and I think you will too. Love you . . . both. I'll try again later this week.

I'm dumbstruck.

How am I going to go about my life this week and not wait by the phone for April and Bubbe? I strip off my dirty clothes and find a decently clean towel. I shower with pinballs knocking around in my brain, unable to follow any thought all the way through.

When I get out, I put on clean clothes, sit on the bed with my hair wrapped high in a towel, and take a breath, readying myself. I pick up the phone and dial Billie's number first. It rings several times and goes to her answering machine.

"Hi, Billie, Hannah here, yes and yes. I'd love to go to Luna Sea with you on Friday, and I'd love to join you in hug practice. We'll get it right. Okay, talk soon."

I hang up and cover my face with my hands. One down.

I find Molly's number and dial. The phone rings only once.

"Hello?"

"Sam?" I ask.

"Hannah?! Did she already leave?"

"Yeah," I say, wincing with guilt. "I ended up staying at the hotel with her, so I never got your message—"

"But why didn't you call me from the hotel?" she asks. "*You're* the one who invited *me*."

"Because I was a wreck, Sam." I tip my head back to keep the tears from spilling again. "I just found out she has pancreatic cancer and—" I feel my jaw tense and my chin start to quake. Sam gasps. She knows Bubbe, knows exactly what she means to me. "She isn't going to do chemo, so she's only going to last a few months, like maybe six months"—my voice cracks—"and she's already different, Sam, she's thin and she's tired and she looks older."

"No!" Sam bellows. I can hear the hurt in her voice.

"I can't believe it either. I feel like I'm in shock. I'm either numb or I'm crying. Mostly I'm crying all the time. I can't stop."

"What are you going to do?" she asks. I can picture Sam's face. I know what she looks like in this moment, panicked, on the verge of tears, her eyes going bloodshot and giving her away.

"I want to go home to take care of her, but she really doesn't want me to. She made that clear. She told me staying here and living my life is a gift I could give her. And I'm like, what life? She's more important than this," I say, choking on my words. "Time is just going, it's going to run out. She wants me to wait until Hanukkah to come home, but Hanukkah feels so far away."

"What if you fly back and forth every couple weeks?" Sam asks.

"I can't afford that now."

"Why?"

"I don't work for Chris anymore."

"What do you mean? How are you making money?"

"I got hired to work with a painting crew, all queer people," I say.

"No way! They painted our building, right? My friends were talking about that company the other night. That's so cool."

I don't answer the question. I'm stuck on *my friends.* The words sting, even though I've started to make my own. Sam has a life here. I'm just not in it.

"You're still at the Cheese Parade, right?" I ask.

"Yeah, I have it down to a science now, so I'm only working two nights a week. I can rake in five to seven hundred a night easily, now that I know what I'm doing."

"That's great, Sam," I say.

We both go quiet. I look around our apartment. It's so weird she's not here.

"Sam?"

"Yeah?"

"I feel like you broke up with me without actually breaking up with me. And I still don't even know why."

I hear her sigh.

"It's not like I decided, *I'm going to break up with Hannah,* I just feel like you're stuck. You won't go out, you won't meet people, and you kept saying Chris was better than stripping, that she didn't leave you fried. Maybe I just got jealous, but you always seemed fried, like faraway and less fun when you came home."

I think about this for a moment. I wonder if she's right. Working for Chris wasn't as exhausting as stripping, but it was still a lot of pretending. So much of my life has been pretending I'm something else, somebody else.

"Sam?"

"Yeah?"

"Bubbe said this thing, she said being brave is like a muscle. It's not like people *are* brave or *aren't* brave, but if they *do* brave, then the muscle gets stronger and stronger. I feel like I'm starting to *do* brave more."

I hear her sniffling again. "I love Bubbe so much."

Another pause.

"Sam?"

"Yeah?"

"I love you. A lot. And I need to figure out who I am here without you."

16

All week I make a ritual of calling Bubbe in the morning. I go downstairs, pick up a bagel and coffee from Li Wei and bring them back up, sit on the bed, and chat with her for an hour at least. I ask questions about her childhood, about synagogue, about the cats that use her potato bed as a litter box. I'm hungry for every last one of her memories. I need them all. I'm scared to lose the stories she hasn't told me yet.

I've also been busying myself counting down the days until Friday, when I get to hang out alone—well, kind of alone—with Billie. On the days I work, she stops by and checks up on our crew; sometimes she brings us coffee or crackers and the pimento cashew dip, "pink lunch," as everyone calls it. I love the way she listens to people. Takes care of them in all kinds of small ways, from pink lunch to moving Heather's truck for street cleaning. She doesn't make a big show of it. She is what she is. Solid. Kind. Crazy hot.

And I swear to god, she smiles at me longer than she smiles at anyone else. Her eyes do that thing to me.

Friday. *Finally.* I don't work today, so I have the entire day to prepare myself, or wind myself into a tangled ball of nerves, depending on how you look at it. I call Bubbe first thing, but she doesn't answer. I assume she's still asleep, so I water a half-dead plant I found on the street and clean the apartment. L7 blasting in my Discman, I dance while using a ripped T-shirt to scrub the sink, then the tub, then the toilet.

Around eleven, I try Bubbe again, and again she doesn't answer. I didn't worry when I called earlier, but now that it's two p.m. her time, something doesn't feel right. It's foggy out. I pull the window open and let the cool in, sitting on the bed to think. Bubbe didn't mention any Friday plans. When we got off the phone yesterday, she said we'd talk tomorrow. Today *is* tomorrow. What if she fell down and Mom and Rachel haven't come to check on her yet? What if she's lying on the floor in pain? Nothing in me wants to call my mother.

I put my hand on my chest and take deep breaths of cold fog until I can get up the nerve, then dial, pinching my eyes tight when it starts to ring. It rings all the way to the answering machine.

"Hi, Mom, hi, Rachel, it's Hannah. I was just wondering if you're with Bubbe, because she hasn't answered the phone today, and normally, we've already spoken by now," I say, cringing. I know it must bother my mom that I have daily contact with Bubbe and no contact with her. I hang up the phone. Again, I stare into the fog. Pull at it with my lungs. I tell myself there's nothing else to do.

I try Bubbe's phone three more times over the next few hours, getting more and more panicked with each call. At three thirty, the phone rings. I dive for it, knocking it off the cradle, catching it before it hits the floor.

"Hello?" I ask.

"Hannah, it's Rachel—"

"Oh my god, thank god!"

"Bubbe is in the hospital and Mom's there with her," she says.

My heart, which has been stuck in my throat, now slides low, filling my stomach.

"Last night Bubbe's leg was bothering her—it was all swollen, and we planned on taking her to the doctor today, but when Mom went to get her, she was completely confused and barely speaking and couldn't stand up at all," she explains.

"What? Like she had a stroke?" I ask.

"They think she had a stroke, but she also has a blood clot in her leg and a small one in her lungs too."

"What are you even saying?" I ask. "Why would she have clots? She has pancreatic cancer, not some kind of blood-clotting problem."

"They said pancreatic cancer put her at risk for all these blood clots," Rachel says.

"Is she going to be okay?" I ask.

"What does 'okay' mean in this situation, Hannah!?" she snaps, her voice suddenly shaking. "Without the clots and the stroke they only thought she had a few months! All of the doctors told her not to get on a plane, but she was set on flying out to California to see you. She wanted to tell you herself, in person. Do you know how badly I wanted to tell you? I would have left it in on your answering machine, I don't care. We wanted her to ask you to come here but she wouldn't. Because she knew, Hannah! She knew you wouldn't come home to see her if she just asked without telling you she was sick. You only ever think about yourself!" Her voice cracks and she cries out loud.

"Are you saying the trip gave her blood clots?" I ask, crying with her.

"I'm saying the trip put her at risk for clots!" she yells.

"You said the cancer put her at risk!"

"They both—"

"Rachel, please!" I cry. "I have to come home now. Tell Mom I'm coming home."

"*You* tell Mom you're coming home!" she says. "Grow up and tell her yourself!"

"She's mad at me!"

"I'm mad at you too! You won't talk to us. You're so busy thinking about yourself, you never think about what it's like for us." Her voice cracks again. "You've never called back when I call. Not one time. Have you ever thought about how cruel that is?"

I swell with guilt. "I'm sorry, Rachel! I'm sorry. The only reason I don't call you back is because I might have to talk to Mom if I call," I say.

"That's so pathetic. I don't care if your relationship with Mom is hard. You think mine is so easy? You can still call and say, 'How's the weather, can I talk to Rachel?' You could have mustered up a two-second conversation with her to talk to me. Do you ever think about all I've had to put up with for your sake?"

I wipe my nose on my sleeve. I always thought she had it easy.

"Please, Rachel, I'm sorry. I really am," I say, listening to her cry. "I'm coming."

When I hang up the phone, I stare out the window. None of this feels real. I bend my knees into my chest and bite one to check, leaving an oval impression of my teeth. Not evidence enough. I dig my nails into my forearms to check again, but the pain arrives late. Muted. I lift out of the top of my head toward the ceiling and then out of the room, above it, where I expand into something broad, boundaryless, soft like a cloud. I pick up the apartment and look inside, as if the ceiling were made of glass, a diorama with a girl in her underwear sitting up in bed. Tangled burgundy hair, mousy roots, knees pulled against her chest, arms wrapped around her knees, face turned toward the window, a half-dead plant on the sill. I watch her get up and rifle through the drawers of the dresser, pulling on a pair of tube socks with green and yellow stripes, black jeans, an oversized black hooded sweatshirt. She puts on a beanie from the floor and a jean jacket with a down vest over it. From the closet she retrieves a sock thick with cash and pushes it into her vest pocket.

She grabs her keys and opens the door, stepping out and shaking in the cold. The shaking brings me back. I'm on the stairs when I begin to feel my legs again. How I can move them underneath me. I tell them to move faster, and they do what I say. I experiment with my hands. I tell them to push the heavy door open, then the metal gate too. It clanks shut behind me. I tell my arms to swing at my sides. They do it. It's me. I'm here. I head to the travel agency at Union Square to buy the first ticket home.

Part Three

Long Beach,
New York.
November 1996.

17

It's five thirty a.m., and I'm standing under a TWA arrivals sign at JFK, waiting for Rachel. She promised to pick me up, but as the Buick approaches, I shield my eyes from the headlights and see my mother's face in the driver's seat, the sight rattling my heart like an alarm bell. I'm completely unprepared. I throw my duffel in the back and open the passenger door, scanning her as I buckle my seat belt. She has heavy eye bags, and her mouth is stuck in a frown, but it's a raw frown, not an angry one. A broken frown.

Patting me on the thigh, she says, "Hannah, let's let it all go for now." Her voice is thin, torched. "We have bigger fish to fry, so let's try not to argue."

"Okay," I say, unnerved by her kindness. Is she softer now? Or shattered? I feel something for her I can't name and rest a hand on her shoulder. "I love you, okay?" I say.

She glances at me. I see the whites of her eyes are snaked

with red. "I love you too," she says, returning her gaze to the road.

As we head back to the house, Mom describes Bubbe's rare coherent moments when she responds appropriately to a question or simple direction. How each time it felt like turning a corner out of a dense fog and seeing a path forward, only for the fog to cloud in thick again. They were completely lost to each other all night. Yesterday she let a carousel of visitors into Bubbe's room, and now she wonders if it was all too much. I feel the stab of not being one of them. Bubbe woke at three a.m. moaning and holding her abdomen, so they started her on pain medication, which seemed to be helping. Her blood tests revealed her liver was worse off, likely from the cancer, and we wouldn't know if her stroke symptoms would improve until they did or didn't.

"I just need to be with her," I say, pulling my knees in and resting my feet on the seat. My mother gives me a look, and I drop them back into the footwell and turn toward the window. I can't bear to hear any more about Bubbe. It feels like it's all my fault.

Driving through Long Beach is eerie. It looks the same but feels removed, like a picture of a place instead of the place itself. November is bringing its cold, salty wind through the naked trees, and they tremble, evenly staggered on the sidewalk. On Lincoln we pass Moshe's Deli, Classy Nails, Rudy's Wash N Fold. I crane my neck to see if I can spot Rudy inside, finishing off the folding before the door jangles with the first customer. Long Beach is the same but different. Or Long Beach is the same and I'm different. It isn't a noose anymore, not a knife or a cage. It's a beach town, with a sleepy main strip. The only weapon Long Beach holds now is Bubbe's absence. An ache in the place she's been gouged from.

When my mother unlocks the door to our house, I walk into a museum. How long has it been? Only a little over four months? It looks like a movie set, the couch intentionally sunken in the middle and the Shabbos candlesticks intentionally tarnished. I go to my room. If I can call it that? The little white desk is untouched, with knickknacks and old pictures scattered across it. I pick up a photo of Sam and April on a bench at the boardwalk, a seagull standing between them. I laugh looking at it, remembering how long the seagull lingered, and how Sam said, "Okay, don't tell anyone, seagull, but Jessica Lombardi saw Jeff Schneider's nuts up the leg of his shorts at the waterslides, and she said they're a really weird color." We died laughing when the seagull found Sam scootching closer far scarier than Jeff's nuts and took off, flying high above the beach and out of sight. It feels like a lifetime ago, but it was only about two years. I put the picture back and sit on the edge of my bed. My room is smaller than I remember. The window looking out to the backyard still calls to me, but it's a quieter calling. The frame glows like an exit sign in a theater. But I don't need to lie in bed wishing I had the nerve to climb out of it now. The world is so much bigger than this place, and I've already left out the front door.

Rachel's head appears through the cracked door, and I stand up and swing it wide to greet her. We hug, my face buried in her hair.

"You totally sent Mom on purpose!" I whisper in her ear.

"I did not!" she whispers back. "When my alarm went off, she came in and said she was going to pick you up, which was crazy because she spent all night at the hospital. What did you want me to say?"

I pull back to get a good look at her. She gives me a half smile, a sad smile, then looks away.

"Rachel, I'm sorry," I say again. I need her to know how sorry I am. I feel more homesick standing in front of her than I ever did in California.

"I don't want you to be sorry," she says, shaking her head. "I want you to be different—"

"But I can't be different!" I say, my eyes instantly blurring with tears.

"You don't know what I mean when I say that, Hannah!" she yells. "I need you to stop telling yourself everyone here hates you and rejects you, because we don't! I don't hate you, Hannah. I need you. For months all I could think about was how Bubbe and Mom always said, 'Hannah needs you, Hannah needs you.' My whole life I heard 'Hannah needs you.' But I need you too!"

I watch her eyes go bloodshot.

"What could you possibly need me for?" I ask, dumbfounded. "When I'm here, you're constantly trying to keep the peace between me and Mom. You make sense here and I don't, I can't—"

"Don't tell me I make sense here. You never ask how I feel!" she yells. "You make sense to *me*, Hannah!" She glances down the hall before she whispers, "You think I don't fantasize about wandering off somewhere new without all this obligation? Someone has to stay here with them, and you always assumed it would be me."

I'm speechless. I always thought things were pretty easy between Mom and Rachel. She was constantly yelling at *me*, not Rachel. Not often anyway. But maybe the only easy thing was for me to assume Rachel was content with a life I wasn't. She was never as loud as me, but she was pushed, and she fought for us all the time. Rachel scraping pancake batter into the trash; Rachel begging on behalf of both of us to stay in public school, to wear regular swimsuits, shorts in the heat of summer; Rachel putting her body between mine and my mother's every time tempers flared, keeping it there while I fled. Rachel, who stayed while I fled.

"Rachel," I start, but then go quiet. What can I say?

"We lived this together," she says, pointing her finger to the ground. "We're the only two people in the world who lived this." Her eyes spill now. I pull my sleeve over my fist and wipe her face. I want to tell her not to cry. It hurts to watch.

"I'm sorry, Rachel. I get it now, and I'm really sorry." I wipe her face again, pushing her hair out of her eyes.

"I don't want to hear any more fighting!" My mother appears in the hallway, car keys gripped in a fist at her chest.

"We aren't fighting," Rachel says. "We're making up."

She eyes us for a moment. "Good," she says. "Come on, Hannah. I need to get you to the hospital before I lose steam."

Bubbe is alone in bed when we walk into her hospital room. Her gown has slipped from one shoulder, leaving a breast exposed. She's dismantling the phone on her bedside table, holding the receiver in one hand and the mouthpiece in the other, a tangle of wires stretching between them.

"Mom!" my mother yells from the doorway as she enters. Bubbe jumps like a child who's been caught drawing on the walls, the crayon still held tightly in her fist. I notice an IV on her forearm secured with tape so the tubing is threaded in at the elbow out of her sight. A bag of fluid hangs on a pole above her.

"I can't figure out how this thing works," she says, looking back down at the wires. My mother turns to me, exasperated.

"See?! This is why we can't leave her alone for even thirty minutes! Everyone says, 'It's okay, the nurses are there to look after her,' but are they?" She gestures around the room. "No. Nobody here. And the minute she's alone, she's up to something." Her cheeks are flushed, her eyes wide and wet. My mom is a child too, her grief and exhaustion turning so quickly into fits, her fists balled tightly at her sides.

"Bubbe," I say, sitting down next to her, pulling her gown back on and tying it at the neck. I watch her eyes study my face, but does she recognize me? "Bubbe, it's me, Hannah."

She lifts her palms like she's unsure but then takes my head in her hands and tips it toward her to kiss my forehead.

"A kiss on the keppie," she says.

My mother leaves to sleep for the day, telling me she'll drop Rachel off at four to take my place. Then Rachel will be replaced by Bubbe's neighbor at seven, and then she'll return at ten for the night shift. When I offer to take the night shift, she says she needs someone who will be able to stay up all night with Bubbe and she's the only one who can do it. I consider reminding her I worked at a twenty-four-hour diner—Bubbe must have relayed that lie—but think better of it. She's not rational. The necessity to never fall asleep, and the idea that she's the only one capable of it, is beyond me, but I know better than to disagree with her. We agreed not to fight. In essence, I agreed not to disagree with her. I try to surrender myself to it. Soften the resistance I feel rising in me at every turn. It's temporary. Everything is temporary.

Once alone with Bubbe, I close the door and return to my place on her bed.

"Do you know who I am?"

Her palms lift again. It's not a yes or a no, but it's the only answer I'll get. My eyes well and spill, and I lay my head in her lap, gripping her at the hips to hide my face. She doesn't seem to mind. She still smells like Dove soap and detergent. She pats my shoulder repetitively with one hand, occasionally dozing off in a snore.

Various doctors and nurses come in and out throughout the day. I learn she isn't eating because she didn't pass her "swallow screening," which means she inhales small amounts of food and water into her lungs each time she tries to eat or drink. Bubbe's oncologist warns me this will eventually lead to pneumonia. When I ask how they fix the swallowing problem, she tells me we need to have a discussion as a family. She says to feed her we need to either place a tube in her nose that leads to her stomach or insert a tube through the wall of her abdomen directly into her stomach. My face must give me away.

"It's important to think about what interventions she would want if she were able to advocate for herself," she says, tilting her head to one side and pushing her glasses up her nose.

"She told me she signed papers," I say.

"She hadn't completed the process. The DNR/DNI order was placed: do not resuscitate, do not intubate. That means we know she didn't want CPR if her heart were to stop, she didn't want us to attempt to restart her heart with a defibrillator, and she didn't want an artificial airway placed, a breathing tube. But she hadn't yet completed her advance directive or her living will, which are much more detailed documents. So, family will have to make these decisions for her."

I look down at Bubbe, her face turned toward me, snoring with her mouth open, her gray curls pressed flat and greasy. *She wants a bottle of brandy and her wheelchair shoved into the snow,* I think to myself, and then I look up, wondering if I said it out loud. The oncologist is staring at me with her compassionate eyes. I look away.

When I'm alone with Bubbe again, I get in bed with her all the way, ducking under her IV line and wrapping my entire self around her waist to sob. At one point she lifts my chin and wipes a tear from my cheek, rubbing it between two fingers like a scientist.

"What's this called again?" she asks.

"Tears," I say.

She shrugs and lifts her eyebrows. I lay my head back down and she returns to the repetitive patting on my back. Maybe it's good she doesn't recognize tears. I'm leaving wet circles all over her hospital blanket. I feel like an enormous whale of a baby.

I doze off a few times and keep landing in a place between sleeping and waking. I see Bubbe in flashes, kneading challah directly on the kitchen counter, flour dusting the floor around her. Then reading in bed, her glasses low on her nose, the macramé wall hanging in the shape of an owl with wooden bead eyes behind her. Then the time she took Rachel and me to Nathan's hot dogs. She took a few pennies from her purse and left them on the seat of the yellow booth we'd been eating at. "Some good luck for other children to find," she said as I eyed them with jealousy. I see her standing in the bathroom, opening the Altoid tin that holds the baby teeth of my mother, my sister, and me, so she could place the canine I just lost inside. "Now when my little puppy bites, it won't hurt," she said, winking at me.

At some point, I wake to a nurse checking her blood pressure and wiping Vaseline on her lips with a gloved finger. I watch her position Bubbe's pillows and throw another blanket over both of us. She reaches under the covers to adjust Bubbe's small legs, folding another pillow between Bubbe's bony knees, before she moves to the IV pump to program it with two thumbs. Bubbe sleeps through it, snoring softly. The sight of a stranger offering this particular tenderness makes me overflow again. I'm full of the ocean. I can't possibly hold it back. My eyes blur and I turn away, pretending to fall back asleep.

Somehow the hours slip and it's already four. When Rachel arrives, I'm standing in the corner, my back to Bubbe, stuffing saltines in my mouth, which the nurse gave me when she realized I hadn't eaten all day.

"What are you doing?" Rachel asks.

I turn around and watch her drop her bag on the chair.

I take a moment to swallow, then whisper, "I'm trying to eat without making Bubbe jealous."

We both look over at her. She's snoring with her mouth wide open.

"You look messed up," Rachel says.

"I can't stop crying, my eyes are broken," I say.

"It's not your eyes," she says. "You should see Mom. She's seriously broken too. She sleeps like three hours a night. Mostly she's been nicer with everything that's been going on, but then she can turn out of the blue and be crazier than ever, so watch out. She just tried to pick a fight with me."

"About what?" I ask.

"My socks."

I look down at Rachel's feet. She's wearing white Reebok shoes with one short athletic sock and one blue dress sock.

"That seems like a move I'd make," I say, pointing to them.

"Well, I guess I'm becoming a real wild card and not doing my laundry," Rachel says. "You've got to go, Mom's waiting downstairs in the car for you."

"The doctor says we have to decide about a feeding tube," I say as I gather my stuff and kiss Bubbe's head. I notice her tongue is dry in her mouth, dry and webbed with deep grooves.

"Bubbe doesn't want a feeding tube," Rachel says.

"I know," I say, leaving before my eyes well over again.

When I get back to the house, I tell my mother I need to nap and crawl into my twin bed, pulling the blankets over my head. I think about calling Sam. She's the only one besides April who could understand what kind of animal this is. This house, this wild Bubbe grief, the way I'm walking on eggshells with my mother. But will it feel good or terrible to hear Sam's voice right now? I fall asleep before coming to any conclusion. I wake a couple hours later to Rachel popping her head in to ask if I want brisket the neighbor brought over. I sit up. My eyeballs ache. I press the heels of my palms into them.

I can smell the brisket from my room. The scent lures me into the kitchen, and I lift the lid off the pot. It's bubbling in a rich broth with carrots and onions, and I bend my face into the steam and inhale. I haven't had brisket since Passover. Bubbe loves brisket. On Passover Bubbe and I always had at least one meal called "a taste," standing in the kitchen together before sitting down for a painfully long seder.

My mother, Rachel, and I gather around the table looking haggard, bedraggled, like we've been out at sea in a storm.

"Is there a reason it's so dark in here?" I ask, noticing the overhead lights are off, one floor lamp glowing in the corner.

"Look, I've had a headache for days," Mom says, her fingers pressing into her temples.

"Okay, that's fine," I say.

"I had a long conversation with the doctors," she goes on, "and tomorrow they're going to put a feeding tube in until she's able to swallow again."

Rachel and I look at each other. I tear a piece of challah in half.

"Mom," Rachel says, "Hannah and I don't think Bubbe would want a feeding tube."

She looks up at Rachel. "When she said she didn't want a tube, she was talking about a breathing tube! The feeding tube will only be in until she regains the ability to swallow."

Rachel's head drops. She stares blankly into her bowl. My mother's eyes move to me next, demanding agreement, and mine follow suit, dropping to my bowl as well. How can I find the right words? Words that won't start a fight?

"Are you two meshuga?" she asks. "She's going to starve to death in no time if we don't do it. Do you want her to starve to death when she could get better?"

"Bubbe didn't want any intervention that would give her time but not quality time. She said that really clearly when she came out to see me," I say. "She said she didn't want to be kept alive if she was bedridden, or confused, or hurting."

"Bubbe doesn't know she might get a few good months if she can recover from this stroke," she argues. "She's improving every day, and it's *my* job to make decisions with her best interest in mind."

"Mom, she's starting to get jaundice because of the cancer in her liver," Rachel says.

"I know that, Rachel!" Mom says, exasperated. "But they thought she had three to six months without chemo, and I want that for her. I don't want to watch her starve to death!" She goes back to her brisket, shaking her head. "God help me with you two!" she mutters. "I'd better not have a stroke."

We eat in silence, all of us staring into our bowls. I look

up at Rachel. She looks so sad. I tap her foot with mine under the table, but she doesn't respond.

"Let's talk about something more uplifting," Mom says. "Hannah, tell me about the synagogue you've been attending in San Francisco. Have you made any friends or met any nice young men?"

I feel my eyes go wide. Rachel looks at me with wide eyes too.

"I actually haven't met any Jewish people," I say.

Now they both look at me, surprised.

"I mean, there are synagogues, I just haven't made it to one . . . yet," I explain, glancing back and forth between them. I feel myself digging deeper into a hole.

"You promised me," Mom says gravely. "You gave me your word."

"I'm going to go," I lie.

Silence.

"I've met other people who were raised religious, just not Jewish. I've been hanging out with an ex–Jehovah's Witness!" I say, laughing.

Neither of them laughs with me. Rachel tips her head down, looking at Mom with just her eyes.

"Oy, Hannah," Mom says, putting down her fork and knife. "And you're fond of this guy?"

I nod, unsure how else to respond.

"He may be nice," she continues, "and he may be handsome, but you have nothing in common with a Jehovah's

Witness, former or not. There is nothing more offensive to me than a bunch of Jehovah's Witnesses sending their children to the doors of Jewish homes trying to convert them."

I think of Billie, small Billie, perfectly dressed with her hair braided too tight. I think of her lifting her little finger to press each doorbell. Little Billie with such an oversized heart, such an oversized responsibility on her shoulders.

It was just last night I returned from buying my plane ticket and called Billie to cancel our date, blustering through an account of Bubbe's visit, the cancer, the stroke, phone pinned between my head and shoulder while I tossed clothes into an open duffel bag.

"That's so awful," Billie said. "How can I help you?"

Thrown by the question, I accepted her offer to drive me to the airport, before I caught my face in the mirror.

"I look like shit," I said, wiping my nose with my shirt.

"I love shit," she answered.

After we hung up, the conversation looped in my head. *How can I help you?* Who says that? Billie does. It's exactly the kind of thing she would say. *I love shit.* I sat down and grinned into my hands.

Now I feel myself burning with my mother's quick appraisal. What could she possibly know about Billie? What does she know about me?

"You don't know who I might have something in common with," I say, too irritated to keep my mouth closed any longer.

My mother shakes her head back and forth, her eyebrows lifting to mock me. She's looking at me like I've been duped. I'm suddenly furious. Sick of pretending.

"She's not a he, she's a *she*. I'm gay," I say, whipping the words from my mouth like a switchblade. She flinches, and her fork clatters to the floor. Rachel's head jerks up, alert to every word now, her eyes jumping between us.

"Nonsense!" my mother barks, pulling her napkin from her lap and balling it in her fist before throwing it on the table. "You are not, Hannah."

"Not nonsense," I say, "for real, I'm gay, and I'm Jewish, but I'm not Jewish like you."

"You are Jewish like us, Hannah!" she yells, gesturing to Rachel and herself.

"I'm Jewish but I'm not going to synagogue, and I'm not going to be out looking for a Jewish guy or even a Jewish girl. I'm going to like whoever I like," I say, pushing my chair out. "And I'm going to be Jewish however I want to be Jewish."

"That's enough, Hannah! You can't know you're gay if you've never had a boyfriend."

"I don't need a boyfriend to know I'm gay," I say, gripping the arms of my chair.

"What then?!" she yells, throwing her hands up. "You're going to have a girlfriend? You're going to have a Jehovah's Witness girlfriend now?" She scoffs. "You're crazy. You're out of your mind, Hannah!"

"*You're* out of your mind, Mom!" I yell back at her. "You

think there's one way in this entire world to live and you've figured it out? And look how great it makes you feel! Are you happy, Mom? Because you seem miserable—"

"*You* make me miserable! *You* make everyone miserable!" she yells, her chair screeching as she shoves it back to stand up.

"Hey! Hey!" Rachel tries to interject.

"Don't you dare come here after disappearing for months to wreak havoc!" Mom yells. She moves to lean over me with hot breath and a finger pointed in my face. "And don't you dare say a word of this nonsense to Bubbe!"

"I already told her when she was in California!" I yell back. "You don't have a say over my relationship with my own grandmother. It's ours, it's not yours. Bubbe and I are close because she can *see* me for who I am, Mom! She's not stuck on wishing I was somebody else. I'm not who you want me to be! Okay? I'm never going to be who you want me to be! Bubbe knows I'm gay and she doesn't need *you* to protect her from me."

I watch her eyes flame. "Feh!" she screams over me. And then she spits. I flinch and close my eyes and feel it land, hot and wet in my hair.

"Mom!" Rachel yells.

"Out!" Mom snaps, her whole arm lifting to point to the front door. "She can stay at Bubbe's house," she says to Rachel. "She's not staying here." She turns and storms from the room. We both jump when her bedroom door slams. I press my palms against my forehead, trying to breathe, and feel the spit sliding on my scalp. I spot my napkin balled on the floor, reach for it with a shaking hand, and bring it to my head. Rachel's hand meets mine, taking the napkin from me to dab the wet spot.

"I'm sorry, but she's not in charge of me anymore," I say, my chin trembling.

"She shouldn't have done that. You didn't deserve that."

It's quiet, and I wonder what Rachel thinks of me, how she sees me now that she knows.

"Rachel," I start, but I don't know what to say next.

"Don't worry. I already knew you were gay," she says.

I look up at her, wide-eyed. "What? How?" I ask.

"I started reading your journals before you left for California," she says.

I bite my lip and pinch my eyes shut. I should be mad, but somehow I can't be. "Then you know waaay too much about it." I shudder.

"You could have told me," she says.

I open my eyes and nod, although it's hard to believe it.

"I mean, I wanted you to. I wanted to know you thought of me as someone you could tell."

"I didn't think I could tell anyone."

"Well, you were wrong," she says, squeezing my shoulder. "What did Bubbe say?"

"She said she was scared for me, but she would work on it," I say.

I watch Rachel's eyes well again.

18

Staying at Bubbe's is like lying in her lap. She's here but not. I take a York Peppermint Pattie from the crystal candy jar in the living room and eat it as I walk around her house, alone but not alone. I sit in her shower seat, pick up her Dove soap, and smell it. Open the medicine cabinet and rattle the teeth she keeps in the Altoid tin. I look through her books and then lie on her bed, holding her pillow and pressing my face into it to inhale the smell of her hair. I open her jewelry box and pull out her small gold locket, pry at it with my thumbnails to see the baby pictures of Rachel and me inside, before putting it on and tucking it under my T-shirt.

After I get settled, I go through her fridge and toss out her rotten food: lox and cottage cheese, an open can of pineapple, a bag with a slimy head of romaine in it. Then I head out walking to the Stop & Shop on East Park Avenue to pick up some groceries of my own.

When I turn left on East Park, I see a young pregnant woman. Belly just big enough to stretch her shirt and keep her from buttoning her coat. She's walking toward me in ripped black Levi's and Doc Martens, and my eyes glide up to her face. It's April. *Pregnant* April. April with no eyeliner on, her black hair showing a couple inches of light brown roots.

"April!" I yell.

She stops in her tracks and stares at me. "What the fuck, Hannah!" she yells back before we run into each other's arms. She's rough and strong and rocking me back and forth, her belly pressed firmly against mine. We can't stop laughing. When I pull back to take a long look at her, she's still laughing, her eyes damp, her face flushed. She looks rosy and full and like the most beautiful April I have ever seen in my life.

"You're pregnant!" I yell at her.

"I know! And I'm sober too!" she yells. "I'm doing it! I'm four and a half months sober and five months pregnant!"

"Shut the fuck up!" I yell at her, grabbing her shoulders with both hands.

"*You* shut the fuck up!" she yells back. "What are you doing here? Is Sam here with you?"

"I came back because Bubbe has pancreatic cancer, and then she had a stroke and she's . . ." I think for a moment and land on the blunt dismal truth. "Pretty much dying."

"Oh my god," she says, bringing a hand to my arm. "I'm so sorry, Hannah."

I swallow and will myself not to cry. "And Sam's not here with me," I go on. "We aren't really speaking that much right now, but I need to call her about Bubbe. I just keep putting it off."

"Why aren't you talking? What happened?"

"Oh my god, April, it's such a long story," I say.

"Bubbe was always so nice to me," she says, her eyes turning heavy. "I need to hear *all* the long stories."

April links her arm in mine. She follows me to the store, then back to Bubbe's, where we sit on the couch together. We've talked nonstop on our walk, and we're showing no signs of slowing down. I tell April everything. *Everything* everything. I tell her about Sam and me, the whole thing from our first kiss to our secret plan. She tells me she knew. Not the part about the secret plan but the part about the secret relationship. "How could I not have known?" she asks, rolling her eyes. I tell her about the road trip and the girls in Reno who gave us cocaine and how hard it is to get a job in San Francisco and about sleeping in the van by Ocean Beach. I tell her about Mr. Patrick and the apartment and seeing the lit-up leg and how we started stripping and what making buckets of money feels like after having so little. And I tell her about Chris and the drugs and the terrible night with the mushroom sex and Sam taking off, and I tell her about meeting Billie and the crush I'm brewing and about painting the Victorian up on Fountain Street. I tell her about sweet Little Danny and Tamika and Heather and Anna G. and everyone else who gathers at Zeitgeist for happy hour on Fridays and how it feels to be surrounded by queers like me. I tell her about Bubbe's visit and learning about the pancreatic cancer and coming out, and I tell her about the stroke and flying home and my mother spitting in my hair and sending me to stay at Bubbe's house. I'm telling her everything, emptying like a tub with the stopper pulled. April laughs at the funny parts, hooks my arm or holds my hand when it gets hard, but mostly she just listens. She listens like it's just facts and not failures.

April tells me she'd already moved from pills to dope before we left. She'd started spending time with Jeremy, her dealer, and slept with him one night in late May because she knew he'd give her free dope if she did, but then she missed her period, found out she was pregnant in the bathroom at Walmart a week after we left. She tells me about getting in touch with the school counselor from our high school even though she wasn't a student by that point and how completely raw and naked she felt asking for help. She had planned on getting an abortion but then changed her mind thinking about her own mother, all the ways it went wrong, what it would be like to do it right with her own kid. Her foster parents didn't know about the dope, but she'd been disappointing them left and right as a result, and she couldn't bear the thought of telling them she was pregnant. So she left home with a plastic garbage bag instead. The counselor drove her to an inpatient treatment program where they detoxed her carefully, checking the baby's heartbeat regularly. She tells me about getting a job at Dunkin'

Donuts and moving into an apartment with one of the girls from her twelve-step program and how they do it day by day, hour by hour. And how she feels important pregnant, and what that important feeling feels like, as if she is wanted and needed when nobody has ever wanted or needed her. I cry in my hands when she says it.

"What part are you crying about?" she asks.

"*I* want you and *I* need you," I say. I move closer to her on the couch and loop my arm in hers. "But to be clear, not in a gay way," I say, smiling.

She doesn't smile back. "Hannah," she says, "you were the person I was the closest to in my whole life, and you left me." I watch the corners of her mouth quiver.

"I know. I'm sorry," I say. "I'm really, really, so sorry."

"I know you're sorry. I just don't want you to leave me again. I want you to be here for this baby, even if you live in California."

"Like be the baby's aunt?" I ask.

"I want you to be her godmother," she says, sitting up.

"I'm Jewish," I say, "I don't even really know what that entails."

"Like be in her life, and if something happens to me," she explains, "if I get hit by a truck or something, I want you to take her. I just can't ever have her go into foster care."

"Wow," I say, "I feel like that's so big and I'm so young."

"We *are* so young, but that's okay because we know what it's like being young," she says. "Maybe that's worth more than people think."

The next morning I arrive at the hospital and find my mother in a chair by Bubbe's bed, her face in her hands. When she lifts her eyes to meet mine, they're puffy and red, no longer furious.

"Hannah," she starts.

I immediately put up my hands. "Mom, don't. I don't want to do that again. Let's just agree not to talk. We shouldn't talk about anything but Bubbe."

"I'm trying to tell you I'm sorry," she says. I look at her, the apology catching me off guard. I don't know how to respond. I glance over at Bubbe, asleep, propped up on pillows. "I shouldn't have spit on you, nobody should be spit on. And sometimes I am miserable."

"Mom." I shake my head. "I shouldn't have said that."

"But my faith is not what makes me miserable. I don't have your father, but I have Hashem. I raised you two with Hashem and Bubbe. I couldn't have done it without either one."

I nod, not knowing what to say.

"I want you to come speak to the rabbi."

"Mom—"

"We could go to the rabbi together. I can't help you if you shut me out. You haven't called me since the first week you left. Not once. If you ever have a child," she says as she glances up at me, and I know what she's thinking, "if you ever have a child, you will know how much you sacrifice—"

"Mom, I don't know what kind of apology this is. I don't want to talk to the rabbi. I just want to coexist. Even if you sacrificed everything for us, I can't owe you a daughter I can't be. I can't do it, Mom." I hear my voice cracking. "I can't do it, so please stop demanding it of me!"

We look at each other. My hands begin to shake, and I grip them together. I don't hate her. I hurt for her. She thinks I've broken her, but she was broken before me, her sharp edges cutting everyone around her. She's not my fault.

Her furrowed brow loosens, and she shakes her head, looking away from me toward Bubbe.

"I told them not to put in the feeding tube," she says quietly. "They told me this morning that her cancer is spreading quickly, and her liver is failing, and that it would make sense to move to hospice."

Bubbe is sleeping with her mouth wide open, her lungs making a crackly sound with each breath.

"They had a lot of nerve telling us three to six months without chemo," she says, shaking her head. "If they had been honest, she might have chosen chemo."

"Mom, they weren't lying. They didn't know. Bubbe said no one could really say."

I move toward Bubbe and wrap my arms around her, burying my face in her neck.

"Bubbe?" I whisper. She stirs, puts her hand on my shoulder, and begins the rhythmic patting again.

"I don't know how to watch her die," Mom says. I lift my

head up and look at her. Her chin is quaking, tears running down her face.

"I'll do it, Mom," I say.

She looks at me, this time with tender eyes. "That's too much for you."

"It's not," I say. "I can do it."

"I'm not cut out for this, I had to do this with your father, and it's very difficult to face again," she says, shaking her head back and forth.

"It's okay, Mom," I say, extending a hand to her. She moves closer to take it in her own. "You don't have to. I'll do it for us."

The hospice team comes to meet us, including a nurse named Meg, who will be handling most of our home hospice visits. She has a wide, kind face with big eyes, long gray hair parted in the middle, and she doesn't wear makeup. She looks witchy in the best way, and we smile at each other in some kind of recognition.

"My job is to support you as a family, because this is really a transition for all of you," Meg says, looking back and forth between Mom, Rachel, and me. I glance at my mother and see her eyeing Meg distrustfully. Meg seems to catch her resistance too and shifts her approach, addressing Rachel and me instead.

"So, you can call me when you need support with her medical needs," she says, a warm smile spreading across her face, "or if you need to just lose your mind for a moment, cry about it, vent about it, I'm here for that too."

She's smiling at me like she knows Mom's tricky. I smile back. She's the best kind of witch. The psychic kind.

At the end of the discussion, Bubbe grips the bed rails and pulls herself up to sit.

"I can go now?" she asks.

We all look at each other, surprised.

"Yes, Bubbe," I say. "We're taking you home."

Rachel and I drive Bubbe home in the Buick while my mother picks up a slew of medications we'll be using to keep her calm and comfortable, to prevent constipation, to thicken the liquids she'll drink so they're safer to swallow, to moisten her mouth and lubricate her eyes.

We transfer her from the wheelchair to her bed, getting her settled with a pad under her, a foam wedge behind her back, and pillows supporting her arms.

"She looks like a queen," Rachel says as we stand back, surveying our work.

"I *am* a queen," Bubbe says.

Rachel and I laugh. We laugh at Bubbe the queen but also at the absurdity of this whole thing. There are no rules. She might be nonresponsive in one moment and completely lucid in the next. She might have only one more day or another whole month. What planet have we landed on?

My mother brings food and medications and pulls out

Bubbe's maroon enameled TV tray. She sets it on the left side of the bed, lining everything neatly on it, before she sits at the table to write up a medication schedule. When she's done, she tapes it to the mirror above Bubbe's dresser, then she moves to the edge of her bed to recite the Mi Shebeirach, her closed eyes leaking onto her blouse as she rocks back and forth.

By eight I find myself alone with Bubbe. Alone together doesn't make any sense, but it makes perfect sense with us now. I pull all the cushions off the couch and make a bed on the floor next to her.

In the morning, I wash her face and hands with a washcloth and dress her in her blue floral housedress, the one she's worn every summer as far back as I can remember. Once when I was little, she took me to the grocery store and introduced me to a skinny woman with a face like a turtle who forcefully attempted to shake my hand. I remember getting scared, grabbing the edges of that blue dress and whipping it over my head. I could feel her hands on my shoulders and hear her apologies to the woman for my behavior, and in the blue light that filtered through her dress I could see my hands, white knuckled on the shiny metal of her leg braces, the Velcro straps pulled tight around her thighs. I pressed my cheek against the hip of her white briefs.

The dress is the same but looser now. She swims in it, and I'm too big to hide underneath it.

Meg told us to change her diaper every couple of hours

and turn her side to side to help prevent the pressure ulcer she developed in the hospital from getting worse. I pull the pad out from underneath her and put a new diaper on her the only way I know how. I imagine April's future baby when I do it. When I lift her legs and wobble her side to side to get the diaper under her, she laughs like we're doing something hilarious instead of humiliating. If she could have seen this moment two weeks ago, she would have asked me to buy a gun, load it up, and shoot her, but does that matter now that she thinks it's funny? If a tree falls in the forest and nobody is there to hear it, does it make a sound? But *I* can hear it. I'm here doing things to her she never wanted. She's here, unrooted, roots exposed, lying on the forest floor, untethered.

I put on Dave Tarras, the Yiddish-American folk musician she played on holidays, and I sit down next to her. She perks up a bit and tries to dance with her shoulders. I laugh and bounce my shoulders with her, snapping my fingers just like she always did to this song. I keep dancing even when she slows, her head tipping back to sleep again. Her gray hair is flat on both sides now. I lean in and kiss her on the keppie. She smells like hay and lavender. Blue housedress. Summers in Long Beach. Driving in the Buick to deliver hot babka to a friend. The instant black coffee she drank every morning.

Days move. Friends and relatives come to sit with her from time to time, and I wait impatiently for them to go so we can be alone together again. I want her for myself. When we're alone, time turns to soup and sloshes this way and that. When people are over, it feels like it's running out.

I'm sitting on the edge of her bed eating oatmeal. I keep wondering if she came out west to say goodbye to me, ask me to help her die, knowing how soon I would be put to the test. I'm pulled from my thoughts when Bubbe leans forward and opens her mouth. I stare at her, not sure what to do.

"I'm only supposed to give you thickened liquids. I'm not supposed to give you food because it might end up in your lungs," I whisper.

"I don't understand you," she says loudly.

"You might choke on it, Bubbe," I say. She swats at me, leans back, and closes her eyes, falling asleep again quickly.

When Meg arrives, I tell her what happened and she says, "You can give her small bites of soft foods along with thickened liquids if she seems to want them. It's all about what she wants now."

I go into the kitchen and microwave a yam, scoop the soft orange meat into a bowl, and mash it with chicken schmaltz. I bring it to her bedside. She reaches her hand in my direction.

"You can offer her a small bite," Meg says again.

I lift it toward her mouth, but she doesn't open it. With her extended hand, she gestures a circle around me.

"Uncoil," she says. I'm confused, the spoon of yams still extended. I decide to play along.

"Like a snake?" I ask.

"No, no, no," she says. "It's a sweater."

I look at the spoon of yams and then down at my body, trying to understand what she means. I need to understand what she means. I look at Meg, desperate for a translation.

Meg moves closer and puts a hand on my shoulder. "It's okay. Don't try and place meaning where there isn't any. She's confused and is going to have difficulty choosing words and expressing her thoughts and feelings. That's it. That's all it is."

Bubbe's abdomen swells over the next several days, and she moans and holds it when it's within an hour of her next scheduled morphine dose. I call Meg from the pink wall phone in the kitchen. She tells me to increase the frequency of the doses to every three hours. There's also the option of having the fluid drained, she explains. It sounds barbaric and I wince at the thought.

"How much longer will this go on?" I ask.

"No one can say," Meg says. "A day? A week? If she's getting enough fluid and a few calories in, it could be as long as three weeks, maybe even four."

"She would hate this," I say.

"Death is a part of life," Meg says.

"She doesn't hate death. She would hate diapers and lying in bed with her abdomen swelling while I fuss over her."

"You're doing an amazing job, and you're so young to be doing it."

I want to tell her that's beside the point.

"God, how do you do this every day?" I ask.

"The same way that you're doing it," Meg says. "Because it's important work that needs to be done. And I'm capable of it."

When I get off the phone, I repeat Meg's words with my face in my hands at the kitchen table. "It's important work that needs to be done and I'm capable of it. It's important work that needs to be done and I'm capable of it." Then I walk down the hall and into Bubbe's room and sit next to her on the bed. She opens her eyes and looks at me, then lifts her hands up into a shrug like, *What do you want?*

"Bubbe, I'll do whatever you want me to," I say.

She looks at me blankly.

"I mean I'll do what you asked me to," I say.

I look for any sign of recognition.

"I'm not going to shove your wheelchair in the snow or hit you with a pan or shoot you."

I look for any sign of fear, anything that would tell me not to do it.

"But I'll help you die, if you still want me to," I say.

She just looks at me. She doesn't flinch at the word *die* like I do, but she doesn't nod in recognition either.

"I need you to tell me you still want me to help you, Bubbe!" I say, holding her face in my hands, "Please!"

She doesn't say anything. I throw myself down in her lap and sob again. I sob loudly. I can't protect her from hearing my broken heart, and she can't protect me from its breaking.

She pats my back, and I cry until I have nothing left and fall asleep.

When I wake up, I see she is asleep too, mouth open, snoring. I peel myself from her and return to the kitchen to call Rachel and Mom. I tell them I feel like she's dying and I want them to come over, but really I'm tricking them into saying goodbye. The tricking part feels awful, wicked, almost evil.

They arrive together and Mom scurries around tidying the already tidy house. She adjusts the meds on the TV tray and tells me I should have put a sheet down before I put the couch cushions on the floor to make my bed, because now they are filthy. Absolutely filthy. Then she goes to the linen closet and finds a sheet to fix my mistake. Rachel cries while she combs Bubbe's hair until it's wild with frizz, and then stands back.

"There, isn't that better?" she asks. I can't help but laugh through my tears, and when Rachel looks over at me, she laughs too.

Mom leans in to kiss Bubbe's face, and Bubbe puts her hand against Mom's cheek and says, "Shayna maideleh, shayna maideleh." I've never heard her say it to my mother. I thought it was something only said to children, but when I look at my mother's face, I see she is a child, her eyes big and broken. She pulls back and cries, looking up toward the ceiling, her teeth biting into her lower lip.

Rachel puts an arm around her, and I watch from the doorway.

"I think I'm going to go back home if that's all right," Mom says.

She kisses Bubbe on the head and then walks toward me. She puts a hand on my cheek, then presses her forehead against mine and begins to recite the Hashkiveinu. I wasn't expecting it and my heart pounds. It pounds with her proximity but also her prayer. Her intention. This is how she can love me. She is praying for my protection through the night. That I will lie down in peace and rise in the morning with strength. I soak it up like a sponge. I pin my lips between my teeth so I don't cry out loud.

When she's done, she kisses my cheek again and moves past me toward the front door. Rachel wraps an arm around me and wipes my tears with the back of her hand.

"I can take care of Mom," she whispers, "you just focus on Bubbe."

I nod. It's what I want too.

"Alone together again, Bubbe," I say when I hear the door close behind them.

She begins her rhythmic patting on my forearm. She doesn't belong here. She belongs in some perpetual summer somewhere. I have to imagine that's where she'll go.

I find the morphine bottle on the TV tray. I can push through my fear. She knew we were both capable of pushing through fear or she wouldn't have asked me. She thought I was strong enough. How much morphine does it take to kill a small grandmother? The absurdity of the question makes it echo in my head. I take a full dropper and hold it in front of her mouth. She opens up wide, surprising me. She's looking in my eyes as I squirt it into the pocket of her cheek. Within a minute, her pupils spin down to the size of two black peppercorns, the full ocean of her gray irises exposed. They're beautiful. I know it's the morphine, but I imagine she offers them to me intentionally, and in their gray, I can see my reflection clearly. It dawns on me that this was the parenting Bubbe gave to me. The gift of holding up a mirror so I could see myself, not wondering why I couldn't reflect her own image back to her. Now that I have turned to mush again, I think of my mother wringing her hands in her house, blocks from this bedside, and for a moment I can feel all the tenderness I can't normally feel, for a parent, for a child, who is doing the best she can, who has done the best she could, and still, it hasn't been good enough.

"I love you so much, Bubbe," I say. She lifts her chin and opens her mouth again. Does she have any clue what I'm doing? I take another dropper full and tuck it into the pocket of her other cheek. She swallows and opens her mouth again. Does she think I'm feeding her? Is she hungry for food and life and I'm tricking her? Feeding her the poison apple while she is so naïve? I empty another dropperful in her mouth. Her eyes lose their focus, going wide at the window in front of her as if she sees something.

"Bubbe!" I squeak, putting down the morphine and holding both of her shoulders, suddenly desperate. Her eyes have gone vacant. Her mouth opens as if she's going to speak, and she pushes out a wet breath. I hear it gurgle in her throat and I panic. Can I reverse course and save her from myself?

Myself. Herself. The cancer. The stroke. The clots.

No.

I lay her back down, take another full dropper, and squeeze the whole thing into the back of her mouth. Is this enough morphine to kill a small grandmother? I kneel on the bed with my head on her chest and my arms wrapped around her. My heart pounds heavily for the both of us, and my eyes wet her shirt.

After a few minutes I find myself alone. Not alone together anymore. Kneeling with what's left. A body. How does it work? How has she slipped from it and where exactly has she gone? She's gone to perpetual summer, I tell myself. Urine soaks the pad underneath her, and my knees are hot and wet where I kneel beside her. My ear is pressed against her chest. I'm listening for a beat I won't ever hear again.

What would I do for love? She was right about me. Brave. I would do anything.

19

Mount Ararat Cemetery. Lindenhurst, New York. Almost a hundred mourners stand huddling like tally marks. The trees above us are bare, knuckled like skeletons. I stand shivering between my mother and Rachel, April behind me, looking gothy pregnant in a long black velvet dress, Doc Martens, and a black faux-fur coat, dodging my mother's gaze. I push a stone deeper in my throat. I don't have any tears today. They are absent when expected and present when inconvenient. Or as Meg explained, when she came over after Bubbe died, "Grief isn't linear. You've grieved while caring for her. Dry eyes are just dry eyes, let go of the story you're telling yourself." I gave her a weak smile. She didn't know I had just killed Bubbe. Or at least I think she didn't know. The story I was telling myself was that I was a cold-blooded killer who'd just offed her own grandmother. But in better moments, like this morning as I stood brushing my teeth in front of the mirror, I caught my own eyes and cried with relief. Relief that she's free from the burden of her declining body. I was able to see myself the way she saw me, strong enough to give her the gift she wanted.

The rabbi recites the Kaddish, and the voices all around call back *Amen.* I close my eyes. The sound of the Kaddish moves me, the swells in it, the way it's handed back and forth from the rabbi to the mourners. The way it reverberates, circling around us, holding us up so we don't fall down.

"Yitbarach v'yishtabach, v'yitpa'ar v'yitromam v'yitnaseh, v'yithadar v'yit'aleh v'yit'halal sh'mei d'kud'sha, b'rich hu, l'eila min-kol-birchata v'shirata, tushb'chata v'nechemata da'amiran b'alma, v'im'ru: amen."

When the service is over, we wait in line shivering to take our turn shoveling a scoop of dirt over her casket. The chill of the shovel seeps through my gloves, and my forearms ache. I drop my eyes to the program while we wait, a picture of her in her fifties on the front, and under it, *Eva Rivka Galinski, May 5, 1914—December 2, 1996.* Eva Rivka Galinski had a name. Her own name. She was Bubbe to me, but how many people had she been? And to how many? I've already been many things to many people. Our lives only overlapped for eighteen of her eighty-two years. A quarter to her, an entire lifetime to me.

After the funeral, we head back to Bubbe's to sit shiva for seven days. People come in and out bringing food. The rabbi reminds me I'm always welcome back and I nod, chewing on an apricot-glazed chicken thigh and covering my mouth with my hand. From the way he's looking at me uneasily, I'm pretty sure my mother told him about the whole gay thing. I excuse myself. I excuse myself left and right, every time I'm cornered, over and over again. I find myself hiding in the pantry, sometimes in the bathroom, sometimes wandering the driveway. This isn't grieving for me. It's a performance I'm no good at. I'm finding that grief is a solitary animal. It prefers to prowl at night. It certainly won't come out when hunted.

I've been trying to call Sam a couple times a day since Bubbe died, but no one ever picks up, and when I reach the answering machine, I feel completely incapable of leaving a message. I'm so used to no one answering that when Sam finally does, I'm caught off guard.

"Hello?" she asks for a second time. I glance around the kitchen. Bubbe's neighbor and my mother are whispering in the corner, and two older women I vaguely recognize are moving stuffed mushrooms from a baking sheet onto white serving trays at the stove.

"One sec," I whisper, trying to figure out what to do. I'm tethered by the pink cord. I stretch it from the wall-mounted phone into the pantry, pinching it in the door as I close myself in. I feel around for the dangling pull chain and light the space with the bare bulb overhead.

"Hannah? Why are you whispering?" she asks. "Where are you?"

"I'm in Long Beach in Bubbe's pantry. She died, Sammie. I'm sitting shiva."

I hear her gasp. "No!" she yells. And then softer, "Oh my god. Bubbe. I'm so sad." I hear her voice waver as she starts to cry, before her frustration surfaces. "Why didn't you call? I should be there."

"I've been trying to call you but nobody ever answers."

"Why didn't you leave a message?" she whines.

I clench my teeth. I have no patience. "Sam, I wasn't going to leave a message on Molly's machine telling you Bubbe's dying! I don't know Molly, and I don't exactly feel great about her. And last time I called, Luz didn't even know who I was. She didn't know my name, Sam. I've been taking care of Bubbe, not obsessing over what you might want, or what you think I should do—" I stop myself there and listen to the sound of her sniffles, waiting for her to bite back, but she doesn't. There's a long silence.

"Did she die in pain?" she asks quietly.

I think for a moment, rub my neck with one hand. It would be risky to tell anyone, even Sam. I'm not ready to anyway, even if I could. Maybe I never will be.

"No, she was on a lot of morphine," I say, clearing my throat. "I know she wasn't hurting."

"How are you so calm?" she asks. I imagine everyone in this house, the rabbi with his wire-framed glasses, the neighbor resting a cold hand over mine while she offered condolences, the women with the stuffed mushrooms, matching smock aprons over black polyester, and I wonder the same thing.

"I can't feel it surrounded by all these people, but at night—" I feel a pressure behind my eyes, in my throat, and stop for a moment. "It was so hard when she was sick that after she died, I felt calmer. I'm relieved for her."

Sam sniffles again on the other end of the line.

"Can I tell you something good?" I ask.

"Please."

"I've been hanging out with April."

"April?"

"Yes, April. She's sober and almost six months pregnant now, and she's doing amazing. She has a job and a sober roommate, and she looks healthy and beautiful."

"What?!" she squeaks. I can hear the smile stretching across her face. "She must have gotten pregnant right when we left! That's crazy. I'm totally shocked." She's quiet a moment. "But I'm so happy for her." She pauses again. "Bubbe's gone, and April's sober and pregnant," she says slowly, to herself more than me.

"So weird," I say.

"So weird," she agrees. "When will you come back to San Francisco?"

I think for a moment, twisting the cord in my fingers, imagining the apartment, Billie, the crew.

"You're coming back, right?"

"Yeah, I want to come back. I need to come back. I'm just at the beginning of doing San Francisco how I want to do it."

"What does that mean?" she asks.

"I just got that painting job, so I was kind of forced to meet people, and I wish I could have done it sooner, when we were together. I'm not terrible at people after all . . ."

"You're so funny," Sam laughs. "Of course you're not."

"On the inside I definitely am." I feel my expression softening; I'm surprised by Sam's easy rebuttal. *Of course you're not!* my brain repeats, as if it has been obvious all along. "So I guess I need a little more time here with April," I say. "And I want to go through Bubbe's stuff before it gets demolished by the rest of the family—" I hear the rabbi's voice beginning the Mourner's Kaddish in the living room. "The prayers are starting, so I think I have to go."

"Okay, but . . . I just want to say, I'm sorry, that I didn't—" She stumbles, clearing her throat to start again. "I'm really sorry about Bubbe. I know, I didn't do that great. I haven't done a lot of things great. I love you. I want you to know I really love you. You're my family, Hannah. And I just want to figure out how we can be together, even if we aren't together."

"I love you too, Sam. You're *my* family too. We'll figure it out."

I pry open the pantry door and drop the phone back on the receiver. Standing for a moment staring at it, I listen to the Kaddish swell, and just underneath the prayer, I hear Bubbe's voice. "Young women quarrel like lovers!" she chuckles. "Silly girls. But you'll work it out! Az men muz, ken men, no?"

If you have to, you can. Beginnings and endings. Endings and beginnings. I can uncoil like a sweater and make a new shape. I can loosen and change. Stretch and expand. Begin and end. Then begin again.

Seven days of shiva feels like an eternity. The house is the most packed with people when the rabbi comes in the evening, then eventually the crowd whittles down to only Rachel, Mom, and me by ten. They leave by eleven, and I wander room to room beginning tasks, abandoning them midway to start others, completing none. I unpack Bubbe's bag from the hospital and find her shoes. She only had one pair at a time because they were so expensive, custom-made for her feet. They're tan, one with a two-inch wedge for her shorter leg, the other smaller and wider for the foot that was curled like a fist. I walk them across her bedroom floor on my hands, grinning, before I line them up, press my forehead against the toes of both shoes, wrap my arms around the heels, and wail violently. When I'm done, I get in her shower, wash with her Dove soap, and belt out "Tiny Dancer" by Elton John—"the short guy with the glasses"—at the top of my lungs, before I crawl into her bed and cry myself to sleep. I've never felt so manic.

On the last night of shiva, I'm relieved. I feel oddly triumphant, like I've successfully completed a weeklong military-style boot camp. A weird one where you're trained in small talk, eating continuously, and mirroring long, sad faces. When Rachel and Mom head home for the night, I press my back against the closed door and waggle my arms over my head in celebration. Then I find Billie's phone number. It's almost midnight, and it's quiet in Long Beach, but it's only nine p.m. in California. I lift the receiver and dial, then stretch the cord into the pantry, closing myself in, even though the house is empty. I'm too nervous for the wide-open kitchen, I need the pantry to hold me in so I don't explode. The line rings only once before she answers. "I was hoping you'd call," she says after I say hi—she recognizes my voice. Her words slide through the line right into my chest and turn my heart into liquid. I close my eyes. She was hoping I'd call, and I hear it in her voice, the warmth, the gentle way she asks questions.

I tell her Bubbe died a little over a week ago. I tell her about Bubbe taking apart the hospital phone, about the conflict around the feeding tube, about Meg the witchy hospice nurse. She asks if I got to say goodbye, if Bubbe could understand, asks how I feel today. Then she asks if I was with her when she died.

I sit myself crisscross on the floor of the pantry.

"Yeah," I say. Every time I'm made to think of that moment, I have to see the cinch of Bubbe's pupils, the sweeping expanse of gray. I have to open the front door for Meg, the knees of my pants wet with Bubbe's urine, and walk her back to Bubbe's soundless bedroom. See how Bubbe's expression had gone morbidly shocked: eyes open and unfocused, mouth agape. Meg using two thumbs to close her eyelids and tucking a rolled-up towel under Bubbe's chin to hold her jaw shut, just until rigor mortis set in, she explained.

"You don't want to talk about that part, do you?" Billie asks.

"I guess not really," I say. "I can say it was hard. But we were okay even though it was hard."

I tell her I was sitting shiva for the last week, but my words tangle in my mouth, and I end up saying I was "shitting siva." We both crack up, and I correct myself again and again, ears flaming.

"I hope you're feeling better now," she says. My cheeks feel like they're going to split open from laughing so hard after only crying for weeks.

"So, what's 'sitting shiva'?" she asks when we're finally calm.

"It's where you stay in the house and everyone comes over and brings food and visits you while you mourn," I say. "And then the rabbi comes and does a little service in the evenings."

"That sounds like it could be really sweet," she says. "Is it?"

"I think it would be, if I didn't feel like the biggest gay weirdo here. And if I was capable of mourning in front of other people. And if the other people were people I actually wanted to hang out with. Then maybe."

"Hmm," she says, "I see how it could go either way."

"It doesn't help that I've had to wear an ugly calf-length black skirt, and tights, and an itchy starched blouse of my sister's. My mom really didn't want me in jeans and a sweatshirt, which I get, and I didn't have anything else here. But it sure doesn't help with the 'I'm a big phony' feelings."

"That sounds like what I wore for years," she says.

"Seriously? I don't know what the 'closeted Jehovah's Witness teenager' look is."

We compare notes. Billie had tights that sagged low in the crotch, black Mary Janes with a sensibly low heel. I try to picture Billie's head stuck over such modest godly garb. I put us side by side, paper dolls in our calf-length black skirts and tucked blouses. I take her hand in mine.

There's a lull in the conversation. "So, how's work?" I ask, jumping to fill it.

"It would be better if you were around," Billie says. I bite my lip and try not to giggle. "Oh, and Little Danny found you a fake ID. It was his roommate's, but she moved to Portland. He found it under the couch."

"Ooooh! Now I can go to all the bars with the big kids," I say.

It's quiet.

"Tell me more things," she says softly.

"Like what?"

"Anything. Everything."

"I can't give up all my dirt when I'm trying to play it cool with you," I say, squeezing my temples in my hand. I'm glad she's not here to see she's got me in a constant shade of tomato.

"Cool is overrated, and what's all this dirt?" she asks.

"Not dirt," I say, "just . . . you know how you get used to being closeted, and then other shit ends up in there too? And then, at a certain point, you don't know what to keep in there and what to take out."

"Try me," she says.

But what can I say? And what can't I say? I'm afraid of scaring her away.

"Okay, first, believe it or not, I'm gay," I say.

"Zero points for that. Too obvious from day one," Billie says.

"Really?" I ask, honestly surprised. "It was obvious when you met me outside the apartment building?"

"Besides the part where you told me I looked like River Phoenix? Yeah, you made serious eye contact. You can spot femmes by their eye contact," she says. "Usually, straight girls are dodgy. Maybe they're worried I'll crush out on them. But any femme, even if they're dating my best friend, is going to look me in the eyes when we talk."

"So, I gave you *femme* eyes?" I ask, still trying to figure out exactly what femme is.

"Yeah, you gave me femme eyes," Billie says.

Another pause.

"Give me real dirt," she says.

"Okay," I start slowly. "What if I told you I stripped for

a while when I first got to California?" I ask it like a question, unwilling to commit.

"Then I'd say, all right, how was that for you?" Billie says. "I mean, a lot of the dykes in San Francisco have stripped at one point or another. Anna G. did for a while. And Little Danny used to turn tricks."

"For real?" I ask, stunned. "My roommate, Sam, who I moved out there with—well, she's more like an ex-girlfriend, kind of a best friend—she's not my girlfriend anymore, to be clear," I say, stumbling, and Billie laughs. "We just ran out of money, and we had to figure something out quick."

"It doesn't have to be a whole thing for you if it isn't," she says. "Straight people think queers do sex work because they're morally bankrupt or something, but queers do sex work because they're not going back where they came from, and cities are expensive. It's just math."

"Math," I repeat. "It *was* math. But it's actually working really well for Sam. She's so good at it and it doesn't bug her."

Another pause.

"Now *you* give me some dirt," I say.

"Oh," Billie starts. "Okay, did you know I have three younger siblings?"

"Okay, that's not dirt, but it does explain why you can handle running a painting crew, and why you're so good at dealing with all these personalities and little dramas."

Billie laughs. "Yeah, probably."

"Give me something better."

It's quiet.

"Can I say something but not go into it? Like we can talk about it later when we know each other better, but I'd just say it and for now we'd leave it at that?"

"Intriguing," I say. "Deal. I won't ask a single question."

"Okay. So. I had an abortion when I was eighteen." She says, "I just realized I was your age. That's so weird."

I pinch my lips between my teeth, not speaking, like I promised. But I want to slip through the phone, read her face. I want to know exactly what this means to her, the weight it carries, or doesn't.

It's too quiet now. "I can't say *anything*?" I ask.

"You can tell me you're pro-choice." She pauses. "But only say that if it's true for you," she adds.

"I *am* pro-choice," I tell her. "I'm basically pro-choice about everything, ever."

"Phew. And now let's move back to *your* dirt?"

I want to empty my pockets for her, but I'm surprised to find I have little left with Bubbe's death off the table.

"The only interesting one I have left is that, for a couple months"—I pause, considering my words—"I had sex for money. With an older dyke," I add.

"You had sex for two months straight?" Billie asks, feigning shock. "That's impressive. That's almost as good as shitting all that siva."

"Stop it!" I laugh. "Never talk about shitting siva again!"

"All right, all right," she says, chuckling her way to a sigh. "So . . . are you done having sex for money?"

"Yeah—well, she's done with it," I say, stumbling. "But I was really done with it too. It was just hard to leave because it paid so well. And I had to take a major pay cut when I started painting, but I actually like painting, and I love the crew, and wearing regular clothes, and acting like myself. So yeah, I'm done."

"Okay, to be honest, that one was a little surprising," Billie admits, "but only because it was with a dyke."

I feel myself squirming in the silence that follows.

"Honestly, Billie, did I just creep you out?"

"No, you didn't creep me out at all," Billie says. "You *can't* creep me out, I don't think."

"Maybe if I tried?" I joke.

"*Maybe* if you tried."

"Would it creep you out if I told you I was super crushed out on you?" I ask, feeling the boldness of the question in my chest.

"No," Billie says, her voice going soft. "Not at all."

"I'm super crushed out on you, Billie Rodriguez," I say, leaning my head back, grinning at the pantry ceiling.

"So does that mean I get to take you out on a date when you get back?" Billie asks. "I would call it a date this time, pick you up, and take you somewhere."

"It *does* mean that."

"Maybe if the date goes well, I could hold your hand?" she asks.

"You can hold my hand."

"And if it goes really, really, really well"—she pauses—"I could kiss you?" she asks, her voice gentle. Easy.

I swallow. "That's a little X-rated for a first date," I tease.

"So, that's a no?"

"You can kiss me, Billie. You can kiss me anytime you want."

20

A couple of weeks later, the terrible task of purging Bubbe's house begins. Shelves and shelves of books, records, tchotchkes, midcentury paintings, handmade blankets, serving dishes with their very own quilted warming covers. And we can't just get rid of things. We have to open every book, check the back of every painting, turn over every stone in the yard, searching for secret compartments filled with gold jewelry and stacks of twenty-dollar bills inside. So far we've found four decoy books full of cash, two domino-sized gold bricks wrapped in a tablecloth inside a stockpot in the basement, and a nest of gold bracelets in a cookie tin on top of the fridge. How she got it up there, we'll never know. All of this irritates my mother to no end.

"If this house had burned down, she would have lost almost everything! I always told her that. And all that squirreling away only makes our job so much harder now."

"Mom! She was squirreling everything away for *us*! It

was for *us*!" Rachel says, her face reddening as she flips through a stack of books. We both stare at her, surprised, before my mother turns to me and lifts her eyebrows.

"What?" Rachel asks, looking back and forth between us. "It's true."

It *is* true. And it silences my mother's incessant complaining, at least temporarily.

April comes over to help me sort early one Sunday morning before everyone arrives. I've decided to take a few things without discussing it with my mother, who is intent on processing every item through family court.

"Here," April says, grabbing a tote bag from the pantry, *The Disability Rights Education and Defense Fund* printed in red across it. "I'll follow you around with this. She was your grandmother just as much as she was your mother's mother."

I nod even though I'm sure my mom would find a way to disagree.

I pack up the macramé owl wall hanging above the bed, put a Star of David pendant on a fine gold chain around my neck and tuck it under my T-shirt with Bubbe's locket. I take a black-and-white picture I find of her at twenty-three, my mom bundled in her arms, standing in the snow on the front lawn of this very house. I take her lavender perfume with the swirly seventies label, the Altoid tin of teeth, and an unused bar of Dove soap from under the sink. I take her blue housedress and her swim cap with the chin strap, the one she wore in the pool at the Rosemont Lodge. When the bag is full, April double-knots the shoulder straps and stuffs it under the bed.

As the weeks move, the house clears, and when it's time for the furniture to go, my mother asks, "Why don't you spend your last few days at home?" as if she weren't the one to send me away in the first place. I tell her okay, but on that first night back in my old bedroom, I find myself lying awake pondering the word *home.* This isn't my home, I conclude, I always knew it wasn't. What *is* home? It's nowhere, which means it could be anywhere. It's wherever I am.

I'm home. And Bubbe's inside of me. I knead the revelation until it's warm and pliable. Then let it sit, rise like bread.

The night before my flight, it's snowing, and I walk over to April's to say goodbye. She greets me at the door in a bathrobe, waist belt tied high under her breasts. Shivering, I step into the warmth of her apartment and feel the skin on my cheeks prickle as I take off my puffer.

We make peppermint tea and sit on the couch with our feet lined up in front of the space heater. She lets me put my ear against her naked belly, but I tell her all I hear are her guts gurgling.

"How do you know those are my guts and not the baby's?" she asks.

"Those are big guts," I say. "Your big guts."

"I always thought I had big guts."

"You do," I say.

"I wish you could come back after she's born, to meet her right away. I read in one of my baby books that newborns imprint on the people who hold them and talk to them in their first few weeks of life."

I think for a moment, imagining April with a new baby and no family to speak of. "Maybe I can," I say. I wonder who will bring her food and hold the kid while she showers. If I had a baby, I'd have to fight my mother off with a stick. Even if she doesn't understand me, even if she's difficult in a thousand ways, she would still be there. It would be impossible to keep her away.

"What do you do with a newborn baby when you need to shower?" I ask.

"I asked the nurse at my last prenatal visit that question. It's not just showering. What about washing the dishes and taking out the trash? She told me I'll need to put the baby in a car seat and keep her in whatever room I'm in, so I guess she's probably going to spend a bunch of time buckled up."

It sounds reasonable, but it also sounds lonely and hard.

"I'll make it happen, I promise," I say, vowing to myself at the same time. "I'll come back for a couple of weeks. I'll find a way. This is my godbaby after all."

"Yay!" April says, pumping her fist. "You're going to get imprinted with me!"

I wrap my arms around her shoulder and lean my head against hers. She rests her hands on my forearm. "Remember when you gave me your sunglasses at school because I was crying?" I ask. "You were always there when I needed you, and you knew better than to make me talk about it. You're a really good friend, and I know you're going to be a great mom."

"I hope so, but it's not that simple, Hannah," she says. "I know my mom planned on being a great mom. But she couldn't do it. I need to stay humble and take it hour by hour. I need to stay consistent with my meetings. I don't get any guarantees."

I turn to look at her. Her face is open, tender. Of course, she's right. Nobody plans on losing their kids to foster care. But isn't she different? Or at least I have to think she's different. Doesn't she have to think so too?

When it's time to leave, I hug April and lean in to talk to her belly. "See you on the flip side, peanut," I say, and then I walk down the steps and we wave one last time before she closes the door. April *is* different. I don't have to think it. I have to know it. I know it. I walk home through the streets, the snow falling slowly, almost delicately, around me. It shows itself clearly in the skirt of light from the streetlamps. I think about April the whole way. I wonder if her sobriety is as fragile as a snowflake. Or maybe her sobriety is the light illuminating all the fragility that was already there.

In the early morning, my mother warms up the Buick while it's still dark, and by the time we're pulling out of the driveway, the blue dawn is emerging. It makes the snow look blue too, blue and sparkly. As we're driving down Lincoln, I can see the breath of each pedestrian hanging in the air in front of them like empty speech bubbles. It's quiet and cold and I didn't think I would miss weather like this but now I think I will. I already do.

"Mom?" I ask, turning toward her.

"Yes?"

"When April has her baby, will you bring her some food and hold the baby while she showers?" I ask.

She glances at me. "Do you think she'd feel comfortable with me? She never talked to me much when you two were in high school."

"That's because *she* thought *you* thought *she* was a bad influence on me," I say.

"Well, she was right, I did think that," she says, shrugging.

"I think she would be grateful for any help, and your offering would make her more comfortable around you," I say.

"I can do that for you," she says, glancing at me again.

"Thanks," I say, a little surprised.

We sit in silence for a moment before she says, "Someday I want to do that for *you*. I want to help you with *your* baby." She pauses. "I'm worried I'll never get to."

I look at her, the way the corners of her mouth point down without her knowing.

"Mom, please don't decide now that I'm not having kids ten years from now just because I'm gay."

She doesn't say anything.

"Ten years is a long time away, a lot can happen in ten years," I say.

I see her consider this. I wonder if she's hoping I might grow into somebody more familiar by then, somebody with a husband and grandchildren to offer.

"The first hurdle is that I don't even know if I want kids, so it will probably take ten years just to figure that out," I say, hoping for a smile. I don't get one.

We pull up to Departures and she turns off the engine.

"Listen. I love you, Hannah," she begins. "God loves you, I know that too. I have tsuris up to here," she says, tapping the top of her head.

"Mom, that doesn't help either of us—"

"I'm not trying to help, I'm trying to explain!" she says, her brow furrowing.

I wait a moment, but she doesn't go on. She sighs deeply. I watch as she unbuckles her seat belt and reaches into her coat pocket, pulling out a white envelope, extending it toward me.

"What is this?" I ask, reaching for it.

"It's from Bubbe."

I look at her, confused.

"When Bubbe was first diagnosed, she worried about

how you would take it. She told me she wanted you to have five thousand dollars of her money right away when she died so you didn't have to worry about missing shifts at your waitressing job. She wanted everything to be a little easier for you in San Francisco for a while. So, here you go. Five thousand."

"Bubbe," I say softly, feeling her here, as if she were telling me herself. My eyes burn for a moment, but instead of tears, I feel the heat moving down into my chest, warming me.

"I love you, and I worry for you," Mom says, patting me on the forearm.

"I love you, and I worry for you too, Mom."

I watch her eyes well. And then we lean in and hug each other. She holds the back of my head in her palm. I feel her mean it; she does love me. And I mean it too. I do love her. I don't know how not to. She's impossible, but she's *my* impossible.

"Thanks for driving me," I say as I swing the door open and drag my duffel out from the back.

She sighs. "That's what mothers do," she says, smiling weakly. "We care for our children regardless of what we get in return."

Our eyes catch again. She doesn't understand how her words land. How easily they can drag us back into familiar territory. I won't go with her this time. I push the door closed without saying a word. I do it carefully, so it doesn't sound like a slam.

Part Four

San Francisco,
California.
January 1997.

21

Scooby pulls up to Arrivals, Sam's hand flapping out of the driver's window with excitement. I swing my duffel into the back and climb in. It's January but it might as well be May. The air is clear and warm, and it feels about sixty degrees. I strip off my coat and sweatshirt while I sing, "Sammie! Sammie! Sammie!" Seeing her in person makes my heart clench in a way I wasn't expecting. She gives me a wide grin, so big her eyes crinkle up. We lean in and hug sideways, before I buckle myself in.

Sam steers with one hand and pulls a banana from the dash, offering it to me.

"It's for you, Hannah Banana."

I give her a curious look and take it from her.

"Is it weird I brought you a banana?" she asks, the corners of her mouth curling.

"Super weird, you weirdo," I tease.

I called Molly's a few nights prior to tell Sam I was coming home. We ended up talking about Bubbe again for almost an hour, exchanging some of our favorite Bubbe habits: Bubbe's stockpile of discontinued Pepsodent tooth powder, the toddler-sized serving of cottage cheese and canned pineapple she ate for breakfast every morning, the way she took a highlighter to her *TV Guide* the moment it arrived in the mail. Talking Bubbe with Sam was like soaking in a warm bath. "A Bubbe bath," I joked. Sam's memories were a place I wanted to visit when I was back in San Francisco. After Bubbe, we shifted to chatting about everyday things as if there had never been a wedge between us. Sam told me about her new obsession, collecting vintage fifties cardigans with pearly buttons, then went on a rant about how wimpy Californians are the second it starts raining—"Even a drizzle and they're panicking, but then they don't even carry umbrellas!" It had felt good to talk about light, normal stuff with her again, and at the end of the conversation, she'd offered to get Scooby from the beach and pick me up at the airport.

"How were the last couple days?" she asks as she merges into airport traffic.

"Okay, I guess. We finished sorting through Bubbe's stuff, and I got to see April a couple more times."

"What do you think April would say," she starts, flipping her head to look behind her as she pulls onto the 101 North, "or I guess, I mean, what would she feel if I called her?"

She glances over at me quickly.

"I don't really know," I answer, peeling the banana.

"So, I shouldn't, right?" she asks.

I pause to chew. "I didn't say that. You should call her. You have nothing to lose."

She considers this.

"What's been going on with you?" I ask.

"Really? You want to know?"

"I mean, how about you don't start with a dating thing," I say, tossing the peel on the dash.

"Well, I just applied to SF State. For next fall. I realized I should do something productive with all my stripping money and all the time it gives me, so I was like, *I'll go to college!* Like, why not?"

"For what?" I ask, wondering if Molly's in college and if that's what gave her the idea. "I mean, what would you major in?"

"I don't even know, but if I'm not broke, it won't matter, and I can just pick whatever I'm into and not stress. I know that probably sounds random," Sam says, glancing at me again. "We were so anti-college when we were in high school, but do you ever think about it now?"

"I wasn't anti-college, I just needed to get out of Long Beach before I could think about anything else. Bubbe wanted me to go to college," I say. "But I didn't really think about it until this trip when I was working with her hospice nurse, and I felt like, that's a job that's really important, and I think I could do it."

Sam frowns. "That sounds so depressing."

"Suffering is depressing. Taking care of her was the least depressing part of the whole horrible depressing thing," I say. "It was the only part that felt good."

When we get to the apartment, I open the door and find it spotless, with new alive plants on the windowsill and dresser.

"Did you do all this?" I ask.

"Yeah, I thought you should come home to something nice," she says. I smile at her. I've been worried about what it would feel like to be here, alone in the apartment again, unsure of how long I can afford it without Sam, but standing here inside it, it feels good. Mine. Homey.

"Since when do you know a thing about plants?" I ask, walking over to the one on the dresser with pale almond-shaped leaves.

"I'm learning. Luz is teaching me how to propagate from clippings we collect around the neighborhood."

"Who's Luz? Never heard that name before," I tease. She sticks her tongue out at me.

"I washed your sheets and put some food in your fridge," she says, opening the door to show me.

"That's so sweet," I say.

"I mean, I *do* love you," she says, sitting down on the bed, "as weird as it is we aren't together."

I look at her. I wonder what she wants from me when she says it.

"Do you want to tell me how it's going with Molly . . .

and all the other girls you're making out with?" I ask, turning to the plant on the windowsill.

"I thought you didn't want to talk about dating things," she says, putting air quotes around *dating things*.

"I need to get used to it at some point."

"Okay." She kicks off her boots and sits cross-legged on the bed. "I'm not sleeping with Molly anymore—I mean, we only did a couple times anyway—and I'm looking for a studio of my own. I never meant to move in with Molly and Luz. You and I just needed a break . . ."

"*You* needed a break," I clarify.

"Okay, yeah, I needed a break, and she said I could stay with them for a bit . . ." She glances at me, then looks away quickly. "I still kinda like Molly, and I definitely still love you, and I also just want to be alone, or just free . . . it's complicated. Maybe I'm not good at being with people, but I'm also not good at being without people . . ." She trails off. "Do you think I'm terrible?" she asks, looking up at me.

I sit down on the bed next to her and push her hair off her shoulder. "I can't ever think that," I say.

"Do you think we'll ever get back together, Hannah?"

I consider this for a moment. "It feels like no, but maybe at some point, who knows?"

Sam leans her face into her hands, then pushes her fingers through her hair all the way back to her neck. "I can't call you my best friend, not all the way yet, and I can't say you're my ex-girlfriend because you're too important to be called an ex, and of course we're obviously not girlfriends anymore, so it's hard to say what you are to me, what we are to each other," she says.

"You don't have to fit me into a category. We're queers. We get to make up the rules or have none, we get to do and be whatever we want."

"That's true," Sam says.

"I have a crush on someone else too," I say. "I know you probably have like ten crushes, but it's kind of a big deal that I have a crush on anyone other than you because you're literally the only person I've ever had a crush on."

Sam smiles and glares at the same time. "Who is she and how did you meet her?"

"She painted this apartment building. That's how I got the job."

"Wait. No way. The tall boyish one? Or the one with two braids?" Sam asks.

"The tall boyish one. Did you meet her?"

"No, but I saw her outside the building." Sam's glare returns. "Am I not your type anymore?"

"Sam, I don't have a type! This is literally my second crush."

"I can't imagine you going on a date-date," Sam says.

"Why?" I ask.

"I don't know."

"Her name is Billie—"

"Well, that sounds a lot like Sammie," she teases.

"Well, she isn't like you," I say, my teeth sinking in. Hurt washes over her face. "I'm sorry," I say.

"It's okay," she says with a shrug. "C'mon, tell me what she's like, I can handle it."

"Are you sure?" I ask.

"Yeah, I can get excited for you. Let me *try* anyway." She sits up straight to show me.

"Okay, well, obviously she looks like River Phoenix—"

"I don't know about that," Sam says.

I give her a look. She gives me a sheepish one back, before gesturing for me to continue. "*And* she's calm and steady and has amazing lips and eyelashes, but also this really nice jawline, and she thinks before she talks, you can tell. She doesn't talk a ton, but when she does, it's like she really means it, and her smile is like so . . ."

I try to gauge Sam's expression. "Melty?" Sam asks.

"Yeah," I say.

"Have you hung out?"

"Not alone, but we're going on a real date on Friday. Her friend's bar is having its opening night and—"

"I'll be there," Sam says.

"I'm not inviting you!"

"No, I'm *already* going to be there. It's called the Lexington. It's going to be a dyke bar, like an actual seven-days-a-week dyke bar. It's going to be a really big deal."

"Oh," I say. "Is it going to be weird if you see me on my date?"

"Molly will be there too," Sam says.

I pretend to gag.

"Hannah, let's just push through the weird," she says.

I look at her. We've been through so much together already.

"I can try if you can," I say.

"I'm going to help you pick out your outfit," Sam says.

"Really?"

"Is that weird?" Sam asks.

"Yes, it's weird, but we can be weird."

"Yeah, we're weirdos," Sam says, "this is totally normal for weirdos."

22

"Boo!"

I yelp and whip around, and there stands Billie with a big grin on her face. It's Friday afternoon, my first day back with the crew, our first date scheduled for tonight, and here I stand, filthy in a respirator and gloves, sanding a window frame that looks out over Market Street. I switch from stunned to a phenomenal shyness, a *monumental* shyness, my heart fluttering in my chest. We've been talking on the phone for weeks, but it's the first time I've seen her since she dropped me at the airport in early November. She's wearing her orange beanie with her hair, longer this time, sticking out the bottom like the first day I saw her, her eyes gleaming at me. I'm frozen. Maybe she senses my awkwardness. She moves to relieve me of it. Pulling the respirator from my face, taking the sandpaper from my hands, pulling my work gloves off by the fingertips, and throwing all of it to the ground.

"That's better," she says. And then she opens her arms toward me. I step into them and put my forehead on her shoulder, and she wraps them around me.

"Are we the same height?" I ask, lifting my head up to look at her.

"You might be an inch taller," Billie says. "But how 'bout we say: same height."

"It *feels* like we're the same height," I say.

"What else does it feel like?" Billie asks.

I want to answer with something so right, so cool, so perfectly hot, but my brain stumbles. I take her hand and put it on my heart, which is thumping away in my chest. "Do you feel that?" I ask.

"Yeah," Billie says, smiling.

"That's for you," I say.

Billie wipes my forehead with her sleeve.

"Am I covered in sweat and paint dust?" I ask.

Billie nods. She brushes my right cheek with her sleeve next. And then she leans in to kiss the spot, her hand still on my heart. Now I feel lusty in a way that makes me want to trick her, turn my mouth toward hers before her lips hit my cheek.

"Oooooooooh!" I hear from behind her. "Busted!" Heather yells.

"What?" I hear Tamika ask from around the corner.

"I just found Billie kissing on Hannah," Heather yells to Tamika.

"Oooooh!" I hear Tamika yell back.

"Are you fucking kidding me?" Little Danny's voice swings up an octave, his head popping into view. "What?! When?!"

Billie turns toward Heather, shaking her head. I can see she's red. I bend down and grab my respirator.

"We have to talk about the house over in Glen Park," Billie says to Heather, while Little Danny mouths to me, *We'll talk later.*

"Are you trying to change the subject?" Heather asks, throwing her hands up.

"Most definitely," Billie says, walking toward her.

But before she rounds the corner with Heather, she turns back to me and smiles. Her eyes smile too. My whole being smiles back. I pull my gloves on. I go back to sanding, my chest singing with electricity. A few minutes later I see her below, leaving the building and heading to her car. She opens the driver's-side door, but before she gets in, she looks up toward my window, shielding her eyes from the sun with one hand, waving with the other. I wave back. And then she slides in, pulls the car out, and I watch her disappear up Market Street. I feel high. I feel delirious. Our first date. Tonight. I'm counting the minutes until I get off work.

In the evening, Billie picks me up in her Plymouth Valiant. I get in and slide across the bench seat toward her. It smells like coffee and Old Spice in here. I'm wearing the outfit Sam helped me pick out: a short jean skirt, a studded belt, and a silver metallic tank top with Bubbe's necklaces tucked inside. Sam circled my eyes in black liner and told me I had to top off the look with my black knee-high boots and a jean jacket even though I worried it would be too much denim. She was right, though—jean on jean is hotter than it sounds.

"Hi," I say.

"Hi," Billie says back to me.

She looks amazing. She's wearing a white button-down and a suit jacket. Her hair is practically to her shoulders now, but greased back away from her face so I can see her jawline, her cheekbones, her thick brows, the flutter of her eyelashes, her lips. I want to stare at her just like I did the first time we met outside my building.

"Hi," she says again, grinning. "You look beautiful, Hannah."

"You look . . . ," I start. I'm guessing she doesn't want to be called beautiful, but my brain can't find the right word to describe her. ". . . really good," I say. I think there isn't a right word in the entire English language.

"You can say *handsome* or *cute* if you want. I mean, that would work for me," she says, and we both laugh.

"You look handsome, Billie," I say shyly, and then scoot closer to kiss her on the cheek, before resting my hand on hers. She tips her head forward, leaning it on the steering wheel. She feels it too. We both feel it. We're magnets pulling toward each other. It's undeniable.

Billie takes me to a place called Country Station Sushi near Eighteenth on Mission. Apparently, it was a burger joint that used to play country music but morphed into a sushi place at the hands of one of the Japanese cooks. It's a place of contradictions, decorated with a chandelier, and plants, and tall stacks of CDs. Boyz II Men is playing when we walk in. Billie and I turn to each other when we recognize the song at the same time.

"I feel like I should ask you to do the couple's skate with me," I say.

"Roller skating or ice skating?" Billie asks.

"Hmmm." I think. "Let's go with roller skating."

Billie wipes her forehead with the back of her hand like she's totally relieved.

When we sit down, we grin at each other in silence.

"Hi," Billie says.

"Hi," I say back to her.

"Hi," Billie says again.

"Hi," I say back to her again.

I don't tell Billie I've never had sushi before, and I can't say if I like sushi or not because I eat it under the spell of her, swimming in the high of her.

Billie tells me about Puerto Rico and the part of her family who are still there, none of them Jehovah's Witnesses like her parents. She tells me about a drink called coquito, how she snuck sips of it on Christmas when she was twelve, and about her mediocre Spanish, and how she's trying to improve with Spanish-language CDs while she paints.

I tell her about frei versus frum and teach her Yiddish phrases that tumble out of her mouth like pebbles when she tries to shape them. I tell her about gefilte fish and liver and onions and pickled herring, and all the foods that make people gag but make me warm inside, reminding me of Bubbe's kitchen.

After dinner we head up Mission Street to Nineteenth on foot, the backs of our hands occasionally brushing, silly grins pinned to our faces like kindergarten art. I'm starting to realize that Billie might have been serious when she said, *Maybe if the date goes well, I could hold your hand? And if it goes really, really, really well, I could kiss you?* There's something shy and slow about the way she moves around me. It makes me feel bold. I want to provoke her, get too close, poke at her, see what she does.

The Lexington Club is on the corner of Lexington and Nineteenth Street between Mission and Valencia. When we turn up Nineteenth from Mission, we immediately see and hear a swarm of people and motorcycles outside the bar. The sidewalks are full, and yellow cabs keep pulling up in front and dumping more people out.

"Whoa," Billie says as we approach.

"Can we get some gum first?" I ask, stalling, a twitch of nerves balling up in my stomach.

We stop at the liquor store across the street. Even the liquor store is full of dykes. But when I see them smiling at us, my nerves untangle, fall loose, my spine straightening. We smile at each other like we know the secret. We smile at each other like we finally own the night. Which we kind of do.

As we cross the street toward the bar, I look up and see

a beautiful new neon sign with *Lexington* in blue, above *Club* in red. I can't believe it's all for us. I look around. Queers, queers, queers. I couldn't have dreamed this up when I was lying in my twin bed in Long Beach. I wish I could snap a picture of it, take it back in time, tuck it between my mattress and box spring, like a souvenir in reverse, so I could have had something to hold on to.

It's the first time I'm using my new fake ID, and there's a girl with dark curly hair, deep cleavage, and a flashlight sitting on a barstool at the entrance. I swallow.

"I know her," Billie whispers to me. "It's fine."

We get in line, Billie behind me. When I hold out my ID, the girl shines her flashlight on it, looks up at me, nods hello to Billie, then looks back at me, raising her eyebrows before motioning us in with her chin. "Phew," I whisper in Billie's ear.

The inside of the Lexington is painted a deep red, and there's a bar to the left with two columns on either end running all the way to the ceiling. There's a green pool table smack in the middle and a jukebox on the far end near the bathroom. The place is almost pulsing, packed with shaved heads, skater-boy haircuts, piercings glinting in the low light. Dykes dressed like the T-Birds in *Grease*, dykes with bright red lipstick and slips worn as dresses, dykes in leather pants and electrical-tape X's over their nipples, Little Danny in the far corner in a sequined cocktail dress. There's so much leather, and sequin, and denim, and lace, and hair grease, and fishnets, and cleavage, my eyes blur with it.

I feel a tap on my shoulder and turn around to see Sam with Molly tucked halfway behind her.

"Hi, Hannah!" Sam says, squeezing my arm with a slight dig of her nails, her gaze moving expectantly between Billie and me. Molly's mouth is drawing an awkward line across her face, and she nods in my direction, quickly averting her eyes.

"Hello," I say back slowly, trying to figure out how to navigate the introductions.

"I'm Billie," I hear Billie say next to me.

"Oh, sorry," I say. "Billie, this is Sam, and Molly." Molly shifts from side to side, pushing her glasses up her nose and tucking her pink hair behind her ears. We stand around staring at each other, with frozen half smiles, until Billie jumps in to save us.

"Hannah and I were just going to say hi to our friends from work over there," Billie says, gesturing to the crew, who have taken over the far corner of the bar. "Want to come meet them?"

"Oh," Molly says, her expression softening, "I know Little Danny! We were in the same band for a minute."

Sam and I walk behind Billie and Molly and make faces at each other like *Blargh, that was awkward.* But once we get over to the crew, everyone shuffles together, and I introduce Sam, while Molly catches up with Little Danny. Billie buys us drinks and I marvel at the way she asks me what I want before she gets it. Then I marvel at marveling at something so basic. I watch Tamika flirt with Sam, just out of earshot.

Tamika's arms are crossed over her chest, her eyes crinkling at the corners while they debate something absurd, I'm sure, knowing the two of them. I love watching Sam flirt back, her hands on her hips, doing her loudmouthed teasy flirt. *I love her,* I think to myself, the feeling light, like a pop of confetti. Anna G. comes in for a "a quick hello," kissing both my cheeks like she's French, before leaning in to hug Billie. Her quick hello turns into a very academic, slightly drunk deconstruction of the lyrics of "Kiss from a Rose" by Seal, while Billie and I chuckle and nod, catching each other's eyes to agree. On what, I'm not totally sure, but I'm certain we do.

When Anna G. wanders off, Billie leans in and says to me, "I'm going to run to the bathroom." Her mouth is close. I feel its proximity and turn toward her.

"Can I come with you?" I ask.

"Like, come in and pee with me?" she asks. I immediately hear how weird it sounds for a first date.

"Yeah?" I say sheepishly. "Too weird, too soon?"

"Not if you promise to turn around while I pee," she says.

"Deal."

I hook my arm in Billie's and we head to the bathroom. Luckily there isn't a line, and a girl wearing red-sequined devil horns comes out and holds the door for us. We find ourselves in a single-stall bathroom painted bright blue on the inside, no larger than a closet.

"I'm pee shy," Billie says. "So you're going to have to look away and talk the whole time too."

I face the blue wall next to the sink. "Talk about what?" I ask.

"I mean sing."

"Sing what?" I ask. "You might not want to go on a second date if I sing."

"Try 'Kiss from a Rose.'"

I clear my throat. It doesn't help. I do a terrible rendition, off-key, humming the words I can't remember, until I hear the toilet flush.

"Can I stop now?" I ask.

"I was waiting to see how long you'd go for," she says as I turn around to see her buttoning the top of her pants. She looks up. "I didn't say you could turn around!"

We swap places and I go quickly while she washes her hands.

"I guess I'm not pee shy," I say.

"I love that you aren't shy," she says.

"Whoa, whoa, whoa," I say as I flush the toilet with the tip of my boot. "I'm not shy?" I ask. I pump the soap dispenser with one hand. She's standing behind me now, and our eyes meet in the mirror.

"Do you see yourself as shy?" she asks. "I see you doing whatever you want, and saying whatever you think, don't you?"

I shake my head, then I stop to hold her gaze. "But maybe I should adjust how I see myself."

"I'm *clearly* the shy one," Billie says, as if there's no questioning this.

I smile at her, reach back for her hands, and wrap them around my waist. She puts her chin on my shoulder.

"I like this," I say quietly, looking at our reflection. "I like you being the shy one, Billie."

She presses her body against my back and moves her mouth to my neck. I feel her teeth. A bite. My heart taps in my chest.

There's a knock at the door. "Hello?!" a voice says.

"Almost done!" Billie yells.

"No, not almost done," I say quietly, turning around to lean my butt on the edge of the sink and wrap my arms around her shoulders. My hips are against hers, and the smell of her, and my mouth close to hers, makes me flush, the heat drifting into my thighs.

"I don't want to kiss you for the first time in this bathroom," she says.

"But why not?" I ask.

"Um, because it's a bathroom," she explains, pressing her forehead into mine.

Now there's a pound on the door. We untangle; she turns toward it, unlocking the silver bolt. Then she reaches back to take my hand as we head toward the crew. Her hand is warm and strong, and I'm made of lust. I want it. Her hands all over me and all the *it*s she could possibly think up.

Sam is still with Tamika, now closer, leaning in to hear what she's saying, catching my eyes as we approach.

A minute later, Sam yells over the din to me, "Can we go have a cigarette?" Billie's hugging a green-haired woman in a purple pleather dress and a dog collar. She introduced me, but I couldn't make out her name.

"I'm going to go have a cigarette with Sam," I yell at Billie.

"What?" Billie yells back. I gesture smoking a cigarette, then point to Sam, then point to outside. Billie nods, reaching to squeeze my hand before I follow Sam. We push ourselves toward the entrance, dump out into the cool air, both of us compelled to expand, lift our arms overhead, sweep the sweaty hair from our necks.

"Jesus, it's like a can of sardines in there," Sam says, pulling a pack of cigarettes from her back pocket and offering me one. I tell her I'll just have a drag of hers. She puts it in her mouth, hands me the lighter, and cups her hands on either side, her face glowing over the flame as I light it.

"Were you and Billie just making out in the bathroom?" she asks, smirking.

I give her the same smirk back. "I wish! She wouldn't kiss me in there. She doesn't want our first kiss to be a bathroom kiss."

"No bathroom kisses. Oooh, how old-fashioned."

"She's actually very old-fashioned, in the most random ways, and then completely not in others."

She passes me the cigarette. "Well, you and Billie are cute together. I can tell she likes you."

I take a drag, eyeing her through a thread of smoke. She's wearing spearmint ChapStick, I can taste it. "You think?" I ask. She nods with confidence. I feel myself beam.

Pushing our way back in, I grip Sam's arm to stay close. I can't believe this many dykes even live in this city. I see Dusty from the coffee shop in the corner and she waves. She remembers me. I wave back. She's sitting with a gorgeous girl with a sleek black bob and red lips. A blue Mohawk fans by, momentarily obscuring my view. When it passes, my eyes catch on two girls dressed like fifties pinups kissing in the corner. I lean into Sam. "This is meshuga!" I say in Bubbe's voice.

"It really is," she yells back.

When I slip in next to Billie, I hook my arm in hers and notice Little Danny watching from the bar like a proud mother, hand on his chest, hearts flooding his eyes.

"Let me fix this," he says, approaching. He unhooks our arms and weaves our fingers together instead, wrapping them tight, and then stands back to admire his work.

Billie leans in. "Is our date going well enough for this?" she asks, dipping her chin to gesture at our hands.

Billie and I leave around one a.m., eliciting groans from the crew and a single squeal and a few claps from Little Danny. I kiss Sam on the cheek and wave to Molly even though we're only standing a foot apart. I can't hate her. I can't care. Sam and I are a lot of things that add up to a big thing, way bigger than Molly. It was never about Molly anyway.

Billie and I head down Nineteenth toward Mission, where the Plymouth is parked. We reek of cigarette smoke and my ears are ringing.

"What now?" I ask, cocking my head toward her.

She looks up at me through her lashes, lets out a shy laugh, then wraps an arm around my shoulder. "Bernal Hill?" she asks.

I put my arm around her waist, tucking a thumb into her belt loop. "Bernal Hill," I agree.

Billie winds us up a dark hill and parks when we get to the top where the road is blocked off from cars on the southern side of Bernal. Climbing out of the car, we find the night much cooler, quieter, up here. Spacious. She creaks open the trunk and hands me a paint-splattered sweatshirt. I take off my jean jacket, put on the sweatshirt, then my jacket back on over it. The sweatshirt smells like her. I want to keep it forever.

As we start to walk, I reach for her hand and pull it into the sweatshirt pocket with mine.

"I've never been here," I say, feeling the calluses on her palms, her short square nails.

"Then we should go to the very top."

The road, low-lit in warm light from the streetlamps, wraps its way around the hill, higher and higher. We ditch it at the top, taking a narrower, crumbling path on the steep side facing the city. From up here, the city is laid flat like a map of itself, glittering in lights. Billie points out Valencia Street, South Van Ness, Potrero Hill, and Twin Peaks. Everything looks different from this vantage point. It's the same city I saw from the roof of our building, the same city Bubbe and I saw from Twin Peaks, but now it's rotated, redrawn, charged up with Billie at my side. We sit down in the dirt.

"Comfy, eh?" Billie asks, lifting her eyebrows.

"Practically a couch," I agree, scooting closer to her.

Billie takes a finger and loops it under my necklaces, untucking the locket and the Star of David.

"I've been wondering what was going on under there," she says.

"They were my grandmother's," I say, looking down at them.

"Then they're extra special," Billie says, holding the Star of David by its points. "I'm sure she'd be happy you're wearing them."

"Maybe she *is* happy I'm wearing them."

Billie looks into my eyes. "I thought white people didn't believe in ghosts."

I laugh. "Yeah, I don't know if I believe in ghosts exactly." I pause, considering. "I guess I'm not sure what I believe in."

Billie tucks the hair behind my ear on one side, then the other.

"I'm ready now," she says.

I look at her, confused. Then I realize what she means.

"Not yet." I stop her, turning my whole self toward her and throwing a leg behind her in the dirt.

"Okay, I'm almost ready," I say, scootching in.

Billie's laughing. "I can see your underwear."

"So?!"

She runs a hand along my shin, grinning. Then I put my arms around her, and she holds my face in her hands, leans in, and kisses me. She kisses me with those lips that are big and soft and shaking a little, that open shyly against mine. I flood with the feeling of it. I flood with the feeling of her mouth, the night, the air, the possibility of it all. The possibility that there might be a place for me, for us, the broader us. A place for you too. The city lights showing you a way in, swinging every door and window open, calling you home. Billie's mouth is on mine, and her hands wrap around my back. I pull her closer. Give her more. I can be a city too. I can open all the doors and windows, and be expansive, full of freaks and possibility. I can say fuck it. I can unfurl, unfold, and uncoil. It's a gift. I can take it and be it and give it if I like. And so I do.

Acknowledgments

To the keepers of my writer's heart: Ann Whidden, Sara Seinberg, Eilis O'Herlihy, and Claudia Sims Black. Thank you for the hours of love and reading and editing and spanking me in the right direction when I flopped on the floor and refused to go on.

Thank you to the many helpers and cheerleaders I've had along the way: Michelle Tea, Kit Haggard, Toni Mirosevich, Andrea Lawlor, Kate Schatz, Melissa Weiss, Naz, Val, Dusty, Mary, Sarah, Michelle, Chloe, my nurse friends, and, of course, meyn shvester, Lisa. There are so many more, too numerous to name.

Thank you to Noelle at Transatlantic for pulling me from the slush pile. Chelene Knight, Amanda Orozco, Alexandra D'Amico, and Laura Cameron for being the kind of agents who take you by the hand and say nice things in a gentle voice while expertly leading the way.

Thank you to my editors, Sarah Jackson and Tarini Sipahimalani, for choosing ~~me!~~ my book. Thank you for your brains, for getting it from the get-go, and for reading draft after draft after draft and somehow *not* poking your eyes out. Thank you to my team at Random House Canada: Sue Kuruvilla, Deirdre Molina, Danya Elsayed, Evan Klein, Trina Kehoe, Polly Beel, Sharon Klein, and, of course, the lovely Catherine Abes. And thank you to my team at Putnam: Vi-An Nguyen, Alice Dalrymple, Aja Pollock, Katie McKee, Jazmin Miller, Shina Patel, Maija Baldauf, Almudena Rincon, Alison Cnockaert, Ashley McClay, Alexis Welby, and Lindsay Sagnette. Holy moly it takes a village.

Thank you to my steady, smart, and extremely good-looking partner, Laurel, and our kids: Cuya, Luca, and Ada. All four of you, my heart outside my body.

And lastly, to the two women who inspired Bubbe. My real Bubbe: Eva Lieberman, a force of nature funneled into the smallest of bodies who taught resilience by example; and S. J. Kahn, who gave me the gentle Jewy lez guidance I desperately needed in my younger years. Both of you live on in this book, and inside of me, so completely. I couldn't have done it without you.

Shoshana von Blanckensee lives in Berkeley, California, with her partner and kids. She is an oncology nurse by day and a writer by any available moment. *Girls Girls Girls* is her debut novel.

CONNECT ONLINE

shoshanavb.com

ShoshanaVB